To Pear

The Best Orgasms Come from the Universe

A novel by

Brandon C. Lay

This book is a work of fiction. Places, events, and situations in this story are purely fictional. Any resemblance to actual persons, living or dead, is coincidental.

© 2003, 2004 by Brandon C. Lay. All rights reserved.

No part of this book may be reproduced, stored in a retrieval system, or transmitted by any means, electronic, mechanical, photocopying, recording, or otherwise, without written permission from the author.

ISBN: 1-4140-6850-6 (e-book)
ISBN: 1-4140-6851-4 (Paperback)

This book is printed on acid free paper.

1stBooks - rev. 01/19/04

Dedication

This book is dedicated to all my friends and all our inside jokes; I hope we always remember the good ones, and continue to come up with better ones.

Introductory Remarks:

When I first started writing this book, I had no specific plan for what I had to say. I decided to say lots of different things, to fill my lack of a single overall message. That's when I realized what I was trying to say. I personally share many opinions with the characters in this book, though not all of them.

The problem today is people are afraid of their own opinions, because people are so quick to judge one another. Don't let this book or any other form of creativity dictate your opinions entirely. Believing anything to be **THEE** **Word** is cheating yourself of life and from your own ideas. Believe in anything you want, as long as you're a happy and good person without causing others unhappiness. Try not to find a meaning in life or the afterlife, it will find you. Enjoy every minute you have; dance, sing, write, paint, make love, make money, give money, eat good food, travel, sleep, and above all else try to stay enthusiastic and pleasant at all times.

"Be happy, so long as you aren't causing unhappiness...believe in what you like, and extend everyone else the same courtesy..."—
BCL 2003

"There are no 'One Way' paths."—
BCL 2003

"We can see color for a reason...If life was black and white, we'd all be colorblind."—
BCL 2003

"Never stand still long enough to let life pass you by."—
BCL 2003

Table of Contents

Chapter: | Page #:

Prologue xi
Chapter One 1
Chapter Two 7
Chapter Three 12
Chapter Four 19
Chapter Five 27
Chapter Six 33
Chapter Seven 38
Chapter Eight 43
Chapter Nine 53
Chapter Ten 59
Chapter Eleven 69
Chapter Twelve 74
Chapter Thirteen 81
Chapter Fourteen 89
Chapter Fifteen 96
Chapter Sixteen 101
Chapter Seventeen 106

Chapter Eighteen	116
Chapter Nineteen	121
Chapter Twenty	126
Chapter Twenty-One	131
Chapter Twenty-Two	136
Chapter Twenty-Three	147
Chapter Twenty-Four	154
Chapter Twenty-Five	161
Chapter Twenty-Six	168
Chapter Twenty-Seven	174
Chapter Twenty-Eight	177
Chapter Twenty-Nine	181
Chapter Thirty	186
Chapter Thirty-One	195
Chapter Thirty-Two	202
Chapter Thirty-Three	207
Chapter Thirty-Four	213
Chapter Thirty-Five	218
Chapter Thirty-Six	223
Chapter Thirty-Seven	228
Chapter Thirty-Eight	235
Chapter Thirty-Nine	242
Chapter Forty	247
Chapter Forty-One	256
Chapter Forty-Two	263
Chapter Forty-Three	268
Chapter Forty-Four	274
Chapter Forty-Five	279
Chapter Forty-Six	284
Chapter Forty-Seven	288

Chapter Forty-Eight 295
Chapter Forty-Nine 300
Chapter Fifty 305
Epilogue 311

Prologue

THURSDAY

"Ok...I start the book out, mentioning all the crazy and horrible things people do to each other. I'll write about the use of the atomic bomb, and the police breaking up rioters by beating them to death, and those sickly people from third world countries, and the twin towers being destroyed. Then right away I'm going to introduce the main character...I think I'll name him Arthur. He'll be in a coffee shop like this one, talking to a woman that is going to dump him. So then, there's some stuff like that, and then...and then he leaves, and throughout the story he meets all these regular, 'normal' people. Like the real life 'normal' people, the ones with strange quirks, or foot fungus, or hang nails, or really big noses that everyone needs to stare at to feel better...you know real people with real problems. So he goes through his life and all these people leave imprints on his life. The real kicker is, in the end he doesn't change; he doesn't overcome any obstacle, except his everyday life. People love stories about people who win, and they are starting to enjoy stories about the people who don't, but no one has ever written about the person that wasn't even in the race. You know what I mean, a regular person, that doesn't accomplish anything tremendous and doesn't fail either, because he never tries to change the world. Just a normal guy with a normal life...I think it would make a great book. So what do you think?"

CHAPTER ONE

Boris looked at his friend a long time, thinking about what exactly he was being asked. He leaned back into his chair and stroked his brown beard. If smoking was allowed in the coffee shop, he would have surely removed his pipe from his pocket.

"Well, Nick...I ah..." Boris finally began, with his usual slight Russian accent poorly hidden in his speech. "It sounds, unsubstantial. People don't want to read about a guy that does absolutely nothing in the story. It doesn't have anything to it."

Nick shook his head slightly up and down a moment.

"Well...well...ah um...well, it'll really be better once it has some meat to it. I just gave you the basic flow," Nick stuttered. "The book is really going to be characterization; it's about people. It's not about just the main character."

"You remember that I write fantasy more than philosophical literary fiction," Boris started. "I might not be the best person to ask about this; I haven't written drama in a long time."

"Well that's the thing, it's not a drama. I'm inventing a new writing genre. It's about people..."

"Right, and that's what a drama is..."

"But Boris, it's about people; it's not about just their lives and their motivation. It's about the interaction and the overall momentum of people," Nick explained extravagantly with all the gesticulations possible.

"What in hell are you talking about?" Boris exclaimed.

Nick set his cup of milk down and put his head in his hands. He shook his head and began to drag his fingers across his face, as if trying to rub it off.

"I don't know. Isn't there some way you can help me? You've always given me great advice in the past."

"Give me a moment to think," Boris sighed.

Boris drew in a long deep breath, as if he were taking his last before his predestined death of petrification. Then he pushed his long, straggly, muddle of hair behind his head, leaned forward, and rested his chin on his palm. This was a ritual Nick knew well. Ever since middle school, he would always come to Boris for writing aid. Now, a long time after high school and well past college, Nick still came to his long time friend for advice, at least on writing. Boris was an award-winning writer; seven of his eight books hit the bestseller's list, almost before the ink on the pages dried. He had also written six movies, two of which earned him high critical acclaim.

Nick watched his friend with a conflicted admiration. Both men sat motionless in a state without utterance. Boris, with his unkempt hair, appeared to be an ancient marble statue, shaped by some seventies hippy who had wanted to create a representation of <u>David</u> and Jesus, yet still keep the rebellious notion of the times, by giving him a grungy appearance.

Nick never confronted his friend, although he believed these long silences to be some kind of test, some sick, twisted, bizarre, and semi-genius way for Boris to feel superior. He knew as soon as he moved or spoke, Boris would conveniently come up with the answer to the relatively simple request for aid. Nick also knew...that Boris knew...that Nick could never stay silent with his thoughts for long. So Boris would wait; wait for Nick to concede in their game of silence. The longest Nick ever restrained himself was one hour: one hour without conversation, without moving, without living, only thinking. He believed restraint to be a dirty word.

Nick could feel each second go by as Boris stared off into his imaginary void. It helped him to think more about what Boris was pondering than his own thoughts.

"I wonder if he's thinking about his book. If I were him, I'd be thinking about my book. If I were a great writer, (wow I'm hungry) I don't think I could stop thinking about my book. Well, maybe I am a great writer. Or at least I will be (I think my leg's falling asleep). So, why aren't I thinking about my book? I should be thinking about my book. My book's great, it's so real...I mean, why do characters have to overcome or learn something? My people are real. Real people don't overcome that much. In fact mostly everyone quits before they even come close to overcoming anything. Just because some people have great life experiences, doesn't mean I or anyone else has to have a world altering life. I wish I could work on my book; I need to work on my book. I need to work on my book," Nick went over in his head.

Finally, Nick just let go, sighed, and shifted his weight.

"So Boris, did you think of anything?" he asked.

"Well, I think you should write some of the meat of the story, and then let me see it," Boris began. "What happened to that movie you were writing?"

"What?"

"That screenplay...Blue Bingo Chips, did you finish it?"

"Oh, yeah, I finished it."

"Wow that's great, are you going to let me read it?"

"Sure..." Nick stopped and looked to the entrance of the congested little coffee shop.

A mammoth man entered, ducking his head under the little bell on the top of the doorframe. He stood nearly seven feet two inches. His shadow engulfed several clusters of people as he maneuvered his thin legs through the crowd. Everyone in the small coffee shop was a writer of sorts, and he was no different.

"Fredrick is here..." Nick shuddered, rolling his eyes.

"Damn phony," Nick thought. *"He claims he's a writer, because he's published a couple sports novels. The great Fredrick Screll, sports legend."*

"You don't like Fredrick?" Boris questioned.

"The only real reason he's even a best-seller is because he's a famous basketball player. He thinks he's something great because people read his name and then buy his book; I bet half of them don't even open it, unless they're having him sign the inside. It's disgusting and depressing," Nick exclaimed. "The man has the intellect of a piece of chalk."

"I hear he's going to be getting another book published soon," Boris started. "I hear it's not about sports."

"Oh great, here he comes."

"Hey, what are you guys talking about?" Fredrick inquired with a voice which went straight through Nick.

"The meaning of life," Nick responded.

"Don't say "oh yeah basketball right"...don't say it...don't say it... don't say it..." Nick repeated to himself.

The Best Orgasms Come from the Universe

"Oh yeah, right," Fredrick said.

"He didn't say it...wow, that's—" Nick began to think.

"Basketball, right," Fredrick continued.

Nick looked down at the table, staring deeply into his glass of milk, trying desperately not to scream.

"Yes...Fredrick...basketball..." Nick replied.

"Wow, cool, can I join in?" Fredrick pleaded.

"Well, actually Fredrick," Boris started, "we were talking about Nick's new book."

"Oh, wow, cool; I'm writing a new book too. It's called Desperately Dodging the Balls of Life," Fredrick explained. "It's about a man who just quit playing baseball, and now he's trying to live his life without it. But the best part is, he left by choice; he was still at the height of his game, so the story's about the 'Big Why.' You know what I mean, like why did he quit so early, and why did he quit when he loved the game so much, ya' know?"

"No I don't know, that's why you're writing the book, 'cause if I knew why, I wouldn't need to read it," Nick sighed.

"Right," Fredrick chuckled. "But anyway, what's your book about?"

"Life, in a non-sports sense," Nick answered. "It's about people, how they interact, how they judge others, and how life *really* is."

"Whoa, sounds like one crazy ass book," Fredrick stated.

"Well it will be," Nick said. "Listen, I would love nothing else than to discuss my book to a further extent, but unfortunately I must excuse myself. I need to be at work in an hour."

"Well, good luck with your book Nick, you know I always look forward to reading your work," Boris said, standing up.

"I'll see you later," Nick announced. "Fredrick, it's always a pleasure."

Nick got up from his chair, shook Fredrick's hand, and embraced Boris in a hug, before leaving the coffee shop. The little bell on the doorframe rang as Nick entered the outside world.

CHAPTER TWO

It was a drab, cold, and wet Thursday; Nick's favorite kind of the day. The sun seemed bundled comfortably within the teabag gray sky. The city street matched the color of the infinite clouds above, making it seem as if the cars and people were walking on nothing at all. The skyscrapers appeared to only be support beams holding up a thick fog waiting to pounce on the already unhappy faces of the people below. The sidewalks were filled on all angles with inhabitants, all of them within their own worlds, staring at the people in front of them, as they all walked at one pace. Each of their expressions displayed a different version of how horrible they thought their lives to be.

Nick daydreamed on what exactly they were all musing over. He pretended to himself, that he could hear all their thoughts at once. All of them were telling their story about life, love, hate, pestilence, poverty, fear, drunkenness, lust, and of course, guilt. Above all else, he could see the guilt, it was tattooed across their countenances, and it seeped in streams out of their pores. All of them second guessing themselves about religion, or their jobs, or their love lives, or more likely, their sex lives. Nick looked from face to face.

Soon he found himself developing entire stories around one expression. One man clutched his brief case as if it held the secret of life. Nick could see the sweat from the man's hand rolling off the handle of his prize.

"The man's name is Brutus Macky," Nick thought. *"He ate a bran muffin for breakfast, and walks to work every morning, including weekends. He combs his brown hair to the right side of his head, just like his Dad. His father's name is John Macky, he named his son Brutus, because his roommate back in college had a dog that went by the same name, and John just loved that dog so much. However, John always used to say Brutus was named after his great grandfather. When Brutus found out the truth, he hired a hit man to kill his father, and the roommate, and the dog (if it was still alive... which it wasn't). He always loved his father, and had nothing against dogs either, although if his superficial supermodel wife found out he was named after a K-9, it would ruin her already fragile career. Just like his Dad used to say, 'Always put your woman first,' and that's all Brutus did. The suitcase, which he held so readily, contains the only evidence of the transaction. Once he gets to his little office on the twenty-sixth floor of the corporate building on Plum Street, he's going to confess the entire thing on his suicide letter, and then blow his brains out with the forty-five in his bottom desk drawer."*

Nick finished his idea just as the extravaganza of people stopped at a crossing sign. The bright florescent orange words, **Don't Walk**, kept the crowd at bay. The mob held their ground, halted on guard, as they quickly acclimated to their new predicament. They all tried uncontrollably not to renounce to the somnolent beast, which so stubbornly did not wish to rush to work. For if the creature inside were let out for even a moment, they would all procrastinate even more about going to work. If they didn't rush to work soon enough, they might get fired, or worse, miss out on getting the **Big Deal**. Within mere minutes of these poor deprived people's lives, a fracas began to form in their minds. By the end of the workday, this petty mental quarrel would turn into a full-fledged state of pandemonium.

At home they'd undoubtedly either try to elucidate, in their own minds, what in the hell they were doing with their lives, or they would mask their yearning to exist, for the desire to "survive." "Surviving" by detaching themselves from their lives. To alleviate their self-inflicted pain, many people would turn to drinking, cigarettes, sex, food, or drugs. Others turned to their kids, and filled them with the antithesis of what hope really was or what it should've been. This helped to raise a future generation of unhappy, single-minded earthlings.

Some people turned to God in a bellicose manner, and combat prayed. Wishing or begging God to change their lives for them. A few prayers asked for nothing and just expected God would do it. Although not all of believers, the true ones knew better, they knew to just thank him for whatever crap they'd been thrown and work with what they had. Nevertheless not everyone had God, and not everyone wanted God, or any other belief for that matter, including Nick. Well, saying Nick believed in nothing is unfair. He was a firm believer in the idea of happiness, living because he wanted to.

This helped to make the monotonous gray days more appealing for Nick. The dank colors of life helped to bring out the reds and pinks. Thus the soggy, misty, moist days helped to expound upon Nick's already colorful exuberant nature, which made him feel as if he were larger than life. He studied the people individually, speculating that none of them knew the truth found in love, honor, passion, happiness, hope, enthusiasm, and humor.

"What is wrong with you people?" Nick bellowed in his head.

Nick saw Life as an old homeless man sitting slumped on some street corner. He knew Life was an entity, which people overlooked. Possibly a couple people threw **Him** some spare change now and again. Nick hoped through his personal lack of complaint that Life would tip his raggedy hat in his direction. Life seemed like a second voice in his head. *"You people should be imbibing life. You should be unrelenting towards it in fact."*

Maybe Nick was being narcissistic and vain, though he would've gladly lied and admitted to either, before he'd have called himself a facsimile of anything ordinary. He walked with undeniable confidence. The way Nick viewed it was, if you're not going to be happy, he'll be happy for you.

And obviously, though not without common suspicion from the people who walked the streets the orange crosswalk's words **Don't Walk** turned off and were replaced by the holy white word **Walk**. As if the deity of the traffic lights waved his mighty hand over the street corner, the unspoken duress of the crowd passed from Nick's current corner and moved to the diagonal sidewalk. And the people closest to the crosswalk stepped down onto the road and began to lead the pack once more to the almighty workplace, Nick among them. He smiled to himself and swiftly waded through the horde, attempting to reach the front of the pack. His increased pace was not due to any time schedule or the need to rush, but the desire not to follow the predetermined pace of the masses. More than his loathing of conformity, Nick hated the idea of predestination or predetermination by anyone else but himself for himself. Even the littlest thing, such as a forced walking pace by a crowd bothered him. The idea that he didn't have control over his life plagued his mind.

The Best Orgasms Come from the Universe

As Nick emerged from one cluster of people to a more open section of the sidewalk, he noticed Brutus Macky cross the street and enter a building. Just for a chuckle, he glanced to the name of the street, which read: Plum Street. With a grin to himself, Nick turned the last corner reaching his office building, where he'd spend his day coming up with ideas to further his father's old business.

CHAPTER THREE

Nick entered the building twenty minutes early. The structure housed his business, left to him by his father. His father's father was a self-made millionaire. The company he started handed out radio air, selling time in an era when radios were the only thing available. Nick's grandmother was a voice actress. When the depression struck, Nick's family diversified into a movie theatre. Back in those days movies were one of the only successful legal businesses. Nick's grandmother married his grandfather and their corporation boomed. They had seven children, six boys and one girl. Four of them died in World War Two. The other three were too young to serve. Like most patriotic boys, Nick's father and uncle collected old railroad spikes, to help the men overseas by providing them with good old rusty steel.

Later, after the death Nick's grandparents, his aunt, uncle, and father inherited the business, which changed into a filming equipment warehouse. When the Cold War stuck, Nick's uncle got scared. His uncle did the research, and found that if a nuclear war were to occur between the US and the Soviet Union, that Australia and New Zealand would be the last places affected by the radiation and other catastrophes induced by nuclear weapons. It was then

The Best Orgasms Come from the Universe

Nick's uncle sold his shares to his brother, and moved to New Zealand to become a Kiwi filmmaker. When the Cold War panic ended, Nick's uncle was already a successful film producer, and wanted nothing more from the business. Nick's father gained full control over the company when his sister became a lesbian and didn't want her sexual preference to ruin the corporation. She believed her private sex life would tarnish the family's and the business's name, so she went down south with her lover and disappeared. She too sold her shares to Nick's father.

Nick never really knew any of his family, except his father, who was deft in being a controlling perfectionist. His father's only bliss was in his son's equal unhappiness. Nick always thought it was ironic how his father wanted more than anything else for his son to be the pinnacle of all his teachings, by becoming exactly like him. It wasn't until his father was on his deathbed, that Nick forgave and thanked him, for showing him exactly what he never wished to become. His father looked at Nick as if he were a venal employee, who sold the company secrets for a shave and haircut. The old man had a look as if he'd just been extirpated from all he knew and held true. It was then that the actual ironic thing occurred; Nick's father smiled to himself as if he had premeditated the exact moment for his entire life.

Nick's father looked up and said, "Good you altruistic little prick…"

Then he died. Nick didn't cry; he wanted to laugh. He just stood there, feeling liberated; as if everything virulent clenching at his soul was lifted. Nick's youth washed away along with his diffident nature, which was replaced with a feeling of infallible pride. All the meaning to Nick's teenage life was filled with a bittersweet forgiveness towards the world. The sudden and unbiased mercy, hurt, yet in a way it felt good. Nick later called it his long awaited, unexpected, life orgasm. He refused to say his father's dying words changed him, because they didn't. Nick's life didn't change; he didn't just become happy. He always had joy inside of him. Nick simply rediscovered happiness. Before his father's death, he was merely a virgin of life, then after being laid by the universe, he realized the basic meaning of life. He understood that as soon as people stop expecting something from life or the afterlife, they'll discover or rediscover happiness, and then it's all worth it. His world began from that point on, with a permanent feeling of repose.

Upon walking through the revolving doors of the company, Nick was met by Curt and Mick. Both of them scurried forward like little pug dogs waiting for doggy biscuits from their master. Both of them looked flustered as they approached Nick, although Curt and Mick always looked anxious. More likely they were just in a regular mood and couldn't alleviate their expressions.

Both of them together didn't have an obvious aggressive bone in their bodies. Nevertheless beneath those mauve and teal suits, repressed under their assenting personalities, they reeked of a Mephistophelian nature. Nick wouldn't have been surprised in the slightest if they were both leeches for Lucifer himself, created to sap out the sanity of everyone they met. Curt and Mick knew Nick's father, and part of the inheritance contract Nick signed before taking over the company stated that he could not fire either of them unless the entire board agreed. He often visualized his father joining a Satanist cult so he could summon the two of them to torture his son after his death.

"Hi Nick," Curt exclaimed pushing his perfectly circular glasses up against his face.

The Best Orgasms Come from the Universe

"Nicolas you're early; you're never early," Mick added.

"*Nicolas, I hate when he calls me that. I wish I could fire him,*" Nick thought.

"Why are you early kiddo?" Curt questioned.

Nick hastened his gait, trying to get to the elevator.

"*I wonder how many pieces I could shatter your glasses into...*"

"You're not being very voluble this morning," Curt continued.

"*If you don't stop talking, I'm going to choke you with your own tie...*"

"Nicolas, we have news about the Emerald deal," Mick announced.

Nick turned around out of obligation, awaiting the mandatory information.

"Well Nicolas..."

"Why do I need to tell you every day to stop calling my Nicolas?" Nick questioned. "My name is Nick, just Nick."

"Well that's not what your father called you," Mick retorted. "And there was a time when you called me Uncle Mick."

"My mother named me; on my birth certificate it says Nick, not Nicolas," he answered. "My father called me Nicolas, because he hated the idea that I didn't have a full Christian name. And as far as the whole uncle thing, I was forced to say that by my father."

"Oh...now, now Nick, you don't need to get testy," Curt smiled.

"*I want you to spontaneously combust...*"

"Anyway...Nick, Mr. Carper, sent word, that he is interested in purchasing all the filming equipment, for his next big movie," Mick explained.

"Great, is there a copy of his inquiries in my office?" Nick asked.

"Why, yes of course—" Mick began to say.

"Good I'll read it in my office, if you'll excuse me," he stated before turning around to head to the elevator.

"Bye Nick," both men said as he walked off.

The elevator reached the twentieth floor and the doors opened. Nick stepped out into a long hallway. Employees milled around going about their daily activities. Making his way to his office, Nick greeted everyone with various forms of salutations. Outside his office, at a small desk sat Mary, his secretary.

"Good morning Nick."

"A very good morning indeed, Mary," Nick agreed.

"Mr. Carper's company has sent a notice about his movie deal."

"Thank you Mary," Nick said opening the door to his office.

"Can I get you anything?"

"Just a glass of milk, thank you Mary."

Nick sat quietly in his office looking over Mr. Carper's inquiry, letting his eyes slowly glaze over. Gradually he leaned back in his chair. With a quick kick of his feet, he sent his desk chair into a spin. The world around him collided into itself, as the light from outside mixed with the browns in the room. As his chair came to a leisurely stop, he leaned farther back, seeing the upside down image of his office, and the figure of a man standing in his doorway.

"I'm glad to know my boss spends as much time working as I do," the man said setting the glass of milk on Nick's desk.

"Hello Bruce," Nick responded, still leaning in his chair. "What's going on?"

"Oh I'm just stopping in," Bruce began. "Mary asked me to bring in your milk."

"I've known you for thirteen years Bruce; you never just 'stop in'," Nick countered.

Bruce didn't hear him, or wasn't listening. Nick rolled his eyes and sat up.

Even after thirteen years, Bruce and Nick's conversations never exceeded the realm of the three W's: weather, work, and women. It always seemed strange to Nick, that those three subjects were the only things Bruce, and most men for that matter, felt comfortable talking about, even after thirteen years. To Nick, thirteen years of almost daily contact and mutual friendship would have sparked at least a few more diverse topics of conversation. Instead, it was something to the effect of, "Wow, the weather sucks today," "How did **–insert name of deal here—** go?", "Guess who I had sex with last night," or some derivative of the previously stated.

"I'll never get over how much I love your office," Bruce started. "It's so...roomy, and what a view! Wow, speaking of the view, it looks like it's going to rain out there."

"Yeah...rain..."

"You know, it's the end of May and we've only seen three days of sunshine. I think April was sleeping on the job..." Bruce commented.

"Why are you here? Say something interesting or go away!"

"...I really hate all this rain," Bruce continued.

"If it wasn't raining, you'd complain about the drought!" Nick's head screamed.

"Don't you agree Nick?"

"Well, there's no real use complaining about that which you cannot change," Nick replied.

"Ha ha, funny..." Bruce began halfheartedly. "So any way, do you want to go eat brunch?"

"What time is it?"

"Almost eleven."

Nick drank his entire glass of milk in one chug and turned to look at Bruce.

"I already had a grapefruit for breakfast," Nick said.

"A grapefruit, that's not a breakfast," Bruce retorted.

"It's better to eat something than nothing. It's the most important meal of the day."

"Well it may be the most important meal of the day, but if everyone ate breakfast, what would happen to brunch?"

"True..."

"I'll tell you what, let me treat you to a bagel at Persephone's Books and Bagels; I know you love it there."

"That's bribery...and I'm your boss," Nick began, giving the thought of food a second chance.

"So is that a no?"

"Don't think I don't know what you're doing. You want to leave the office to go eat, so you don't have to work, and you think since the boss is with you, you won't get in trouble for not doing work. I swear if you weren't my friend I'd fire you."

"It's better to be at the right hand of the devil, then in his path," Bruce grinned.

"Point taken."

CHAPTER FOUR

Nick and Bruce's quest for brunch led them back through the streets. The short journey to Persephone's was filled with Bruce's constant clamor. The bookstore itself was Nick's frequent and reliable sanctuary. Like a church, where Christians go to talk to Christ, Nick went to the bookstore and talked to Persephone. Persephone, like Nick, was a bloated hog for creativity; often times they'd refer to themselves as hardcore religious fanatics of imagination.

When the two men entered Persephone's, Nick instantly felt at home. The entire place reeked of life. He breathed in the fine musk of creative eternity. Each book symbolized another writer's immortality. Somewhere on those shelves was the book of Nick's father. In fact somewhere in the store, all three of his father's books were probably for sale. He paid the quick thought of his father's success little heed and made his way to the back of the store.

In the back of the bookstore was the café, which specialized in bagels. The scent of creativity was complimented by freshly baked breads. Bruce glanced at the round wooden tables, which were all filled with other hungry bagel-snatching intellectuals. Nick looked back to notice Bruce wasn't scanning for a place for the two of them to sit, but rather, he was searching for a sighting of a beautiful woman. A woman he would undoubtedly flirt with. Nick sighed just as it happened; Bruce caught sight of **her**.

Her...that woman guys spot in a crowd of people, the kind that make everyone else disappear. The one who it doesn't matter what you have to do so long as you get to talk to her. Although many things were going on in Bruce's mind, talking wasn't one of them. Unlike in Bruce's simple mind, Nick's head was scattered with a series of thoughts.

"Wow, she's gorgeous and she's in my store...well Persephone's store, which means she's smart, or at least likes the bagels. Is she eating a bagel?" Nick started to think. *"Yup, she's eating a bagel... Gasp! (Wow an interjection, I really need to learn to think better) it's an everything-bagel. That's my favorite kind of bagel, moreover it's... (I can't believe I actually thought the word moreover). Stop it man, it doesn't matter what you think. You're looking at the most beautiful woman on the planet; think about that...stay in the moment. Oh shit, I'm staring...look away before she notices...good...don't look, don't look, don't look. Damn, I'm looking again. I wonder if she's funny. Wait what is Bruce doing? Bruce, don't walk over to her. Don't do it. Maybe if I stare at him, he'll stop. This isn't working; I should do something. I'm going to do something...do something Nick!"*

"Hey Bruce!" Nick exclaimed. "What kind of bagel do you want?"

Before Bruce could answer, Nick was attacked with a barrage of "shh's" from quiet readers all around him. Bruce turned with an odd expression, as did the beautiful woman. Bruce looked at the few paces between him and the mystifying woman. He bit his lip as he approached Nick.

"I don't care...surprise me," he sneered.

The Best Orgasms Come from the Universe

"Well, ah, I don't know what you like. I ah, never buy bagels with you," Nick explained.

"I don't really like bagels; I came here to treat **you** to a bagel because I know **you** like them," he retorted. "Now can I go back to what **I** was doing? Go get the bagels, and I'll give you the money back."

"Are you going to hit on that woman over there?" Nick whispered, glancing in her direction.

"No…"

"Come on Bruce, I've known you longer than that."

"Hey! Hey come over here," Bruce began walking Nick closer to the counter. "Don't talk so loud; she might hear."

"I was whispering."

"You weren't whispering quietly."

"What do you mean I wasn't 'whispering quietly,' the whole point to whispering is to do it quietly. I wouldn't have said I was whispering, if I wasn't whispering," Nick said as quickly as possible.

"What the hell are you saying?" Bruce questioned. "There are different levels of whispering first of all and second of all…" he paused. "I don't have time to get into it."

"Oh no, you started the argument; now prove your point," Nick said looking over to woman again.

"You're such a little kid some times," Bruce glared.

"Watch it, I'm your boss. Now explain."

"There are different levels to everything, including the area of whispering. Take a stage whisper for example. That's what you were doing, you were stage whispering. You have heard of a stage whisper before, right? That's what you do in a play when you're supposed to be whispering, but you still want the audience to know what you were saying. That's what you were doing; everyone could still hear you were whispering, and what you were whispering for that matter," Bruce elaborated starting to walk away.

"What matter?"

"What are you talking about?" Bruce sighed.

"You said 'and what you were whispering for that matter.' What matter are we speaking of, the one about me whispering, or the matter that in a stage whisper the audience still needs to hear you," Nick countered, shifting his eyes to the lady again. This time he noticed her looking back at him.

"Oh no, she's noticed me looking at her looking at me...wait?"

"Ok, what are you talking about Nick? We are not on stage, you were whispering too loud, and I am explaining my reasons for you to be quiet and shut up. We are not actors on a stage, so don't stage whisper; I'm the only one that needs to hear you."

"Well, philosophically speaking we may be just actors on a stage. So maybe in that avenue of thinking, I was whispering in a proper tone."

"We weren't speaking in a philosophical manner," Bruce said through his teeth.

"Perhaps **you** weren't, I simply thought that after thirteen years our relationship would have surpassed small talk and gone head first into deeper discussions. I guess I was moving too fast for you."

"Are you going to let me go talk to that chick now?"

"Alright, but I don't know about this whole 'area of whispering' thing. I think a stage whisper is just a kind of whisper."

"Fine, whatever, can I go back to what I was doing now?"

"Ah, ha so you were going to talk to her!"

"Yes, alright, yes, I was...now can I go do that now?"

"Absolutely, right after you buy our bagels. The truth still remains that I don't know what kind of bagel you want. Moreover—

I mean...besides that, I just don't trust the fact that you're going to pay me back if I buy the bagels."

"I'll pay you back," Bruce pleaded.

"You still owe me eighty bucks."

"From what?"

"From all the other bagels, cups of hot chocolate, lunch bills, and anything else you have said you'd pay me back for."

"Alright! Fine, I'll get the bagels."

"Good."

Nick moved away from his friend and sat himself down at one of the few open tables. When Bruce came back, he glared at Nick.

"She's gone," Bruce growled. "You kept me from talking to her and now she's gone. You wanted her for yourself didn't you?"

"I have a girlfriend."

"So why did you keep me from talking to her?"

"Do you really have to ask that question?"

"Stop trying to answer my questions with questions," Bruce hissed.

"The last time you talked to a girl in anything except a bar, you've made a fool out of yourself. Not only that, you've ruined my chance with any woman I've liked while you were around. Normally, I don't have a huge problem with that, because I don't only meet women with you. But now you're in my home, or at least a place that feels like home. I've known the owner for as long as I've been a writer, and I've been a writer since the age of five. So, if you could do me a favor by not flirting with every woman in here, I would appreciate it."

"You're a funny guy, Nick," Bruce grinned. "It doesn't matter, there are plenty of beautiful woman in the world."

"If that's a yes to my request, then thank you."

"Am I being a hypocrite?"

"You know what, Bruce?" Nick continued. "What I just said, it's not all true. I know this whole dating women thing is just a game to you, and that's fine, I guess. It's just that it isn't often I see a beautiful woman eating an everything-bagel in my favorite place in the world. I've never seen her before, and I just wanted to talk to her before you started in on the flirting. I wasn't really sure what to do because I didn't want to do anything but talk, being that I have a girlfriend and all."

"Dude, its ok, you just have call dibs next time."

Nick chuckled and scratched his head.

"You actually noticed she was eating an everything-bagel?"

"I also noticed she has bluish green eyes, reads romance novels, and plays with her hair," Nick recalled.

"Ok its obvious how you know she reads romance novels and she has green eyes, but how did you notice she plays with her hair?"

"Well she has straight hair, but several strands are really out of place. My guess is she moves her hair with her hand a lot when she reads. I'd think if she did it enough it would become out of place."

"That's weird, man," Bruce said.

"Hey, I'm a writer I need to keep my eye on the details," Nick grinned.

"Could you tell me her cup size?"

"I wouldn't know, I didn't look."

"Man, you're hopeless."

"I have a girlfriend, and besides, I'm a legs man," Nick laughed.

Nick looked down at his everything-bagel and began eating it contently. Bruce scoped the room with his eyes a bit, before cutting his plain bagel with a plastic knife. Nick continued to eat in peace, watching as Bruce smeared strawberry cream cheese all over his bagel. It was then, watching him, that Nick realized that of all the people in the world, he was probably Bruce's best friend. Beyond all thought over the thirteen years, Nick finally noticed, in all Bruce's sheer simplicity, he was a good friend.

In many ways, Bruce was probably Nick's best friend, although not his favorite. It became strange to Nick, that the idea of best and favorite were so interchangeable, especially in the case of friendship. It was then he agreed with himself that "Best Friend" did not mean, "Greatest Friend." The term of "Best Friend" came to mean his truest friend, the one who would stick with him during the best and worst times, and judge sparingly. Nick knew that Bruce would be an honest and fair friend, who'd say what he means. This made Nick realize above anything else, that he needed to put forth the same respect.

"You know, I'm actually kind of surprised how good of a friend you are," Nick began.

"Nick, like you said: 'it's just a game to me,'" Bruce explained. "It's all part of the fun."

"No, I'm not talking about her; I'm talking about you. You're a true friend. I've known you since before my father died, and you've always been a good friend. I've just never really seen it and I don't think I have reciprocated your friendship."

"You're my best friend Nick; you've always been great to me. I don't have many friends. The few I have are just jokers; their opinions don't mean anything to me. You're my true friend, I thought you knew that?"

"No, I didn't. But I don't want to say you're my best friend. I can't say it. Things like that are thrown around, and they lose there meaning. I assure you though, of my real friends you have always been there for me. As far as I'm concerned you are the best of my friends."

Bruce grinned and Nick took another bite from his bagel.

Nick's brunch lasted over two hours. Bruce opened up conversations enough for thirteen years in one discussion. He explained the story of how he had a son, named Burt, who lives in Arizona. He elaborated on his belief in Jesus and his hopes for the future. He talked for an hour and a half all about his ideas on life, and magic, and justice, and law, and politics, and all the other things Nick never believed Bruce envisioned. Nick offered his uncommon views of life, calling himself more pagan than not. As their dialogue wore into midday, Nick soon realized that their chats about the three W's were as much his fault as Bruce's. Nick decided a friendship is as meaningful as you make it.

CHAPTER FIVE

Nick entered into his luxury apartment at around seven-thirty.

"Hello," someone called from the kitchen.

"Hi, I picked us up some Chinese food," Nick announced.

"I thought you were dieting," the call came once again.

"I've already lost thirty six pounds. I don't think a little Chinese food will hurt," Nick responded.

Nick set his keys and wallet on an end table and continued to the kitchen.

"I left a message on your machine," Nick continued. "I guess you got it if you're here."

As Nick came to the kitchen, his girlfriend came to the entrance.

"I can't stay long," she said. "I just need to talk to you."

"Talk?" Nick thought suspiciously. *"I've heard that to many times not to be worried."*

She turned around and sat at a small table in the kitchen. Nick put the paper bag of Chinese food on the counter and sat next to her.

"What's wrong?" Nick asked.

"Nick you're a really nice, great guy..." she began.

"I think I see where this is going," Nick thought.

27

"...and I just love the time we've spent together."

"She's either asking my hand in marriage or dumping me."

"It's just, you're not what I need right now," she continued.

"What do you need, that I haven't done?"

"It's not you it's me..."

"I hate when woman say that! No, if it were you, I'd be the one being the dick, by dumping you," Nick hissed in his head.

"There's nothing wrong with you," Nick said reassuringly.

"Except your dumping me, without a real reason!"

"Well I just feel so bad about this, you're such a great guy," she began.

"Yes you said that already."

"I mean you're nice, romantic, passionate, funny..." she started to say.

"Great playing to my ego."

"...and you're a great lover, it's just..." she continued.

"Just what?"

"Our names don't match," she said hesitantly.

"Excuse me?"

"What? That's the stupidest thing I've ever heard. And that means a lot because I've heard some really dumb things in my time," Nick started. "I mean really why are you breaking this off?"

"I shouldn't need to give any explanation! I don't want to be together!" She said standing up.

"Maybe she met someone else."

"Yes, actually you do. You do need to give me an explanation. If I'm as great as you say I am, I deserve at least that much!"

She started out of the kitchen to the foyer, without looking at Nick.

"I'm leaving," she said over her shoulder.

"Wait, I know what it is, you met someone else," Nick assumed, following her. "You met someone; maybe you were even with him, before now. You wanted to let me down easy, so I wouldn't know."

"That's not...it's not...it's just, he..." she stuttered, in the doorway.

"...Treats you like shit!" Nick said finishing her sentence. "Everyone wants a nice guy, between every couple of dickheads! Well excuse me if I wanted our relationship to be more than a one night stand."

"You know maybe I was wrong," she started, walking out the door and to the now open elevator leading to the downstairs, "maybe you aren't a nice guy, because you can be a real asshole!"

"Good maybe than some beautiful, smart, funny woman will dump her nice boyfriend for me!" Nick retorted as she walked out towards the elevator.

Nick stood in the doorway watching the elevator close and the numbers on the dial change as she went down the floors. He thought at first without words, about running after her and apologizing. Then he realized he had nothing to apologize for. He stood there reminiscing about the cold winter they spent together. He introduced her to Boris, in hopes they would hit it off after her last bad experience. It turned out she was interested in Nick, and not Boris. He dated her all through the end of autumn, the entire winter, and the first half of spring. Beautiful woman always love nice guys for the colder seasons. The idea of being shallow was adopted from men by women after they gained the right to vote.

Nick closed the door and walked back to the kitchen.

"Way to go Nick," he said to himself.

"I hate being a nice guy..." he thought.

Nick sat himself back in the kitchen, with the companionship of the Chinese food. It wasn't long before he stopped rustling through the paper bag with the kung-fu panda on it. He glanced blankly at the bear kicking the bamboo shaft. The panda's devious grin grated on Nick's sanity.

"What are you looking at?" Nick asked.

The panda was unfazed.

"I bet the guy that trained that panda made a lot of money on his book, if he has a book. What am I talking about? If someone trained a panda bear in kung-fu, I think they would have written a book. I should be working on my book."

With that thought, Nick took up the bag of food and headed to his dining room, which was connected to the living room. The opposite wall was made of windows, and Nick could see it had started to rain. He opened the windows just enough to let the cool air in. After letting the air pass over him, he picked up a remote and turned on his CD changer. He could here it selecting a random CD. Most of the music was from the seventies and early eighties. Music was one of the few things he had in common with his father. As the CD began to play, Nick found himself singing along to the song as he retrieved his laptop. It wasn't long until he sat down in his beautifully carved wooden chair at his equally well crafted antique wooden table and began typing. Writing and eating at the same time was a skill he perfected.

While most writers would be disturbed by loud seventies music playing while they write, Nick was actually soothed by it. The music kept his subconscious busy while he wrote. Without the music, his writing would often be outpaced by his ideas, making his stories jumbled and inevitably indecipherable. Every now and again, like most people when they try to concentrate, even the slightest thing distracts him. When this occurs, Nick finds himself singing aloud to a song without recognizing he's doing it, at first. Nevertheless, this break often helps for his ideas to recollect themselves.

Even more than the music, the rain helped Nick, especially in the early morning or late at night. The sound, smell, and overall subliminal feel of the rain filled him with creativity and even more drive to work on his writing. Often times when Nick couldn't get a line the way he wanted it to sound, he'd stop his writing and the music to go listen to the rain. He would listen and look out his window at the streetlights reflected off the puddles. The cars driving by would make a very distinct sound, which always helped him to regain his concentration.

The perfect company of Chinese food, music, and rain, made Nick's creative juices all flow correctly. In the milliseconds before his brain told his fingers to type, he could physically feel the imaginative gem formed by the pressure of his mind, as a diamond or ruby made over millions of years in a dormant volcano. For that seemingly immeasurable amount of time, Nick sensed the cosmos was getting frisky. When creating anything, one should acknowledge life, and its desire for a bit of foreplay. When producing anything, one generates something for his or her partial immortality, whether it's in the form of writing, art, construction, or even childbirth. These things help to extend one's life into that of others.

Creating in itself was one of the key reasons for Nick's personal belief that there is no need for heaven above if you can't find heaven on earth. If you can find heaven on earth, why would anyone want or need a heaven above. Heaven shouldn't be a place of perfection, it should be a place where you have found happiness and can stay to help others reach that point as well. A utopian world, in real life or the afterlife would defeat the purpose of living. Part of the point in achieving greatness, enlightenment, bliss, purity, or any other "higher state" is to do it despite your inadequacies. Why not enjoy life for what is, instead of what you wish it was?

CHAPTER SIX

FRIDAY

Nick wrote all through the night and into the morning. The rain died down, but he could still hear the cars driving over the puddles. Nick was so tired, he wasn't tired anymore. After one single highpoint in his weariness, he could feel the exhaustion pass. He couldn't sleep now if he wanted to. Throughout the night, he went through many stages in his creative process, including one that involved destruction.

During the climax in a good writing pace, a writer can become quite furious by even the most minuscule of annoyances, including things such as, the phone ringing constantly, a dog barking, or in Nick's case, sitting in an uncomfortable chair. The best way for the annoyance to be relieved was to deal with it right away, so as not to get angry or overly stressed-out. Unfortunately, for most writers and especially Nick, once he was in his climax state, he didn't want to stop for anything. Nick, not having been one who usually experiences stress, paid the annoyance of his chair little heed at first. The buildup quickly came to a head when Nick shifted his weight to get comfortable, and found an even more undesirable spot.

The discomfort made the writing progression difficult and resulted in Nick getting up, lifting the chair off the ground, and smashing it numerous times into one of the support beams of the apartment. He did this until all that was left in his hands were two very cracked chair legs.

He entered his bedroom and quickly wheeled out his desk chair. If it wasn't for the stereo system, sound of rain, and wall of windows being in the living room, Nick would have probably worked in his bedroom, like he usually did. Nick continued his writing, getting back into the flow of things in his very comfortable wheelie chair. Within twelve minutes he was back in his constant creative stream.

In the space of ten hours Nick had written two hundred and thirty pages. When he put on the final changes to his rough draft he sang the song that played on the stereo as loud as possible. After he finished writing, he rolled through the dining and living rooms still singing to another song. As the next song ended, he slid his chair to where he placed the remote, and turned off all the accoutrements to his stereo system. The clock on the CD player read seven thirty before he shut it down. Nick rolled to his cordless phone and called Boris.

"Hello? This better be important..." someone answered hesitantly.

"Hi, Boris?"

"Speaking."

"Hey it's Nick, I finished my book. I saved it on a disk, and I was wondering if I could come over with it. I'd have emailed it, but my online service is down."

"It's kind of early Nick."

"You're an early riser, Boris."

The Best Orgasms Come from the Universe

"I was up late last night. I'll tell you what, how about I come over to you?"

"I'm turning off my laptop as we speak. It's really starting to overheat, because I've been writing since about eight last night. Why can't I just come over with it?"

"Well...I ah..."

"This isn't like him."

"I have someone here with me, and well, they are staying," Boris explained.

"Someone's spent the night?"

"Yeah."

"Did the two of you spend the night...together?"

"Yeah."

"Oh, well let me come over, I'd love to meet her."

"Well...you see..."

"What is it Boris?"

"You can't."

"Why not, I've tried to hook you up with someone for a long time and..." Nick started.

"Oh, my gosh, is Boris gay?"

"...Wait Boris, who's over?" Nick questioned.

"A friend...just came over and..." Boris went silent.

Nick could hear something on the other end of the phone.

"Boris, this is going to sound really weird if I'm wrong, but, Boris are you gay?" Nick finally asked.

"No, it's not that...yes."

"Oh..." Nick was speechless a moment. "Well that's great, when did you find out?" he continued excitedly.

"Wow I just made it sound like he was pregnant, that certainly wasn't my intention."

"You're happy about this?"

"Hell yeah. If it's what makes you happy."

"Oh, I ah...don't really know what to say. I didn't expect anyone to be happy about this."

"Are you happy about this?" Nick asked.

"I'm kind of worried, actually. I'm a Christian, and well a lot of people are going to look at me differently now, including God," Boris explained.

"That's bullshit," Nick exclaimed. "Well the part about people looking at you differently is true, but that's because they're ignorant and they all believe love is something simple that can only be applied to 'normal' things. How can they love God, when really God is the pinnacle of abnormality?"

"What are you talking about?"

"Think about it, God supposedly created everything and loves everything. The 'normal' person doesn't love everything or everyone, and since God does, that would technically make him abnormal. If people judge you because of your sexual preference, when you aren't taking advantage of animals, children, or dead people, they are basically flat out wrong. And to say God doesn't love you because of your feelings is not only wrong; it's blasphemous based on their very religion. If God exists, he's going to love you no matter what, and if you believe in heaven, you're going in so long as you are a good person. I think if God does exist, he or she would be crying over what is said or done in his name. The only thing any all-knowing, all-powerful, omnipotent being should want from the so called people it created, is that they are happy without causing anyone else unhappiness. Why would an infinite energy want or need people to believe in it to feel good about itself? People believe in God because they choose to. If God exists, I believe he wouldn't want that. God doesn't want only his or her word passed on; God wants any good words passed on, so long as people get the idea. You're a good person, Boris, and as far as I know, God is not going to judge you because you love a man over a woman. And as far as people go, someone is always going to dislike you, or what you do, or what you say, so don't worry about it. That's what I believe; you can take it for what it's worth."

"Hey, Nick."

"Yeah?"

"Could you run that by me again? I'm trying to write that down," Boris started. "I've known you a long time; have you always spoken in monologues?"

"Funny."

"Do you still want to come by, with that book? You can meet Alfred."

"Sure, let me just get one thing out in the open, I am not gay," Nick announced.

"I know Nick; I'll see you when you get here. We'll print it off on my computer, and go have breakfast."

"Alright, bye."

Nick turned off the cordless and put it back on the cradle. After taking a shower, he left for Boris' home.

CHAPTER SEVEN

"Making Left Hand Turns on A One Way Street from a One Way Street," Boris read. "Well that's quite a title."

"Once you read it, the title will make more sense," Nick explained.

"I think it's a very poetic title," Alfred said.

"Thank you Alfred," Nick replied. "Where should we go for breakfast?"

"Well we could take your novel to Persephone's, that way if I finish it you could show it to her," Boris responded.

"Sounds alright to me," Alfred agreed. "What do you think Nick?"

"Yeah."

When Nick entered the bookstore, the normal smell of creativity was gone. The aroma was replaced with the distinct odor of a congested ancient bazaar. The entire building was crammed full of people. The inhabitants mingled throughout the front bookstore and back café. Several queues of people led to something or another. One group of people which resembled a line was aiming at the registers, where three very rushed looking employees hustled to ring up various orders. All the people inside held one book in particular, although Nick could not make out what it was. Another line forged toward the café counter, which rapidly distributed free half bagels to whoever wished one.

This gathering of people was a tradition Nick never experienced on the receiving end. Some called this congregation a book promotion, an activity which most published writers knew well. A grouping of people all arriving to have the book you wrote signed for them. It was an experience Nick loathed all because he had never experienced it. He could sense the excitement of some successful creator. Nick's instinct told him it was a first timer, a virgin to success in writing. He knew this because of the crowd. This mob in particular, was the group that usually only came to a new writer's signing.

"*The vultures,*" Nick thought. "*They just want the book, in case the author becomes famous. They don't care about the work.*"

Nick recognized Boris' lethargic expression. Boris was recalling his first publication, his first book, a collection of what he called "American" poetry. Nick was there when Boris was given immortality. The gaze on Boris' face was like no other. At the time it seemed to Nick as if his friend had just seen all the meaning in his world. The experience was something like when a dog or cat is in heat, when their primitive imagination has just kicked in. Nothing in the world mattered for those few seconds in Boris' life. That short time was just for him, and it would be held in his subconscious forever. Boris had achieved his life goal; his place in the lunch line of history was saved by his soda can. For no matter how insignificant a can may seem, it was enough to hold his place of immortality. From that point on, Boris had a huge weight lifted off his shoulders. He no longer worried about being forgotten.

As Nick and Boris waded through the crowd, they could see the author of the book of the hour. The expression as previously described was found on the author's face as well. From across the store, Nick looked into the author's eyes and concentrated a moment.

"Daren Hill is the oldest thirty year-old in his family. Daren was the runt of his mother's quintuplet delivery," Nick thought of the writer, as he waited in line with Boris. *"His mother was pregnant nine times, having a total of fifteen children, including: six normal births, two sets of twins, and the quintuplet. Daren was always the smallest, and although he shared the age of four other siblings, he was still treated as the youngest, due to his size. He always earned straight A's in school, though he never exerted himself enough to go into honors or advanced classes. Even though Daren didn't hit puberty till the age of twenty, he still acted the oldest. He soon started noticing his bodily changes and grew into quite the attractive fellow. With all the sudden attention of women, Daren soon realized he had a gift with the ladies. With his dashing good looks, superior mental maturity, and his willingness to experiment, Daren quickly became quite the ladies man. He then took full advantage of his talent, and became a highly paid gigolo in France. Three years prior to this very day, he came back to America and began his book about his unique profession."*

Nick stepped out of line and Boris turned to him.

"Don't you want to meet the author?" Boris inquired.

"I don't want to know his name, his book's name, or anything else about him," Nick declared.

"You made him into a character didn't you?" Boris questioned.

"As a matter of fact, I did, his name is Daren Hill," Nick began, "but that isn't why I don't want to meet him. I'm not really in the mood to see **that** expression. I don't want to see it again until I publish my book."

"Ok, but I hear his book is really insightful," Boris said.

"I know. It's about being a gigolo in France," Nick answered. "I'll try to find us a seat."

"Try to find Alfred too, if you can. He seems to have disappeared with your book."

After a short time, Nick found an open wooden table. He sat down and Alfred seemed to materialize out of thin air when he appeared next to Nick.

"Hi, Nick," Alfred announced. "I got the autograph of the author. He's going to be famous."

"Oh...great."

"Do you want to see it?" Alfred asked, removing a large stack of paper.

"No," Nick replied. "Wait, is that my manuscript?"

Alfred flipped the stack over and noticed Nick's title page, which read: Making Left Hand Turns on a One Way Street from a One Way Street.

"Oh dear," Alfred began. "I'm sorry Nick...I've always been a bit of an ass."

"No, its ok, Alfred."

"Here, you keep this and I'll get something else signed."

"Well it's really—" Nick began.

"No, no, it was my mistake."

Alfred disappeared nearly as quickly as he arrived. Nick sat quietly, looking over to the long lines of people. Boris had gotten out of his place to talk to someone he knew farther down the row. Alfred joined Boris' new conversation. Daren was off using the bathroom, so the line wasn't moving. Nick peered around trying to find someone he knew. Then he saw **her**.

CHAPTER EIGHT

"Is that her? It is her...from yesterday," Nick thought. "She's sitting alone, and she's wearing another skirt. I really shouldn't look at her legs; she'll think I'm trying to see her panties (Wow that's a stupid word). Underwear...that's kind of stupid also. Wow, she has great legs...ok it's time to stop looking. Wait...I'm single...and she's alone. Damn she has great legs— Stop it! Ok, I'm going to go talk to her. Is she eating? Don't look at her legs...no she is not eating. At least not that I notice. Maybe it's on her lap— No! I will not look at her legs. I could offer to buy her breakfast. Oh man, she is playing with her hair, I was right, she does twirl her hair. She has great hair...ok you're not accomplishing anything Nick. (I wonder if her playing with her hair means it's a boring part or a really good part in her book) Nick, you don't know her well enough to try to analyze her habits. So go over there and talk to her. Well I don't want to disturb her if she's in a really good part, then again it could be a bad part, and then now would be the perfect time to talk to her. Well she could— No! I'm going over there now. Get up Nick!"

Nick got up from his chair and walked over to her.

"I can't believe I'm doing this, I need more confidence...wait, no I don't," Nick contemplated as he wondered over to her. "I have plenty *o, confidence; I'm allowed to be nervous; this is the most beautiful woman in the world. Oh no, she may be involved with someone. Of course she's involved with someone, she gorgeous. Oh well, it's to late now, I'm here...and more importantly so is she. How long has it been since I saw her? Well let's think...wait I'm here...say something,"* Nick didn't say anything at first.

The lady glanced up from her book.

"Say something...Ni...wait what's my name. Check your ID, no wait that would look weird. Oh never mind, you need to say something, wing it."

"Hi my name's Mick, no Nick, Nick!" he exclaimed. "My name is Nick."

"Good recovery...ass."

"Oh...hi," she said holding her book open. "Oh I remember you, from yesterday. I saw you looking at me."

"Oh no...quick say something funny."

"Yes well they say if you look at someone long enough without them knowing, they'll still look up, because of your energy."

"I think that's the strangest pick up line I've ever heard."

"It's been about twenty-one hours since I saw her last."

"Well I'd imagine you get a lot of them...I mean. Well, it's not exactly a pick up line."

"I was kidding."

"Another fine mess you got yourself into."

"Right...well I just want to talk to you and maybe find out your name. I've never seen you here before, well excluding yesterday."

"Well I know your name, and you don't know mine. I'd say I have the advantage..."

"I don't mind, having a woman above me..."

The Best Orgasms Come from the Universe

"You didn't just say that!"

"Do you always say the first thing that comes to your head?" she asked putting her bookmark into her book.

"Not nearly..."

"I can only imagine the things you'd say if you did," she said grinning.

"It has a mind of its own," Nick agreed.

"Your mind has a mind of its own? Sounds like a serious personal problem."

"The say two heads are better than one, so I'd guess two minds is at least almost as good, and besides there's no use complaining about that which you cannot change."

"Does that mean you don't complain?" She asked. "Because by that logic, you're saying that if you can't change it, there is no use complaining about it. Although if you can change it, you shouldn't complain about it anyway, you should try to change it."

"No, I've been known to complain from time to time."

"Not about the weather I hope, I can't stand when people complain about the weather, it's raining get over it."

"Wow! Nick you need to marry this woman."

"I couldn't agree more," a short pause came over the conversation before Nick continued. "So I was wondering if I could treat you to breakfast."

"What do you have in mind?"

"Well, we are in a bagel shop. Could I buy you a bagel?"

"Yeah, a bagel sounds good."

"Would you like to come with me to wait in line, it could take a while," Nick said pointing at the breakfast crowd.

"Well actually, I'd prefer to wait, I'm in a really good part in my book."

"Wow, beaten by a book," Nick grinned. "I'll settle for you name."

She didn't say anything for a short time.

"Why are you smiling?" she asked smiling back.

"I'm not entirely sure, why are you smiling?"

"Because, that line is pretty intimidating; I think I should probably go with you I wouldn't want you to get lost."

"Shall we then?"

Nick and the mysterious woman, who plays with her hair, walked together to the bagel line.

"She has nice skin. What am I saying...she has nice everything, although specifics always sound better. A name would help?" Nick thought as they reached the end of the line.

"So what's your name?"

"Well, what do you think my name is?"

"What?"

"If you had to guess, what would you guess by just looking me?"

"Let me think a second."

"I'm in a bagel line with a gorgeous woman, with great legs, perfect straight hair, a beautiful smile which I hope I see more of, and the most beautiful eyes I've ever seen. Now she has just asked me to guess what her name is, there is a story here somewhere I know it (why do I feel the need to narrate this experience). Maybe because it's to go to be true, I mean it's not every day you get to treat a girl to an everything-bagel. What am I talking about? I should be thinking about her name. Ok, I should search her eyes; it works in movies all the time. I just look deeply into her eyes, and it will come."

For about half a minute Nick looked into her bluish green eyes, and searched for a name. He grinned a bit, and she smiled.

"Terra...her names Terra, yup that's definitely it, Terra Jones. No you're not making a story about her."

"You look like a Terra to me," Nick stated.

"No..."

"Was I close?"

"Well, sort of, it is five letters and it does end in the letter 'a'."

"Well it works in the movies. So what is your name?"

"Leila, Leila Jones," she said.

"Leila Jones..."

"Yeah, why."

"Oh nothing, that was just going to be my second guess."

"Jones...wow, I'm good."

"So Nick, why did you want to meet me?"

"Because I saw you eating an everything-bagel."

"What?"

"I just happened to notice, that you were eating an everything-bagel yesterday. I just had to meet you. All the meaning in the world can be found from an everything-bagel."

"Well that's a first..."

"No actually, it's not every day I see a beautiful woman I don't recognize inside my favorite place in the world. I come here everyday and I've never seen you before. When I saw you, I had to convince myself that I wasn't daydreaming."

"I want to compliment her. I want her to smile. I wanna say, 'Leila, I just couldn't take my eyes off you from the very second I saw you.' That's such a cliché. I wish I could just kiss her right now, so I'd stop thinking about it. I shouldn't compliment her again so soon, it's not tasteful. I wish this were simple. No I don't...if it were simple, getting to know her wouldn't be as much fun," Nick thought as they continued to talk.

"You think I'm beautiful," Leila blushed a bit.

Nick looked at her again.

"Yes..."

"Well, it's not everyday someone says that to me."

"Really?" Nick questioned. "I would think you hear it everyday."

"You'd be surprised," Leila began. "I'm going to let you in on a little secret, women are starved for compliments and romance these days."

"Funny, it doesn't seem that way."

"I'm only telling you this because, you seem to be the kind of guy that already knows it, and just doesn't realize it."

"You've only known me for about ten minutes, tops."

"I have an extra sense for people," Leila explained. "Are you a romantic, Nick?"

"I try..."

"The thing about romantics is that they're rarely verbally appreciated. A romantic isn't truly valued until he's gone," Leila said.

Before Nick could answer, the column shifted and the two of them arrived to the front of the line.

"May I help you?" the employee asked.

"Oh hi, Andréa," Nick said recognizing her, "two everything-bagels, please. Thank you."

"Only butter on the bottom half, right Nick?" Andréa confirmed.

"That's right. Would you like anything on your everything-bagel, Leila?"

"Cream cheese please, Andréa," Leila answered.

When Nick and Leila sat back at the table, Nick couldn't help but stare at her cream cheesed bagel.

"I'd like to know what women you're talking to, about this whole starving for romance thing. I mean I know women like it, but starving for it...that's a little much."

"It's true," Leila said smiling. "I have some friends who have been dating the same guy for years, and never has he even given her a flower or a box of chocolates."

"Wow, no chocolates!" Nick exclaimed. "The last two girls I gave chocolates to got insulted. You women are vicious sometimes. I felt like they were going to kill me. They started going on for about an hour on how if they accepted the chocolates, it would make them fat."

"Well even if they say they don't want them, they still do."

"Think of it this way, if all guys were romantics, then they wouldn't be special anymore." Nick said. "I'd still like to meet these, strange women though."

"Hey, be careful of what you say, I'm one of them," she smiled, before taking a bite of her bagel. She noticed Nick's eyes wander to her bagel. "Why do you keep staring at my bagel?"

"I'm just trying to stay calm as you butcher that poor bagel. It should be illegal for people to put anything on an everything-bagel. The entire point of it being called an everything-bagel, is because it has everything it needs."

"You put butter on yours," Leila retorted with a grin. "You hypocrite."

"Actually, I only put butter on the bottom half; you see that's acceptable because, the bottom doesn't have as much of everything, but cream cheese, is just plain blasphemous. It's like wearing knee-highs when your wearing a skirt, it's just not right."

"You sound very set in your ways."

"Well some things shouldn't be messed with."

"Like good songs."

"And good books made into movies. Bagels are a big one. I'll forgive you this time because you don't wear knee-highs...you don't right."

"Not if I can help it."

It was then Boris and Alfred walked up.

"Hi Nick," Alfred said. "Who's this lovely lady?"

"Leila, this is my friend Boris and my new friend Alfred," Nick said.

"Pleasure," Boris began. "Are you going to come back to the table, Nick?"

"Yeah I'll be over in a minute," Nick answered before turning to Leila. "I thoroughly enjoyed having breakfast with you Leila."

"Yeah, it was nice talking with you," Leila agreed.

"I'd like to see you again."

"That'd be nice."

"Are you going to be here tomorrow?"

"I don't normally come in on weekends. I usually stop in here either before work, or on my lunch break. I work down the street at a winery."

"Oh..."

"But I will come in tomorrow at around nine, if you're thinking about stopping in."

"Yes...and yes...I will be here."

"Why did you say yes twice?"

"The first one yes was to your question, and the second yes was like, 'yes, this is good,' or vise versa." Nick explained.

"Oh, well I'll see you then, and I'll treat you to a bagel."

"Tomorrow," Nick said walking off.

The Best Orgasms Come from the Universe

"Ok, that worked well, you can fall to the ground anytime now. You have a second date, I mean meeting...well technically speaking, it is a date...we have set a date for our second meeting. It may not be a romantic date. You are going to see her again tomorrow... Leila...she is so...great. I wonder if she's smiling, don't look...it will be so much cooler if you just keep walking. Don't turn around...quick think of big words that will distract your mind...culmination, ambiguous, conundrum, xenophobic..."

Despite Nick's efforts, he peered over his shoulder, and found Leila glancing back at him from over her book.

"You looked...you need to take charge of your life. If you say to yourself, 'I'm not going to do something,' and then you do, you deserve to be punished."

When Nick sat down both Boris and Alfred looked at him with wide eyes.

"Who was that," Alfred asked.

"I saw you flirting," Boris announced. "What happened to that girl you tried to hook me up with. You guys were going pretty strong."

"She dumped me..."

"Oh why?" Alfred asked.

"Her answer was really ambiguous," Nick said putting the emphasis on the word ambiguous. "By the culmination of our discussion, I felt as if I was trapped in some inescapable conundrum...and..."

"Xenophobic...how can I..."

"I think she was xenophobic or something," Nick continued.

"She had a fear of strangers and foreigners?" Boris questioned.

"Yeah, she hated them..." Nick reassured.

"What are you talking about Nick?" Boris questioned once again.

"I'm trying to discipline myself."

"By what, using big words?" Alfred replied.

"Well, there is this thing I do, when I'm trying to stop thinking about something. I think of really uncommon words to take my mind off of what I'm trying not to think about. When it doesn't work, I try to force myself to use them in sentences in the context of my conversations."

"You are a strange man Nick, but I like you," Alfred said.

"Oh, well you can go back and talk to her, while I read your novel," Boris offered.

"I don't want to overwhelm her, I'll wait until tomorrow."

CHAPTER NINE

Boris was a fast reader. He plowed through Nick's entire book, in one hour. He sat at a separate table, to concentrate. Meanwhile, Nick learned all he'd ever need to know about Alfred. Alfred told him about his childhood, his dreams of being a stage actor, and his favorite performances. He described at length his discovery of being gay, and how it affected his father. The last thing to come up before Boris finished Nick's book, was Alfred's fear of anything yellow.

"It's a new disease. I can't touch anything yellow, and if I look at anything yellow for to long I faint," Alfred explained.

"You're kidding right?" Nick asked.

"No, I can't touch anything yellow," Alfred said.

"How do you take a piss?"

"I only drink water," Alfred answered.

"Sounds like a pretty severe phobia."

"Last time I was truly traumatized, was at the age of seventeen," Alfred started. "My Dad thought it was just some crazy thing I made up...being afraid of yellow I mean. So one day he grabbed me and tied me to yellow lawn chair, with yellow colored scotch tap. I went ballistic; I broke my arm and three ribs, trying to get out. I was flailing the entire time, but he...my dad I mean...he was really strong. He tried to hold me down. When I got out, I didn't stop throwing up for six days. Well not constantly, but on and off, for six days. You and Boris are the only two people alive I've ever told about this."

Nick could see Alfred's eyes fill up with water.

"My father was an asshole, but he never did anything like that," Nick admitted.

"It wasn't really the pain that bothered me...he was just so damn, sad. He was a sad old ignorant man."

"It's not your fault, you know that right. You didn't do anything wrong, you know that don't you?"

"My father was a wreck after my mother died. He disowned me after he found out I was gay. He never really liked me. I was never tough enough to join the football team, or smart enough to be in honors. I was his only son," Alfred said and then quickly he changed the subject. "I wonder if Boris is almost done with your book."

It wasn't much longer before Boris returned with Nick's manuscript. Boris sat back down at the table and no one said anything for quite some time. Nick thought he'd have to start off the conversation.

"What exactly are you trying to say?" Boris asked.

"What do you mean?"

"I don't understand your message Nick," Boris explained.

"What do you mean?"

"Stop saying that, I'm just saying that I don't understand what you are trying to say in your book. I don't understand what you're trying to say." Boris repeated. "I don't get the message."

The Best Orgasms Come from the Universe

"Why does a book have to have a message? I mean so long as you have a good story. You write fantasy. Do any of your books have a message?"

"Yes, they do. It's showing a different view, and a different world. The message can be found in the character's actions. However, that's not my point. A nonfiction...well a less-fictional book."

"Less-fictional?"

"When writing a philosophical drama, like this book is, you need a message. A book with philosophy should have an overall meaning to the reader. It makes your story have more depth."

"But in life, not everyone has something deeper to them," Alfred said.

"I agree, and besides my book does have a deeper meaning. The guy in the story doesn't change, because he doesn't choose to change. That's the point. While people show you things in life, it's up to you to change yourself. People try to change the central character, but he chooses not to. He changes his path, but it doesn't matter because he doesn't change himself, thus the title: "Making Left Hand Turns on a One Way Street from a One Way Street.""

"I get it. That's the only time you can make left turns on a red light," Alfred said.

"Exactly, but you have to be turning onto another one way street. The point is there is never just one way to do anything."

"I get it," Alfred began. "I haven't even read the book yet, and I already get it. Do you get it now Boris."

"But there is only one way to make left turns on red lights..."

"Unless you break the law," Alfred chimed in.

"Right...Well, it's a nice idea," Boris said. "I don't think it will sell, but its a nice idea."

"I'd read it," Alfred interjected.

"Yes well, most people don't read about real life anymore."

"I disagree Boris. I think people need more real life, a real life different from their own. They want to read it. People are just too afraid of their opinions these days. So if I must have a message, that would be it."

"Well you seem to repeat that basic message a lot throughout the dialogue," Boris added.

"I did repeat myself a bit; people in real life repeat themselves all the time. People are afraid of their own opinions. There I just did it. I repeated myself. I'm not afraid of being judged, because like I told you earlier today, people are going to do it no matter what you do. I might as well just say what's on my mind. That's the only time my mind gives me any peace. Think about it, the only time you aren't thinking about what to say next in a conversation, is when you speak straight from yourself, and say what you mean."

"I think you're a better promotional speaker than you are a writer," Boris jeered.

"Well, other than all that, did you at least like some of it?"

"Well you know I'm harsh on you, Nick. It's important that I criticize you as bluntly and harshly as possible, so you can improve as a writer. I've always loved your writing, Nick, it's always very…ah …poetic."

"Are you suggesting I'm a flowery writer?"

"Not really, well a little bit. I prefer the adjective graceful; you're a graceful writer. The problem with poetic writing is if it's not in a poem it may sound out of place. I'd never want to see you stop writing. I love your overall idea, and that alone is reason enough for me to read it. Your characters are very real, it's just some of them just don't fit in. I'd get rid of some of them, there are a few too many."

"Well, I'll look it over," Nick said. "I appreciate your help, and respect your ideas."

"I'll read it when I get a chance Nick," Alfred stated. "It's on Boris' computer. I look forward to looking it over."

"I'm anxious to hear your opinion, Alfred."

"You should go and show it to Persephone," Boris said. "Like I told you yesterday, I haven't written any drama since that screenplay a couple of years ago. Persephone is an expert; if she likes it, you know you've accomplished something. She reads all those philosophy books. She prefers real life stuff, so you should take her word over mine."

"I'm going to do that Boris, thanks. I know you two probably had plans, I'm very glad you included me. It seems this book signing is dying down; I'm going to see if Persephone is in. It was nice meeting you Alfred."

"Bye Nick."

Nick sat inside the store for abut an hour, reading over his book. In that time employees went about their business, cleaning and reorganizing. Persephone was nowhere to be seen. After the first hour rolled into the second, Nick realized soon he would need to stop in at his job. He scanned the store one last time and roamed the isles. He caught sight of Andréa and walked up to her.

"Hey Andréa, I was wondering if you'd do me a favor? Could you give this to Persephone when she comes in? Nick asked handing her his novel.

"Well actually, Persephone is at home sick."

"Yeah, I figure as much, she'd have been here for the book signing. Thank you for your help, have a nice day," Nick said starting to leave.

"You too Nick."

CHAPTER TEN

The streets outside were riddled with puddles. The people on the sidewalks and inside their cars looked even more hesitant towards life. Their expressions changed overnight from the slightly droopy, agitated look to a down right glaring discontent. The rain seemed to bring them all the affirmation that anger was the best way to feel "better" about themselves. They all went from just thinking that their lives were terrible, to positively knowing their live were terrible.

Everyone seemed to be walking in dark browns, blacks, and grays. All of them dressed to match their moods. All of them save Nick. He strutted down the street in his bright red button-down shirt and blue jeans. He looked like a pinhole of sunshine leaking out of the "depressing" cloud cover. Everyone stared at him disdainfully, as if he were frolicking in the nude. Nick imagined other people looking at Leila with similar prying eyes, as she passed by in her short skirt.

Nick stopped at his usual small Chinese restaurant. Outside he could see the florescent lit panda. The puddles shined like a pool of paints, reflected from the colored image of the bear. He shuffled inside the pointlessly air-conditioned store. The same monotonous flute music played in the background competing against the sounds of the sizzling woks. Behind the counter, he could see into the grill, where flames leapt all around the metal pans, as the chef flipped the large quantity of pork fried rice.

Nick ordered a pint of wonton soup and went back out into the misty lands of the city.

Persephone opened her apartment door to find Nick holding his bag of Chinese food and his manuscript. She was armed only with a tissue and her pale face, which made his eyebrow raise. Her normally long black hair had reverted to its non-conditioned frizzy state. Her casual magnetic smile was replaced with a plain half grin.

"Good morning Persephone, I heard you were sick. I come bearing gifts. I thought I'd come by with some soup and make some tea."

"I don't know if you want to come in, you might get sick."

"Sick? Sick is a state of mind, besides I don't get 'sick.' I have an almost excessive supply of vitamin C in my system."

Persephone smiled and tried to laugh, which instead made her cough.

"Yeah, you just get headaches," Persephone said. "Come in at your own risk."

She stepped aside and slumped onto her couch in the living room. The furniture showed signs of being her bed for the previous night or two.

"I have some wonton soup and Chinese noodles. The guy at the restaurant always feels the need to give me some free pork-fried rice and an egg-roll. So that's what I have. Oh, and I also finished another book."

The Best Orgasms Come from the Universe

"Really, give to me," Persephone exclaimed enthusiastically, stretching her arms and fingers out as far as possible from her temporary bed.

Nick entered the kitchen with his bag of food and started a pot of tea. Neither of them said anything for about a minute. Persephone removed a pen from her coffee table and opened the manuscript.

"Where's Jack?" Nick asked looking out the opening in the wall from the kitchen.

"He's out on business for the week. I'm guessing your girlfriend dumped you?"

"Yeah, how did you know?"

"You always write a book when that happens."

"Yeah she dumped me..."

"That bitch..."

"No she's not a bitch, she was just unhappy. Where are your bowls? The cabinets empty."

"Check the dishwasher."

"I did."

"Ok, then get two bowls from the china cabinet."

"Whoa, the good stuff. But any way I met a girl."

"Already?"

"Yeah I can't believe I've never met her before, she says she comes in your store almost everyday. We're meeting again tomorrow for breakfast."

"Leila..."

"Damn you're good. How did you know that one?"

"I knew you'd two would meet eventually."

"I wish I'd have met her earlier, she seems great."

"Well everything happens for a reason. It's not fate, it's not your destiny, and it's not luck, it just happened. Now that it's happened you need to let it take its course. I can't wait for you to get to know her, and all I'm going to tell you about her is this, she's read one of your books."

"Really, which one?"

"Big Hill...Little Hill."

"That's a good one, although this one you're reading now, I think is better. So you think we're going to hit it off."

"All I'm saying is I've known you since you were five, dated you for a year, and I'm glad the two of you found each other. Just don't screw things up Nick."

"What are you talking about?"

"I know you don't cheat, drink, abuse, neglect, or even argue. Don't get me wrong those are good things, except for the arguing thing. Sometimes you change your life too much for the other person. It's good for you to argue in a relationship, like aging wine, it will turn to vinegar if you don't wet the cork."

"That sounds more like a sexual reference."

"In a relationship you have to wet a lot of corks to keep it from turning to vinegar."

Persephone always had a way of putting things, so that whomever she was speaking to could understand it. Well, they'd understand it completely or be totally lost. She was so confident in what she was saying. She paused and waited for Nick to come back into the room. When he came back into the living room with two bowls she began speaking again.

"You try to accommodate them so much, you forget yourself, and the relationship dies. The reason a relationship works is because two people are attracted to the other person in more ways then one. If you change too much, the other person may not be attracted to you anymore."

The Best Orgasms Come from the Universe

"I never knew you thought this way."

He set the bowls down and went back for the plate of rice. Persephone blew the steam away from her spoonful of soup, before eating it. Blowing on it didn't help, it was still hot, and Persephone swished it through her mouth, trying to keep the liquid moving. She swallowed just as Nick came back in.

"Listen Nick I'm not trying to be cruel, you know I love you. I love you when we aren't together. You are the most romantic, intelligent, interesting, and funny guy I know. In a relationship you're something that every other woman wants in her man on the inside. Women are funny creatures, as you know," Persephone paused to eat a moment. "The thing is if a woman knows you're romantic and nice when they aren't dating you, they won't need to date you, because they know you'll do these great things without having to be with you. You have to take it slow to start."

"So what are you suggesting?" Nick asked before eating some pork-fried rice.

"Be yourself, and stay yourself. You change too quickly. Don't change to make the relationship better for the other person. If you love someone else, you'll both change for the relationship, not just for the other person. Make sure you can talk to her about anything. If you feel uncomfortable about a topic or a problem, something bad is going to occur. When we were going out, you were worried I was going to judge you."

"I was not," Nick exclaimed in mid-chew of his wonton.

"Yes you were," Persephone continued, half laughing. "You were worried that if you said something or did something I didn't like, I was going to dump you. That is by far your biggest problem, the minute you stop speaking your mind to your partner is the minute your relationship is going to start falling apart. If a person is going to condemn you for your opinion, and treat you differently, then they're not worth your time. You taught me that. You were afraid if I knew certain things about you that I wouldn't love you. If someone loves you, and stops because of your point of view, then they never really loved you to begin with."

"She's right... I hate when she's right."

"I hate when you're right. I really do like her."

"I understand, just be careful, you might just have something real good going for you. Are you going to eat that egg role?"

"No it's all yours."

Nick could hear the teapot howling from the kitchen.

"Do you want some tea?" he asked getting up.

"Of course, Earl Gray, please. What you need from your relationship is something like this."

"What's that?"

"You need to be able to listen to one another, and still be able to make tea, because I know you're still listening to everything I say."

"What's that?" Nick paused. "I'm just kidding."

"You know we never sat together talking about relationships, while we were dating."

"You know what it is," Nick said coming back with two cups of tea. "I need someone to love. I'm not sure I need to be loved. I mean, I love that I'm loving someone else. I'm like one of those fish that live by cleaning the fish tank. I feed off the tank, instead of the food. Most people are fulfilled in relationship by the other person fulfilling them. I'm fulfilled by knowing or hoping I'm fulfilling them. I get worried that I'm not pulling my weight and then I'm no longer fulfilled. I self-destruct by crushing my own chances."

"Just let life take its course. Go to your date—"

"Meeting, it's not a date yet."

"Sorry, meeting. Go to your meeting tomorrow, and don't worry about things like whether it's a date or a meeting. Have a good time and don't worry. She will fulfill you if you let her. I'll tell you this Nick; you fulfilled me when we were dating. You don't have to think about that so much, you are naturally good at it. You have a gift. Although if you aren't fulfilled, exactly what you fear is going to happen. Try to get all you can, without taking anything, and enjoy what you have, not what you wish you had."

"Ok Persephone, I'll try," Nick said.

"Speaking of gift, I don't suppose you could work on my back a bit."

"Sure," Nick said bring a chair to behind the couch.

"This couch isn't exactly the most comfortable bed in the world. I woke up and I couldn't even move my arm or neck."

Nick massaged Persephone's neck and shoulders, as she read his novel. He could always tell if his book had her attention, by how fast she read. If it was a good part, she'd read nearly five to ten pages a minute. Conversely, if it was a bad part in the book, she'd only read two to four pages a minute. Although Nick could not see her face, he could tell she changed her expression by the tension in her neck. He had spent many an hour massaging Persephone's back as she read his various writings. Persephone rarely laughed or sniffled while reading, so Nick learned the pattern of her likes and dislikes by how she moved. When she thought something was funny, her entire neck loosened, when something tense was taking place, she obviously turned tense herself, and when something sad happened she alternated between the two.

When she finished the manuscript, she set it on her lap, sighed, laughed, and then coughed. Nick stopped rubbing her upper back as she turned to him.

"Well?"

"I love it...I want to see this on the shelves of my bookstore. It's fantastic, I love your altruisms; I mean there are a lot of them. I think the title is a little long, but I like it. You really depict you point of view well. Your grammar and spelling still suck, but I'll correct it. The story is like nothing I've ever read before. Well I've read things like it, but not this well written. I feel like I know these people, did you base the characters on any real people?"

"I always do, sometimes more than others. Surprisingly few of them are based on people you know though."

"Listen, we need to get you published. I'll give you the list of some good, publishing editors, give them my name and I can guarantee you'll be published."

"I don't want that Persephone. Well, I want to get published, but I don't want my book to be published for any other reason besides that it's a good book. That's why I write under a pseudonym, I don't want my father's fame, or my business' name, or my connections to matter on why it was printed. When someone picks up my book, I don't want them to look at my name first. I want people to buy my book because it sounds interesting, or because they heard from some else that it's good."

"I understand Nick; it's just that you might want to take your advantages to get your foot in the door. Then you can start doing some damage."

"I can't do that, it's against all that I've ever believed about success. I don't want to succeed unless I earned it completely. I didn't even want my father's business; I just didn't want my father's work destroyed by some board of directors. I never liked my father, but that doesn't mean I let my entire family business die. A lot of people put their time, sweet, blood, and tears into making that company what it is. I have never achieved anything great, by myself.

"That's not true, you achieved happiness by yourself."

"Your right, but achieving happiness is nothing great. It's important, but it's not great. Just because not many people have achieved it doesn't make it great. Anyone could be happy if they truly wanted it. I'm not even saying writing a book is something great. I'm simply saying that if I create a book, that touches other people, then I've left my mark. Like you said everything happens for a reason, and if I can't spread my opinions to everyone else, then there is a reason for it. I want others to find meaning in my work, but the achievement I want to be all mine. I want my great grandchildren to be able to find my book, read it, and know me and more importantly, my ideas. Ideas and experiences are what bring us beyond ourselves in the world."

"Well isn't that more important, than believing you have to do this alone?"

"No, it's the same thing. I need to know that my heritage realizes that I got my word out without any advantages. The only advantages I have are ones I've earned. That's why I won't make a publishing house from my father's business. I'm going to be heard, and I'm going to be heard because I was loud enough, not because someone handed me a microphone. Do you see where I'm coming from?"

"Yeah...I see."

"I still don't entirely agree, but it's your decision. At least let me give you the names of some good publishers. You don't have to mention me. I warn you though; some of them are pretty harsh. Let me hold on to this, I'll correct it. You can retype it and drop it off at the address I give you tomorrow. They usually get the job done quickly so, you'll probably get a call the next day for an appointment. How does that sound?"

"It sounds acceptable," Nick started. "Ok, well then I'm going to get going. I'm glad you liked the manuscript. Is there anything you need before I go?"

"If you could take the garbage when you go, I'd appreciate it."

"Sure," Nick said kissing Persephone's forehead. "I'll see you later today."

Nick gathered up all the trash, before leaving for his job.

CHAPTER ELEVEN

Nick's strolled into his job at around two thirty. Mick and Curt were nowhere to be seen. When he walked across the bottom floor, the two minions appeared from the corners of the room.

"Hi Nicolas," Mick grinned. "You certainly left us hanging, not calling to tell us when you were coming in."

"Where did you two come from?"

Curt fiddled with his glasses, smiling the same pompous grin Mick had plastered across his face.

"I don't want to talk," Nick started. "I just want to go to my office."

"Why are you always so distant?" Mick asked.

"It must be a Friday, that's Mick's day to be the only conversationalist."

"Go away...and stop calling me Nicolas," Nick demanded.

"You're being so hostile," Mick said.

"That's because you are one-dimensional pieces of cardboard, with no lives, no emotion (other than anxiety), and nothing interesting between the two of you."

Nick pressed the button for the elevator, and waited patiently.

"Aren't you going to apologize or something?" Mick said.

"No, I have nothing to apologize for," Nick retorted. "I need you to leave me alone."

"Aren't you having a good day Nick?" Curt questioned.

"Wow, he speaks on a Friday, Mick must be getting tired."

"I was...and I will be once I get to my office...in fact, so long as I can convince the two of you to leave me alone, I might be having a good day once I get on this elevator. Actually if you leave right now, I'd be having a good day again even before I get into this elevator."

"You look tired Nicolas," Mick said.

The doors opened and Nick let the other people exit before stepping inside.

"Bye Nick," Curt said.

"Yeah."

When Nick came to his office door he was greeted by Mary.

"Good morning Nick."

"Good morning Mary."

"Can I get you a glass of milk?"

"Yes thank you, were there any calls?"

"No, but Bruce was looking for you."

"If you could let him know I'm here, I'd be most grateful."

Nick stepped into his office and sat at his desk chair. He could feel his drowsiness take over. That's when a sudden pain hit him. Like having your head stuck between a rock and a hard place, literally. The pain compressed his eyes back into the sockets. The headache struck without warning or reservation. Nick sucked in a quick lungful of air as the sharp stab impaled his brain. The flash headaches weren't nearly as common as when Nick was younger. The causes for these unrelenting flogging of his mind, were due to lack of food or sleep, the over-consumption of liquor, an

The Best Orgasms Come from the Universe

overabundance of second hand smoke, stress, or any combination thereof. Excluding the foremost fact of his hatred for the taste, headaches were the major reason for his reluctance toward alcoholic consumption. The majority of his youthful headaches were caused by the stress between him and his father.

After his life orgasm, stress was never really an issue. Without alcohol or stress, Nick's only causes for his head pain became smoking, lack of food, and in that particular case sleep deprivation. No medication had ever properly treated Nick's pain. Sleeping was the only asylum from his torment. Unfortunately when he had a headache, it had often kept him from sleeping; luckily that pain was only mild, and he could still function. On a bad occasion, he would have become completely bedridden.

Nick closed his eyes and rubbed his temple with his left fingers. There was a knock at the door which sounded as if the world was falling down upon him. Ever color in the room was magnified as he opened his eyes.

"Come in," Nick said under his breath, yet to him it sounded normal.

"Nick? Are you inside?" A woman asked from outside.

"Yes," Nick replied slightly louder. "Come in."

Mary entered with a glass of milk.

"Are you ok Nick?"

"Is that cold?" He asked, pointing to the glass.

"Yes," Mary got out before he took it from her hands.

Nick pressed the cold glass against his forehead. Slowly he took three soft breaths, in through his nose and out through his mouth. After one last deep inhalation, Nick gulped down the contents of his glass.

"Do you have another headache, Nick?" Mary asked. "Can I get you anything, a cold rag, another glass of milk, or maybe a back rub?"

"A cold rag would be just fine, Mary, thank you," he said. "Did you tell Bruce I'm here?"

"Yes, he'll be down in a couple of minutes, let me put on your music."

Whenever Nick's head ailed him, he would always put on classical piano music to sooth himself. Mary walked to one of the walls and opened two sliding cabinet doors, which revealed a stereo system. She pressed a few buttons, and the music began as she left the room.

"I'll be right back," Mary said quietly.

He stared deeply into his wall clock, watching the second hand toddle along.

"I wonder how long Mary is going to take," Nick contemplated. *"My head hurts...think about something else, to take your mind off of it. I can't wait for my date tomorrow. Leila, you are so beautiful...owe my head hurts...and smart...owe my head hurts. It would be nice to be famous from creating my book. I wonder...owe...if I...owe...should bring flowers...tomorrow...OWE! God damn my head hurts!"*

It was then that Mary came back in with a cold rag.

"Here's your rag, Nick," she began softly. "I also brought a bowl of ice water, incase you want to re-soak it. You should just go home."

"Maybe I will, but I need to read that inquiry from yesterday. Once I get through it, and talk to Bruce, I'll go home."

"Ok Nick, you feel better, and if you need anything, you let me know."

The Best Orgasms Come from the Universe

Nick shook his head as Mary left. He applied the cold compress to his forehead, and leaned back in his chair. He let the wet rag cover his eyes as well. Often times, his eyes hurt as much as his head, at least when he was experiencing a flash headache. The head pains were not due to his eyesight, for he had perfect vision.

Nick looked over the inquiry, which stated, that Mr. Carper was interested in making a deal for supplies for his next big movie. The movie he was producing was entitled, The Emerald Bell, thus the title of the deal, the Emerald deal. The document consisted of pointless questions, legal hoopla, and the redundant us of the words, imminent, apparently, and questionable. Nick wrote his name on the seven sets of doted lines, signifying the need for his John Hancock. He was just putting the last touches onto the packet as Bruce entered his office.

CHAPTER TWELVE

"You feel alright Nick?" Bruce asked.

"I just have a headache," Nick said. "What did you want to talk to me about?"

"Oh I was just stopping in to see if you wanted to go to brunch again. We might see that gorgeous woman again."

"I'd rather talk later, I have a headache, and I don't want to get into a conversation."

"Well don't you need to eat?"

"No, I've eaten already, actually."

"Don't you want to see that girl again?"

"Right now I just want to sit and be quiet."

"I know you want to see her."

Nick let out a loud sigh, threw his cold rag into the ice water, and turned off the piano music, with his remote.

"You want to talk, ok, let's talk. As a matter of fact I do want to see her again. Actually, I saw her today, and her names Leila. My ex dumped me last night; I finished a book, saw Leila this morning and asked her to breakfast tomorrow. It's kind of a date thing... more like a meeting, which might lead into a date. Are we good?"

"That's what I love about you Nick. You don't BS your way through a conversation. When someone offers you something, you say 'yes please' or 'yeah thanks,' it's never 'are you sure?' When something comes up, you don't hint at it with silly conversation starters like, 'I saw that girl today.' You just dive right in; you don't make me ask about it. I hate when people try to navigate a dialogue. You actually make people want to talk to you without tricking them with things they have to ask about."

"Well the thing about talking is it's become a game to people. Yeah sometimes I'm forced to use conversation tricks, just like anyone. If you think about it, people are afraid of silence. People would rather argue over something petty than just be quiet." Nick started.

"What does that have to do with anything?"

"Give me a chance to explain. People feel that talking is the only way to get to know someone. If they can't talk and find a common-interest, they will find a common-interest through a mutual-complaint. The worst of it is, when people don't have someone to complain to, they instead turn to a topic they know about. They try to impress the other person with a superior knowledge of a subject…"

"Does this have a point Nick," Bruce interrupted. "Because I don't mind listening to you talk, I just want to know if this has a deeper meaning, I should look for."

"Yes, just bear with me. Now, if the other person has some knowledge of the given subject matter, then they may debate something, rather than let the other person have control of the conversation. So the two given people start kicking around opinions of a subject, judging one another in the back of their minds. If by some chance one person has a very powerful opposition towards the other person's opinion, this might spark an argument. Sometimes even, the fact that the other person won't give up their point or at least acknowledge the other persons thought, an argument may arise."

"Break it down for me!" Bruce said enthusiastically and sarcastically.

"So one person may start arguing their point with a tone, this will intern make the other person reciprocate, due to the natural human behavior of competition. Thus two people may start arguing over a silly topic, because both people would rather voice words than shut up. So they yammer on, without ever seeing the other persons point, because their minds are too clouded, with they're own next comeback. This being the case, their argument and original conversation goes to shit."

"Preach baby!" Bruce exclaimed clapping his hands, before chuckling to himself.

"The two people further their relationship with one another, without ever learning a thing about the other person. Neither of them grows as a person, and neither of them accomplishes anything besides a mutual desire to waste time," Nick finished with a sigh.

"Yeah! I still don't get your point Nick."

"My point is, shut the fuck up, I have a headache."

"Sure doesn't sound like it."

"When I have a headache, my mind works in two settings, really fast or not at all," Nick explained.

"Was that really your point?"

"My point about people is, you can learn just as much from not talking to someone as you can from talking to them. You learn a lot by how people react to silence. Besides that, people look for things to argue about these days. They think if their friends are on their

The Best Orgasms Come from the Universe

side of an argument, than they will be closer. You wouldn't believe the stupid things people will argue about these days. That's one of the things I put in my book."

"You know what I think when I see discussion in a book like the one we just had?"

"Is it going to get you out of my office any sooner?"

"Probably not," Bruce admitted.

"What the hell enlighten me," Nick said.

"I think wow what am I doing reading this when I could be reading a thrilling spy novel."

"That's because you don't read about real life."

"No...well yes, but it's also because I don't really see your point."

"I just explained it to you," Nick sighed. "What don't you understand?"

"I don't believe people will just argue about anything."

Nick shook his head a moment, and then he began to drag his fingers across his face.

"You're not going to let me have some peace a quiet so I can get ride of my headache, are you?"

"Would you let me, if you wanted to prove your point?"

"Yes..."

"That's besides the point...so make your point."

"*What*," Nick stated.

"What do you mean *what*?" Bruce questioned.

"I was just saying *what*," Nick said. "I wasn't asking anything."

"What do you mean? You can't just say *what*."

"Actually you can, I was simply stating the word '*what*.'"

"*What* is a question," Bruce said.

77

"I'm not disputing that. I'm simply saying *what* can be a statement," Nick said calmly.

"No it can't, the word *'what'* can only be used as a question. When you said the word *'what'* you were using it as a question."

"When you think about it, any question can be a statement. I'm stating something. I'm stating that I need you to explain or re-edify something. Although in this case I was not asking what, I'm just saying the word *'what.'* Can I really help that that provokes a response?"

"*What*, is used for a question! You can't just say the word *'what.'*"

"*What*, with a period at the end. I'm just saying the word *'what'*, it's just like any other word in our language. The meaning of the word doesn't matter when you are using it in dialogue. You see while a sentence would be wrong by just using the word *'what'* without a question, using it in speech changes some things. I can say anything I want, it doesn't have to make sense, and I can still say it. For example...*it spam ran jam*. That made no sense, but it was still a statement. *What* can still be a statement, without me using it correctly."

"*What* is used for questions, period!"

Nick grinned a moment and just looked at Bruce.

"You do realize that we are arguing about the word *'what,'* right?" Nick retorted.

"What? Oh..." Bruce said. "It doesn't matter, *what* can only be used as a question."

Nick continued grinning.

"You're a prick," Bruce said.

"People are just dying to argue about the littlest thing. Yesterday we were arguing over whisper. Well that was actually a distraction so you wouldn't talk to Leila."

"Because you wanted her for yourself, you prick."

"At the time I just didn't want you to have her, because I knew what you were going to do."

"What was I going to do?"

"What were you going to do?" Nick repeated. "You were going to talk to her. Then you were going to flirt, if she seemed interested in you, you'd try to make her feel comfortable around you, and then you'd have gotten her number. You'd hang her dry for a couple of days, to try to get her thinking you weren't going to call. You'd want her to know you weren't desperate and then you'd make 'contact.' After that you'd invite her out and try to have sex with her."

"Wow, you know me really well. That doesn't change the fact, that you wanted her for yourself."

"At the time, I didn't want her for myself. I was quite happy with the relationship I was in. Like I said I just didn't want you to just have sex with her. You can learn a lot from a person after thirteen years of listening to them talk. I thought she was pretty and probably smart. She was eating an everything-bagel and was in Persephone's store, I got a little attached to her style. I just didn't want you taking advantage of her."

"So what are you going to do with her, Mr. I'm-Too-Good-For-Sex?"

"That doesn't make any sense, I love sex. I just don't feel the need in taking part in one night stands, that's all."

"Ok fine, so what's your plan?"

"I don't have a plan; I'm just going to see where it goes. I really like her."

"I hate you Nick, which is why I love you. You know I'm just playing with you, right. You called dibs and all. I still don't agree with the whole 'what' argument."

"It doesn't matter about what I thought. Don't you see? I was simply proving a point. People love to argue. It's sad but true...and you know what...I think my headache's gone. Oh wait...no it's not."

"How could you only **think** your headache was gone?"

"The best thing for relieving a headache is not paying attention to it."

Bruce left soon after that point, and Nick finished up his work. The rest of the day went by incredibly slowly, due to the headaches innate ability to make time lag. Nick stopped in at Persephone's house and picked up his novel, as they had planned. He quickly went home and fixed the entire thing based on Persephone's corrections. After saving his work, he went to bed.

CHAPTER THIRTEEN

SATURDAY

Nick awoke at seven am without the aid of an alarm clock. He slid himself out of bed. Standing on his tiptoes he stretched himself as far as possible, before cracking his neck and back. It wasn't long before he ambled into the bathroom and stepped onto his scale, which revealed a number higher than desired.

"I have to stop eating those bagels. Carbohydrates go right to fat, faster than fat does these days. I should start running again. What am I talking about, I hate running," Nick said looking down at the scale, as if he could possibly will the numbers to change. *"Swimming...that's a full body workout. I love swimming. I could swim, and eat well. I'm doing well so far. I've already lost thirty six pounds. Ok twenty six...but still that's a lot. Ok, now it's actually twenty four pounds, I've gained two back. No more Chinese food and no more bagels. Well, Leila is planning to treat me to a bagel, so one more is ok."*

Nick walked into his bedroom and gathered clean cloths. He looked over his selection as he came back to the bathroom. He continued thinking in the shower.

"I'm sure Leila would understand if I didn't want a bagel because I was dieting. I shouldn't tell her I'm dieting. She'll think I'm making it up to impress her. But I'm not making it up; I really am trying to lose weight. It doesn't matter just take the bagel. Although then I'm not being honest with her, because I'm taking the bagel when really I'm trying to lose weight. I'll also be cheating myself, by not losing weight. Ok...take the bagel...it's just one bagel...then go to a public pool and swim off the calories. Yeah...that will be fun. Shit! I just conditioned my hair before I shampooed it."

Nick stopped singing and concentrated a moment on washing out the hair product.

"Ok Nick...now we put on the shampoo...good boy. No...don't start singing in the shower...you'll forget what you're doing. Ok lather...maybe I need to read the directions. Ok, so I take the bagel and work it off later. Wash your hair. I can't believe I'm still overweight...I wonder why Leila is willing to go out with me? Wait, it's just a meeting...Ok now put on the conditioner."

Nick arrived at Persephone's Books and Bagels at eight thirty. He sat pleasantly in one of the store's leather reading chairs and read over his manuscript, which he brought to drop off at the editor's building later in the day. When nine rolled around, Leila was nowhere to be seen. Nick bought a glass of milk and sat back down to read. As nine thirty passed by, he had finished three glasses of milk, and gone over several scenes in his writings. She was a half hour late, which made Nick a bit lethargic of his high school days, when girls would stand him up all the time. He looked around for someone interesting to make a story about, to take his mind off the possibility he was being put on. Unfortunately everyone

The Best Orgasms Come from the Universe

there had already been decreed with a tale, or was too boring to bother with.

Nick sat quietly as nine thirty turned to half past ten. By that time he named all the boring people anyway and began to extend their stories. It wasn't until ten thirty when Nick noticed Leila come to the door of the bookstore. She entered and peered around. At first he hid himself behind his manuscript, peeking his eyes and nose over the edge. He watched her a moment as she glanced down the isles for him, presumably.

The weather outside matched the previous days, in everything except the temperature. Today was slightly colder than the preceding Friday and Thursday. Leila wore an open button down sweater over her spaghetti strapped tank top. Her jeans emphasized her long legs. After laying an overview of the store, she put her hands through her long blond hair and sat down at the café. Nick continued to look at her with a smile. He didn't move, he just sat and looked. It was than, Leila turned to see him. Nick wandered up to her and sat down next to her.

"I guess that thing about sensing the energy is true," she said as he approached.

"I think that's the strangest conversation opener I've ever heard."

"Sorry I'm so late. I'm really glad your still here," Leila said.

"It's alright, you're worth waiting for," Nick smiled.

"You sure do smile a lot," she stated.

"Do I?" Nick inquired, ending his smile.

"No it's not a bad thing, you have a nice smile."

"Yours isn't half bad either," Nick said.

"Wow that's the understatement of the century."

There was a short silence.

"So what's your line of work, Nick?"

"What? I'm sorry I was just enjoying the silence."

"Oh, I'm used to braking uncomfortable silences."

"Was it uncomfortable?"

"I guess not…it wasn't uncomfortable. I was calm. It was a calm silence."

"I like it."

"I supposed you can learn a lot about someone by how they react to silence."

"That's odd; I was just talking to a friend about that yesterday."

"But isn't it weird how silences usually come after someone compliments someone else. It's like the conversation has nowhere to go afterward…"

"So you start a new topic," Nick agreed finishing her idea. "Its kind of strange that insults further a conversation's discussion, yet a compliment ends it. The good ends a topic yet continues the meaning and the bad ends the meaning but continues the topic."

"That's kind of funny."

"I guess if you couldn't tell before, I'm a writer."

"Oh, have you written anything I may have read?"

"Well actually, I've never been published. I own my family business, that's how I pay the bills. I really don't like it, so when people ask, I tell them what I do like. I've been a writer since the age of five. Although, I was talking to my friend yesterday and you came up in conversation. She said you have read a book of mine."

"Who's your friend and what's the book."

"The owner of this store, Persephone. The book is called…ah; I think she said the one you read was, Big Hill, Little Hill."

"I love that book!" Leila exclaimed shocking him. "Your characters were so real. I just loved Andrew Baker and Samantha

Teal. I can't believe I'm meeting the man that wrote Big Hill, Little Hill. How do you write emotions so well?"

"Emotions are easy; fitting them to the people is what's hard. One thing I try to do, it not over exaggerate it. When people cry, they often try to hide the fact that they are crying. I hate in movies when a character just starts weeping. It's unfortunate that people hide their emotions, but if you want to write people accurately, you have to remember that emotions are often masked. In that book, I wanted the reader to be dying for Samantha to start crying."

"But she doesn't cry in the story," Leila said.

"The point of the story is that if people hide an emotion long enough, it might go away. The character of Samantha held in the tears so long, that even after Andrew's death at the funeral she couldn't mourn."

"I'll tell you what, she wasn't crying, but I sure was," Leila began. "What's your new book about?"

"Well it's about a lot of things. I wanted to create a story about people. I didn't want it to be just any other drama. In dramas big things happen as the main focal point, like someone dying, or someone has an affair, or someone has an overwhelming attraction to someone they can't have, or some other possible life altering experience. In my book I wanted to show what real drama is. Day to day life is drama and it doesn't always happen suddenly. Real life altering experiences should be gradual, real changes happens without someone knowing about it. Not only that, but real change happens by choice. This is the little drama, about what happens when people aren't busy saving the world."

"I can't wait to read it. Why haven't you been published before?" Leila asked.

"I want to talk about her...I want to listen to her talk, not the other way around."

"I don't really know I'm trying to get published today actually. I'm putting in the manuscript after we're done having breakfast."

"Speaking of breakfast, I'm hungry, do you want that bagel."

"Actually I think I'll pass, but I don't mind if you eat."

"You're not going to eat with me?" She said getting out of her seat.

"I'm not really all that hungry," Nick answered standing up. "But what about you, where are you from?"

"Well I've lived in the city for about two years. My sister owns the winery so I work for her. I'm her best sales woman. I used to live out in Pennsylvania. My Mom and Dad still live out there. They have a little home in the woods, it's nice."

"Why did you ever leave?"

"I love people. I like living in an area where everyone doesn't know everyone else. I like walking down the street, and not knowing everyone. It makes my life more interesting. It makes me feel as if I could change my life by just talking to one stranger. Kind of like you. You could have been anyone in the world before you looked at me two days ago. Then you became that kind of cute guy that was staring at me on Thursday. If I never saw you again, you might have stayed just that. Instead you talked to me, and now I'm having lunch with the writer of one of my favorite books."

"There's a reason for everything," Nick agreed.

"I've heard that before."

"Persephone?"

"Yup. She's a great woman."

"Yes she is...are you going to order your bagel?"

The Best Orgasms Come from the Universe

"Actually I probably should get going; my dog is at the vet. That's why I was late, my dog broke his leg. I want to go see how he's doing. I really just came by to make sure you didn't think I was just stringing you along."

"Oh, well am I going to see you again?"

"Maybe...everything happens for a reason...and all that. Bye, for now."

Leila started walking off, and Nick stood there motionless for a moment.

"Wait...what's going on...she's leaving again...we barely talked... she thinks I'm cute...hehe."

"So that's it?" Nick asked aloud.

Once again, Nick was beset by an assault of "shh's" from the tranquil readers. All of them turned in sequence to him, and then as swiftly as they attacked, they turned back to their business.

"For now..."

"Can I have your number?" Questioned Nick slightly calmer.

"No..." Leila answered with a smile before turning around. Then she turned back. "Oh, by the way, your eyes look a lot better today. That green shirt makes your eyes look lighter. You look kind of elf-like."

With those words Leila left the store. Nick looked from side to side at Saturday morning readers. He walked to his seat and sat himself into it.

"Elf-like...so I have Elven eyes. That's sexy...I can be the writer with the Elven eyes. Wow...I should start writing fantasy; I'd get a lot of readers. I could write under the pseudonym Elf Eyes. I guess I'm going to have to wait to see Leila until Monday. Monday I'll come in at breakfast, and stay through brunch. Maybe she'll be here. I can't believe I have to wait that long...that really sucks. Wow she looked

pretty. I should have said something. Well I'll just have to save it until Monday...good old Monday. I should go and drop off my manuscript at that editor's building."

CHAPTER FOURTEEN

Nick arrived at the building at around twelve thirty. The building itself had a striking resemblance to that of his family business. He entered the building, and found his way to the front desk, where he was greeted by a petite brunette.

"Good morning Sir, how may I be of assistance?" She asked.

"Hello Mia," Nick said looking at her nametag. "I'm looking into getting a book published."

"Well, we don't normally take unsolicited works. Are you an agent?"

"Ah, no," Nick replied. "I'm just a writer. I was told that I should come here to get published. I heard it was one of the best. According to my sources, the people of..." He glanced over to a business card, being that he wasn't sure of the company's name. "Blier's Tech are very accommodating to newly published writers, and often times get finished with the piece within a matter of a single business day," Nick continued. "Is that correct?"

"Why yes, that's true, Mr...?" Mia questioned.

"Nick, will be fine," he answered.

"Well Nick, you see you have to get an agent to support your publication. Blier's Tech, has a contact list of many great agents who would love to read your work. Would you like me to find you some names?" Mia asked.

"Please..."

"What form of writing do you fall under?"

"Ah, novelist."

"And what genre?"

"Drama, mostly," Nick answered.

"Well, just give the computer a moment, to find some people," Mia started. "Ah here we are, it appears we have several names. We have a Mr. Plaw, his office is on Tran street and a..."

"Thank you Mia," Nick said. "If you could print me a copy of the first five names, that would be great."

"Alright."

After getting the list, Nick made his way to the location of the second name after Mr. Plaw. He entered the building and walked to the front counter. After a short discussion with another young lady named Mia, Nick learned that the office he was looking for was on the twenty-sixth floor.

"Another Mia? This must be some cosmic message..."

He entered the elevator and waited patiently as a crowd of people entered the small compartment. Everyone faced forward, staring at the opening. Nick turned to one side and faced the left wall. The crowd all looked at him obscurely, as Nick faced the other wall. Progressively, as the elevator went up, old inhabitants left and new ones entered. Some people tried to ignore Nick, others continued to have that silly bemused look across their countenances, and a group of three Chinese businessmen joined him, thinking it was customary. When his part time companions reached their floor, he smiled and nodded his head; they in turn bowed politely.

When the elevator came to his stop, Nick smiled openly, turned, and headed out the doors. He was sure the slight alteration in those poor people's lives would strike at least three separate conversations on their lunch brakes. He found himself confronted with another young lady sitting behind a desk.

"Hello," Nick greeted.

"Good afternoon Sir, how may I help you?" she asked.

"Well," Nick started, looking for a nametag, when he didn't find one he continued. "I'm looking to hire an agent."

"You've come to the right place. Well our office represents novelists in literary fiction, suspense, and mystery. Does your manuscript fall under one of those three categories?"

"Basically."

"Well good, if you'd fill out this form, you can leave that and your manuscript with me, and I'll make sure one of our agents gets it. You'll get a call in a couple of days, about meeting with someone. Here at the Vivla Agency, we try to take care of your publication needs as quickly as possible."

"Do all of you desk people practice lines like that?"

"Do I still get informed if Vivla isn't interested in my work?"

"Yes Sir."

"Thank you."

When Nick arrived in his home he removed a carton of milk from his refrigerator and shook it. He could tell it was almost empty, so he opened it and drank without a glass. Nick felt empty. He drank his milk and sat in his wheelie chair without a single real thought. He turned on his music with his remote and drained the carton of all its contents. The music played on, and he didn't sing along. The words just slithered into his subconscious. Nick snapped out of his trance when he attempted to take a sip from his already empty container of milk, for the third time.

He had been sitting there for a half-hour without realizing it. He looked up to his end table, were he set his keys and wallet without noticing. He stood and ambled his way over to his answering machine which flashed an indication of a message. He pressed the play and the little computer voice came on.

"You have three new messages...Saturday...Eleven thirty-two am..."

"Hi Nick, its Persephone. I was just calling to thank you for the soup you brought me yesterday, and to see how your meeting...date ...thing went with Leila. I hope it went well. Obviously you're not around, your probably either still out with Leila or you are dropping off your manuscript at some agents' place. Good luck...give me a call when you can, k' bye."

"Saturday... Eleven fifty am..."

"Good afternoon...oh wait, its still morning...silly me. Well good morning Nick, its Alfred. I read your story last night at Boris', it's really good. You're so talented; maybe you could make it into a play or a movie, and give me a role. Ha-ha, just kidding Nick, but really your writing is so wonderful, great metaphors and alliteration and all that hoopla. Anyway, I hope you have a nice date with that girl...ah she's so pretty, she could definitely be a model or something if she got the right agent. Right well, I'm using up all my recording time, so have a nice day, Nick. Give Boris a call later; we'll have dinner during the week. Alrighty, bye, bye Nick."

"Saturday...Twelve twenty-one am..."

"Ah Nick? Are you in? I guess not, well this is Leila. I love your answering machine message. I got your number from Persephone. My sister's winery is catering an art show at the Stillwater Gallery, and I need to make an appearance on behalf of the business. My sister was going to go, but she can't make it, so I'm going to be going. I was wondering if you wanted to accompany me, as my date. Well give me a call before four or leave me a message if you're interested. My number's 365-2127...The show starts at nine tomorrow and ends at twelve. Well I look forward to your call, bye."

"End of messages..."

Nick's dumbfounded expression did not recede for several moments, before his mind registered the information.

"Wait...I don't have to wait until Monday anymore. She's going to be at an art gallery...and she wants me to be her date. I'm going to be her date...I don't have to wait until Monday. Leila wants to go with me...as her date. I have a date! Wait I need to call her."

Nick fast forwarded to her message, picked up the phone, and dialed her number. It rang three times before someone picked up.

"Hello?"

"Hi, it's Nick."

"Oh hi Nick, I'm Ray. I'm Leila's older sister. I heard Leila asked you to be her date for the art show."

"Well that's what I'm calling about."

"Let me get her. Hey Leila!" Ray bellowed.

Nick jerked his head away as she screeched again.

"It was nice talking to you Nick," she continued. "I'll give you to Leila."

"Ok, bye Ray."

"Hello, Nick?"

"Leila, hi, I'm calling you back about tomorrow."

"Would you like to be my date to the gallery?"

"I'd love to."

"Ok, meet me there at nine; do you know where it is?"

"Yes."

"Good...are you listening to music?"

"Yes."

"I thought so; I love that song you're playing. You've got good taste, I mean everything-bagels, seventies music, and green button-shirts. Tell me Nick, why hasn't some nice girl snatched you up?"

"I guess I haven't found a nice girl."

"You still haven't."

"Well maybe that's the thing. Maybe I'm only attracted to not-so-nice girls. Why hasn't some not-so-nice guy snatched you up yet?"

"Bad boys get boring."

"That's a first; does that make nice guys like me interesting?"

"No, that makes you available," she paused. "That doesn't change the fact that you could be interesting."

"I see...well I'll settle for available."

"It was nice talking to you Nick, I'll see you tomorrow."

"Oh wait, how's your dog?"

"Oh, he's fine, his leg is healing. He'll be back home tomorrow. Do you have any pets?"

"No."

"Have you ever had any pets?"

"Nope."

"That's depressing, don't you like animals?"

"Yeah I love them, it's just I've never really gotten around to getting any, I guess. Pets are a family thing. My friends are my family, and well, they have enough pets for all of us."

"Oh, alright, well, I guess I'll see you tomorrow at the gallery."

"I can't wait."

The Best Orgasms Come from the Universe

The rest of Nick's day sped by in a very uneventful manner. He sat around watching TV and then he convinced himself to do two-hundred crunches before going to bed.

CHAPTER FIFTEEN

SUNDAY

Nick slept in until around midday, before he pulled himself out of bed. He truly awoke while showering, which assisted in his daily process of remembering who and where he was. While still in the shower he could hear the phone ringing. By twelve thirty, Nick was dressed and ready for his day. He entered his living room and hit the button on his answering machine.

"You have one new message...Sunday...Twelve fifteen am..."

"Hello, this call is in regards to the book entitled, Making Left Hand Turns Onto a One Way Street From a One Way Street..." began the male voice.

"Wow, they are fast," Nick said.

"Our only available time slot is today at four thirty. The next most convenient time isn't until the end of next week. Please stop in at four thirty, if at all possible. Thank you."

"End of messages..."

Nick deleted the message and left his apartment. He brought along his laptop, and killed some time typing at the little coffee shop, he and Boris had breakfast at earlier that Thursday. He spent his

The Best Orgasms Come from the Universe

time typing several ideas for a new movie. Then Fredrick walked inside. The tall man peered over everyone's heads and saw Nick. Fredrick raised his hand and waved to him. Nick faked a grin and nodded.

"Hey Nick," Fredrick began as he approached.

"Hi Fredrick," Nick said.

"What's new? Did you work on your book at all?"

"As a matter of fact, I finished it," Nick answered.

"Really, what's it called?"

"Making Left Hand Turns on a One Way Street From a One Way Street," Nick responded.

"Cool," Fredrick said. "What's you working on now?"

"Just some ideas."

"Cool, do you mind if I join you?"

"It's an open seat, be my guest."

"Thanks Nick," Fredrick began. "I was actually wondering if I could get your opinion on an idea I've been kicking around."

"Shoot."

"Well the story is going to be about a soccer player..."

"Stop...stop..."

"What?"

"A soccer player, Fredrick, you have to write something new."

"I am writing something new, I've never written about a soccer player before."

"No, no, you're not hearing me. You need to write about something new. You need to try to write about something other than sports."

"Why?"

"Because if you love sports so much you should have never quit playing basketball."

"I can't go back to basketball, so instead I write about it."

"You quiet basketball by choice...didn't you?"

"No, I didn't."

"You didn't...what happened."

"It's kind of personal..."

"Ok, never mind."

"Well alright, yah see it was after a game the one day and I saw this girl. She was hot; we are talking like drop-dead gorgeous. She called herself Muse, and she wanted me. I mean she was all over me at the party after the game. I could hardly say no. So we had sex. It was the greatest thing in the world, next to winning the entire season of basketball. I mean it was like I had a perfect slice of warm pie, and then she was the pecan ice-cream on top."

"Sounds great..."

"So then I find out she was a minor," Fredrick started again. "She didn't look like any minor I've ever seen. Another team found out about it, and threatened to expose me. Not only were they going to expose me, they were going to pin it on the entire team, because there were other minors at the party. I took the fall for it, and I quit. God, I miss that game."

"I'm sorry Fredrick," Nick said.

"Yeah it sucks..." he paused. "You know what Nick?"

"What?"

"You are really easy to talk to..."

"Sure, I didn't really help you any."

"No, but you listened."

"Well, you are welcome Fredrick," Nick said. "Now about your writing, if you ever want to grow as a writer you're going to need to try new things. It's just like anything in life, you need to try everything, before you know what your best at, and what you like the most."

"Like practicing a lay up even though I usually dunk the ball."

"Sure...that's exactly what I'm talking about."

"So what should I write about?"

"I don't really know. That's for you to decide. I could give you a basic idea."

"Ok."

"Alright, a man named Ron Crab broke his heel."

"How?"

"Well just wait. Ron Crab broke his heel in a biking accident. Winter was coming, and Ron wanted to go on one last bike ride. He crashed into a man in a black windbreaker. The man Ron crashed into broke both legs and both arms as the bike knocked him into a moving car. Ron went to the hospital to see if the man was ok, and the man gives him a package."

"What's in the package?"

"Well that's for you to decide, but whatever it is, people are looking for it; bad people Fredrick."

"Bad people...?"

"Oh very bad, and they kill the man in the hospital. Now they are trying to find the package, so they try to find Ron."

"And..."

"And that's it, you have yourself the beginning to a mystery, suspense, thriller," Nick said.

"And you're going to let me use your idea?"

"It's all yours."

"Wow, thanks Nick."

"My pleasure Fredrick, it comes easily to me. If you practice it will come easily for you as well. I hate to cut our chat short, but I have to get to a meeting."

"Ok, Nick thanks again."

"Bye Fredrick," he said nodding his head.

Nick closed his laptop, without turning it off, and exited the small coffee shop.

CHAPTER SIXTEEN

Nick arrived at the Vivla Agency building a half-hour early and headed for the elevator. At first he was the only person going up, he stepped inside and looked straight up. As the next gathering of people walked inside they noticed his apparent interest in the ceiling. Most of them looked up to whatever Nick was staring at, and found only the ceiling.

"What's he looking at?" one old lady whispered.

"I'm not sure, there's nothing up there," the man next to her said glancing up only with his eyes.

"Except a new aspect on life," Nick thought.

"Maybe he's slow," the lady said, reassuring herself that she was the 'normal' one.

"Surely," the man next to her agreed.

The old, wrinkly woman didn't even look at Nick or the ceiling as she exited. Nick grinned as she stepped off the elevator, heading back into her 'normal,' convenient, boring life. When Nick reached the twenty-sixth floor he smiled at the other people and left. One of the people inside looked up to make sure he didn't really see something above him.

"Ah, you have a nametag today," Nick said looking at the lady behind the desk.

"Hello Sir, you're early," she said.

"Well Kristy, better early than late," he said.

"Your meeting won't be starting for another half-hour, so if you could take a seat."

"Sure."

Nick sat down and imagined what his agent would look like. He pictured a short, plump, balding man wearing a black suit. Nick envisioned entering the office of this man just to have him turn the manuscript down. He visualized the chubby man turning on his radio to sing along with Queen's "Another One Bites the Dust." The agent would sing inharmoniously, jumping onto his desk as he went. He'd pull his shirt from his pants and start shaking his flab in Nick's face as if he were some tribal dancer from Africa. Nick would get up and start to leave, just as the rotund man threw the manuscript into the trash.

"Nick?" said a voice from the office.

"Yeah?"

"Come on in," said the voice.

Nick couldn't help but imagine the agent's double chin, hairy stubble, and shiny head. He entered just as the man sat in his chair. The seat faced out the window and Nick couldn't see his face.

"Please sit down."

He did as the agent asked. The man swiveled in his chair, and Nick's musings about the man's appearance abruptly stopped.

"Brutus Macky..."

"It's nice to meet you Nick," Brutus said.

"Yeah, you too Brutus," Nick replied.

The Best Orgasms Come from the Universe

"Pardon me?"

"You are pardoned."

"No, what did you say my name was?"

"Brutus...Brutus Macky..."

"Well you've got the last name right," Mr. Macky said. "But my first name is Alex."

"Oh."

"Why did you call me Brutus exactly?"

"You just look like a Brutus to me. I'm sorry please let's continue."

"Yes well, it's a pleasure to finally meet you. I read over your novel and I believe it's a...not bad."

"What's wrong with it?"

"Well, there are a couple of things really. One of which is you never capitalized God in your writing, but I edited that for you."

"Ah, no, I meant to do that."

"What?"

"I don't capitalize the word God."

"What do you mean you don't capitalize God?"

"I mean exactly what I just said. I don't capitalize the word God. It's just a word, and I don't believe it should have to be capitalized," Nick said.

"It's a proper noun, you have to capitalize it. God is...well God, it needs to be capitalized."

"Why?"

"I just explained it to you. It would be like not capitalizing your name."

"Well, while I acknowledge the fact that I exist, I don't believe in God, I don't believe I should have to capitalize it. Its acknowledgement, if I capitalize it, it's as good as saying I agree with it."

"Well what about Christian, you capitalized that."

"I acknowledge that Christians are a religious group that hold some kind of precedence in our country. They exist, as did Jesus. If I were writing a novel from the point of view of someone who believes in God, I'd capitalize it. I also capitalize the word Pagan. It's a religious group which people don't always recognize. It should be capitalized also."

"You're weaseling your way around the point. You have to capitalize the word God," Brutus said getting slightly frustrated.

"I find it kind of interesting that you're getting annoyed over this," Nick said.

"You started it."

"I simply don't believe it should **have** to be capitalized. If the publisher we choose doesn't accept that, than I'll just have to change my Introductory Remarks."

"Well we haven't gotten that far yet," Mr. Macky said.

"By the sarcastic tone in your voice, it doesn't sound like we're going to get that far."

"Listen Nick," the agent said. "Your book may insult a lot of people; I don't really know if my agency is going to be prepared for that."

"Excuse me?" Nick said.

"I spoke plain English."

"Yes, but my statement was an indication that you either need to re-edify or repeat your previous statement."

"It wasn't a statement. It was a question."

"Yes it was that also. That's why I'm a writer, and you're an agent."

The Best Orgasms Come from the Universe

"Excuse me Sir?" Mr. Macky glared as he got out of his seat.

"I don't believe someone with such a one-dimensional point of view would be a very good agent for my kind of writing. Excuse me," Nick said with a grin. "See you later Brutus, say hello, to your supermodel wife for me."

Brutus Macky sat back in his chair without relieving himself of his ugly glare. Nick left the office with a smile and realized he would have rather had an encounter with overweight, balding belly dancer.

CHAPTER SEVENTEEN

The streetlights seemed like spotlights on the sidewalk. Nick peered out from the window of his cab. The stars hid behind the ceiling of clouds. The lights from the windows of the skyscrapers looked like small square holes of brightness in the finite darkness of Nick's vision outside the window. The taxi pulled up outside the Stillwater Gallery, and he handed the driver a twenty dollar bill. He stepped out of the vehicle and started up the steps of the gallery.

At first he looked through the crowd of neatly attired people, dividing them into groups and couples. Then he saw Leila. Nick pictured in his mind his life as a movie. He imagined a popular, pop-culture song playing in the background as he watched her. Each reel showed another glimpse of his life as a sappy romantic-comedy. He walked up the steps toward her, admiring the white and gold dress she wore. Her straight blond hair was styled up. Nick was never partial to women wearing their hair up, although Leila seemed to be the exception. His eyes traveled up her back at the patterned lace tying her dress around her. She seemed to turn her head in slow motion, as Nick approached. Their eyes met as he presented her a white rose.

She took the flower in her hands.

"I'm glad I picked the white, it matches your dress."

"Nick, you're wonderful," Leila said. "Everyone, this is my date, Nick. Nick this is Nancy and Jonathan."

"Hello," Nancy said.

Nancy held Jonathan's hand and he said nothing. Jonathan gave Nick an unimpressed look.

"Well, if you'd excuse us I want to show Nick around inside," Leila said taking his arm.

"Pleasure meeting you Nick, I hope to see you again," Nancy said.

"You too," Nick said. "Nice meeting you Jonathan."

Jonathan moved his bottom lip and raised his eyebrow a bit in response.

Nick and Leila entered the art gallery. The entire building was filled with bright chandeliers. Paintings, photographs, sculptures and other assorted works decorated the first room. Hundreds of people walked about the first very large hall of a room. Nick had never been in such a large gallery. The lights in the room fell on the observers like a glowing fog. The high culture people glanced at the paintings from the corners of their eyes. Meanwhile they'd daintily sip their campaign and nibble finely made cheese. Everyone was talking just above a normal, non-stage whisper.

"Quite a turn out," Nick said.

"More than I expected, but not less than the winery prepared for," Leila smiled. "Do you want something to drink?"

"I don't really drink," Nick said. "I get headaches from drinking too much. I might try something later."

"Oh, alright...you know what? You're the only one here that I know besides Nancy and her date."

"Jonathan isn't it."

"That's him," Leila said rolling her eyes slightly.

"What's with him exactly?" Nick asked. "He was very... antisocial."

"He's a lot of things..." Leila started. "He just doesn't like people, and I don't think he liked you getting me the flower. Thank you again by the way, it's beautiful."

"Your welcome, it's nothing really," Nick said. "I'm just glad it made you smile."

Leila looked down and grinned.

"What?" Nick said.

"You're not wearing a tie."

"Yeah, well, me and ties haven't been friends since high school. Even then it was one of those friends you're forced to have, like when you're in grade school and your parents want you to play with your neighbor. At the senior ball in high school some guy who wasn't picked for prom king didn't like it when I asked his date to dance."

"And?"

"And when I wasn't looking he tried to choke me with my tie. He did a pretty good job, before I elbowed him twice in the ribs. I didn't want a tie to begin with, so after that it seemed like a good enough excuse for me never to wear one again. Besides, ties are stupid and have no logical purpose. I actually thought you were smiling at the fact that I said I wanted you to smile."

"Well, that too," Leila said.

Nick and Leila didn't say anything for a short time as they walked the line of artwork.

"So do you know anyone here Nick?"

Nick turned and made another quick sweep of the crowd with his eyes.

"As a matter of fact I know everyone here," Nick said. don't know someone, I make up a story about them."

"Did you make a story about me, when you first saw me?"

"No, because if I make a story about someone, it's harder for me to talk to them and I didn't want that to happen with us."

"Did you ever meet someone you made a story about?"

"Only two people, and we aren't friends."

"Well who's that?" Leila asked pointing at a small overweight man.

"That is Aaron Burduss. He likes ale and mead. His stubble of hair on his chin grows back in full everyday, so he decided to keep it, even if it's not in fashion. That's how he looks at life, he doesn't worry about what people think of him because he is happy with who he is. He jogs every morning, but he still cannot repress his belly. He is a rising comedian. His Irish accent drives the ladies crazy and his sense of humor makes him irresistible. I'd prefer if you don't talk to him. I'm worried he'll steal my date," Nick ended with a grin.

"You have nothing to worry about."

"Am I that dashingly attractive?"

"No, he's just not my type," Leila replied.

"Don't you like comedians?"

"I don't like accents."

"Oh, so what is your type?"

"The scruffy, wannabe rugged, handsome kind."

"I'm flattered."

"That's as good as it gets."

"It's good enough for me."

"How often do you make up stories about people?" Leila asked.

"Several times a day, it keeps me in a creative frame of mind. When I need an idea for a story, I just pull one out of thin air."

te a talent. I used to write when I was younger. id when I was little," Leila paused and got very y, writing isn't an adult profession...it's just it

...just smiled to himself.

"I didn't mean it to sound like writing isn't a real profession," she continued.

"No, it's ok," Nick said still smiling.

"Ok, I need to use the lady's room," Leila said.

"Alright."

Nick didn't like being in the gallery alone. The room was congested. The people all chatted about boring and repulsive things, like golf and the consistency of caviar on their last Hawaiian cruise. Their monotonous, single-minded, collective conversation slowly shifted towards Nick. The threat of being assimilated into their pointless banter frightened him to no end. He quickly darted away toward another line of artwork. He continued to walk along the rows of art, hoping not to be bothered. He found a particular piece he liked and studied it until he heard a familiar voice.

"Nick!" bellowed the voice.

"That sounds like, no, it couldn't be..."

Nick turned around to see a tall man with smooth feather-like hair going down to nearly his shoulders. He appeared well groomed, save around the edges. If someone knew to look for it, you could see the paint under his fingernails. His piercing glance drew people's attention when he spoke, though when he was not talking or holding your stare with his eyes he could easily be overlooked. He was older than Nick in years, though by just looking at him, you would hardly be able to tell. His devious grin lit up his face as he drew near.

The Best Orgasms Come from the Universe

"Nick, I had hoped I'd see you here," the man said. "How long has it been?"

"Griffon, I never expected to see you in a place like this," Nick said smiling, taking his friends hand in his and shaking it readily. Everything about Griffon was loose until need be, and when Nick felt his grasp, he recalled his old friend's hidden strength.

"Wow, it's been like two years. Why didn't you ever call me?"

"You don't have a phone Griffon," Nick retorted. "And it was three years."

"Right...well it doesn't matter, I'm seeing you now. How the hell are you?" Griffon asked.

Griffon reached into his pocket and removed a small zip lock bag filled with something Nick couldn't see.

"I'm great; I'm here on a date. I just finished another book; I need to get published soon."

"I remember you were working on that book, Choke Collars and Mountain Bikes, how did that come out."

"Oh great, I really enjoyed writing that. I have a copy somewhere at home. I'll get one to you. Are you still painting?"

"Want a jellybean?" Griffon offered after finally getting the bag open.

"Sure," Nick said taking a yellow and brown jellybean from the plastic bag.

"Yeah I'm still painting; in fact some of my stuff is being exhibited farther down the line."

"I'm glad to see you're on your feet," Nick said eating the jellybean. "This jellybean tastes really weird; can I have a different one?"

"It's banana, and no you can't. I only buy banana."

"You only eat banana jellybeans," Nick chuckled.

"Yeah my doctor said I need more potassium in my diet," Griffon said with another menacing grin.

Nick didn't say anything; he was never sure if Griffon was kidding or serious because he always had that eerie grin no matter what he said. Griffon could have been eating banana jellybeans for a number of reasons. Nick wouldn't have put it past him if Griffon really thought banana jellybeans had a noticeable amount of potassium, even in large quantities. Griffon was an odd, old friend.

"You really helped me out a lot, back in the day," Griffon began. "You really set me straight; I mean I was a real prick before you came along. I'd hate to think what kind of guy I'd be if you didn't kick my ass that day."

"I glad you don't hold a grudge."

"I was just lucky really," Nick said. "I had the advantage you were drunk."

"I fight better when I'm drunk Nick," Griffon said, and he wasn't grinning. "You really showed me the light. After that night I realized a good fight really helps clear the soul. You know it's a healthy thing for people to flip out every now and again."

"It's kind of hard to flip out and not hurt anyone else, Griffon," Nick retorted.

"Well the trick is to flip out on someone else who needs to flip out. That's what you did for me three years ago. You were all nuts after that girl Persephone dumped you, and I gave you some crap. You flipped out on me, and you made me into a better person."

"You're crazy Griffon."

"Listen all I'm saying is some people can't change slowly. Some people bottle up things inside. I know you had that life orgasm thing after your father died, but not everyone can see when something happens to them. Sometimes someone else has to put it into perspective. You showed me just because I'm the hero of my own story, it doesn't make me right."

"I'm not really sure what to say," Nick said.

"Say...you're welcome..." Griffon grinned.

"You're welcome," Nick said. "Can I have another one of those banana jellybeans?"

"Addictive, aren't they?" Griffon reached into his zip lock bag and removed a small handful. "Enjoy Nick, I'm going to get going. I'll see you around. I'm in town, so I'll look you up."

"Later Griffon," Nick said.

Nick found Leila talking to three tall men. Nick walked up to her.

"Hey Nick...Gentleman, this is my date, Nick," she said. "Nick this is Rod, Allen, and Bret, they're artists."

"Hey Nick," Rod said.

Allen nodded and Bret didn't even look at Nick.

"Well, we have the three types of artists the nice one...the shy recluse kind, and the prick."

"Nice to meet you all," Nick said eating a jellybean.

"Unless he's deaf, then he may not be a prick."

"Nick's a writer," Leila said.

"Wow that's great. What do you write?" Rod asked.

"I write about people and life mostly," Nick said.

"That's all we need, more writing about life," Bret said sarcastically. "As if we don't have enough of it in our own lives, people don't need to read about it,"

"Yup...he's a prick."

"Well it's not for everyone," Nick said. "What exactly is your chosen artistic point of view?"

"I paint, I paint pain," Bret said.

"Hypocrite, you should learn to listen. You can start with your own mouth."

"Pain? Well you do realize that pain is only a part of life?" Leila asked before Nick could.

"Pain is the only thing people can call their own," Bret continued.

"What about love?" Leila said. "Love can take away pain."

"No it can't."

Nick looked at Rod and Allen. He could see that Rod was just waiting to add his opinion to the conversation. Allen looked deeply into Bret's elbow and listened to every word spoken.

"You can if you let it," Nick agreed.

"What do you know about pain?" Bret glared.

"What do you know about love?" Nick asked.

"I asked first," Bret said.

"I know that unless you're willing to listen, someone could misconstrue pain as creative agony. Creative agony is simply when you stop believing in your work. That's what happens when a dark emotion rules a person's imagination. Pain is one way to create, but it's a drug, it does more damage than it's worth."

"You don't know what pain is," Bret hissed.

"Do you?" Allen finally said.

Bret turned around and stormed off. Rod sipped his wine and walked after Bret. Allen looked at Nick and Leila before smiling to both of them. He too shuffled off behind his friends.

"You certainly do know how to scare people off, don't you Nick?" Leila said.

"I'm sorry..." he replied eating another jellybean.

"No, I was about to do the same thing, you just put your words together faster. You practice those lines, don't you?"

"My only practice is from saying it to people who need to hear it," Nick said.

"What are you eating?"

"A jellybean...you want one?"

"No thanks, I don't really like jellybeans. So what do you know about pain? Other than what you told Bret."

"I don't want to sound like I'm complaining about it; I've dealt with it, which is why I'm not like him."

"I asked, it's not complaining. Will you tell me?"

"How would you feel about taking a walk?" Nick said. "It's kind of congested in here, and it's a nice night. It's going to be warm tomorrow, I can tell."

"That would be nice."

CHAPTER EIGHTEEN

Nick and Leila walked down the street, and the cool air pawed at their hair. The clouds began to disperse, exposing the full moon.

"So your mother died when you were really young?" she said.

"I was six, just old enough to remember her and to young to realize what happened. I was also old enough to recall how my father was before her death. He loved her so much; I mean real worship. All I really remember is her long straight brown hair and her humor. She was the only person alive that could make my father laugh. When she died, he did too. I have one picture of her, with me as a baby; one picture to remember her by. My father never talked about her, and he wrote about everything except her. He'd write about depressed people whose lives meant nothing. He hit the public just right with the idea that life sucked and shouldn't be important. He was only masking his own pain. He pitied himself. I can remember his exact words when she died. I was in the hospital room. He said, 'I can't believe this is happening to me.' He never even looked at me. I don't think he ever looked at me after that day. I was told about it by two of my Dad's friends, Curt and Mick. They try to control me even now. Back than it was even worse, they thought that I should listen to everything my dad said, because he knew what life was really about. I almost stopped writing for good because of that first year after my mother's death. That's when I met Persephone...well I knew her, but that's when we became real friends. She was such a tomboy. She was the biggest book worm I've ever met, at nine she was reading and understanding books like Moby Dick and the Scarlet Letter. Persephone and her mother told me that life was full of happiness as well as pain."

"What about your Dad?"

"He wrote a child development book. It was to help parents learn to help their kids. It taught them about what to do if someone died, or divorced, or what to say if your kid asked about sex. I learned what sex was when Persephone explained it to me at the age of eight. My Dad brought business home everyday. He wanted me to be unhappy. Just before he died I forgave him, but I still never knew who he was. His books are all lies, that's why I write what I really believe, so people will know me for who I was when I die. High school and college are different stories, but basically I was an outcast. I enjoyed writing more than people."

"Are you still like that?"

"I've grown out of it," Nick started. "What about you, what did you write for yourself?"

"Stories like yours make mine kind of boring."

"Believe it or not, even though I talk a lot, I actually prefer listening. I want to know your story..."

"Well, I was born in Pennsylvania, as you know. I studied law for about four years in college and changed to sales. I moved out here to work for my sister, Ray, and have been working in the city ever since."

"Wow that's a great story," Nick said sarcastically.

"I'm not much of a writer."

"I know it's not an adult profession," Nick said smiling.

"I didn't mean it to sound like that."

"I know, I'm just kidding."

"It's just, I could never get into writing," Leila began. "I'd get writer's block."

"Writer's block," Nick chuckled.

"What?"

"Well writer's block is a myth," Nick started. "It doesn't really exist, it's a rumor. It's an excuse. People who just write words made it up. Writer's block is when you want to write and have no ideas flowing. Writers shouldn't be having that problem. If they are, then they are merely people who put words on paper. Real writers are vessels of creativity. There isn't a second that goes by when I'm not absorbing feelings, emotions, ideas, and life in general. A real writer takes those things into himself when he writes. There is an infinite supply of it out there. A good writer always has something to write about, if one thing doesn't work, work on something else. Writer's block is when someone isn't paying attention to life around them. If they aren't soaking in life, then they shouldn't be a writer, and if they are getting 'writer's block' more like 'life block' then they aren't a writer."

"That's horrible..." Leila said. "You make it sound as if your way is the only way."

"That's not what I'm trying to say," Nick said. "People can write anyway they want and about anything they want, that doesn't make them wrong or me right. It's just that saying you can't write when you're a writer is like saying you can't move when you're a dancer. The thing is a true writer, is writing all the time, if only in their minds. A dancer, I mean a real dancer, who labels themselves as such, is always moving in their minds. It's like love; it drives you and empowers you. Writing, dancing, singing, running, or even sitting, if that's what is true to you, is always part of you, and in some way you are always a part of it. Even when you are doing nothing at all, you are still part of that thing in some way because your mind is still at work. So you see a true writer would never have writer's block, if they are a Writer."

"So you're a 'Writer' I take it?" Leila said smiling.

"What are you?" Nick asked. "Where is your heart at all the times, no matter what you are doing?"

"I am a...Faerie," Leila answered. "I live for fun...and love."

"Love is fun," Nick said.

"Love is a lot of things, good and bad," Leila said. "I plan to have fun until I fall in love, and then I plan to have as much while in love. Sometimes love isn't fun, sometimes love is hard, and sad, and painful, and sometimes love is even giving up...The best thing about life is the fact that if you keep an open mind, almost everything can be fun. Like that moon, have you ever seen such a beautiful moon?"

"It's full," Nick said stopping with Leila to look at the moon.

"From here it looks perfectly round," Leila began pointing at the moon. "A perfect circle, and yet up close, you start to see the blemishes, in fact the idea that it's perfect, makes people want to look for imperfections."

"Are we still talking about the moon?"

Leila reached down and took Nick's hand in hers. She was quiet a moment, and then she held Nick's hand over the moon, covering its light from both of them.

"I'm just worried that's what love is," Leila said. "When I look at the moon from here, it's beautiful, but what if I was closer to it? What then? Would it still be perfect? What if you love someone so much, and then you start to see all of them. What if you lose sight of your love? What if the journey keeps going and the love stays where you first started?

"Well it's a full circle," Nick said bringing his hand down from covering the moon. "Like love, maybe it has no corners; it just may seem endless sometimes. If you know where you started from, maybe after you explore it more, you come back to the beginning, and love the person more."

"You just can't stop..." Leila said inching closer to Nick. "Maybe it's not worth starting."

"Maybe it's the only thing worth starting..." Nick said.

Gradually the two moon observers came together, and the tips of their noses touched. Leila looked down a bit and Nick moved his head to look into her eyes. She looked up at him and put her hand on his shoulder. Nick moved his index and middle finger down her check to the side of her chin. Their lips touched slightly, but only slightly...The white flower fell to the ground, and Leila put her fingers through Nick's hair. Their lips parted, and as if they'd never experienced a kiss before they came together again, yet this time more readily.

The gallery's opening party raved on, in remembrance...

CHAPTER NINETEEN

MONDAY

Overnight the entire city turned into an orchestra, an opus written by the sun. Everyone's life was altered dramatically by the sunlight. It looked as if the populace had all exacted an epiphany from the world overnight; one giant life orgy, when in reality the light only brought a partial happiness, which would pass in due time. Soon people would find something new to complain about other than the rain, something like the heat or the humidity. People will always find something bad to outweigh the good. Nevertheless for one day, everyone had that laid back feeling of a good orgasm. Unfortunately most of them didn't realize what the day really was. Most of them were too drunk or stoned on their familiar unhappiness to comprehend the sheer magnitude of the cosmos' gift. They were date raped by life and didn't even know it. Nick loved being sober. He knew exactly how rare days like these were. If everyone else knew or more importantly wanted to know what the world had to offer, they would surely become nymphomaniacs, just like Nick. And they would take any chance possible to enjoy a good orgasm from the universe.

Nick couldn't attribute his happiness solely to his orgasm from the cosmos. What truly put the grin on his face was the kiss he shared with Leila. Every now and again a chuckle would slip out of his mouth. He started playing a game with himself, by attempting to force the smile to subside. Even with his greatest efforts, he could not repress the excitement.

When Nick arrived at work he dashed swiftly across the bottom floor to the elevator. The elevator doors opened and he waited for all the people to exit. He kept an eye on Curt and Mick as they chatted to one another.

"Don't turn around, don't' turn around..."

Curt turned and glanced in Nick's direction. The crowd exiting the elevator concealed him from view. He slipped inside and went up to his floor. After ascending to his level, Nick walked to his office with an arsenal of 'hello's' and 'good mornings,' which he waited patently to spring on all his workers. Nick looked forward to receiving a response from his employees on this rare type of day. Although when he wandered to his office, everyone sat in their cubicles with their normal half dead expressions. The few people whose cubicles faced a window had the extra pleasure of being tortured by the sunlight. Even though the sun was shinning more brightly than in the past, it still didn't help them while trapped within the four walls of Nick's building.

He noticed his staff's torment and sheathed his greetings of the morning within his pleasant demeanor.

"Hi Nick," Mary said.

"Morning Mary," Nick said entering his office.

"Bruce is already in there."

"Thank you Mary."

Nick entered his office and found Bruce inside.

"Hey Nick, how are you?"

"I'm great," Nick replied.

"Yeah well it's a beautiful day outside today," Bruce said.

"That it is," Nick agreed.

"So what's on the docket for today?"

"I don't know really."

Bruce continued looking outside.

"It must really suck to have a window office," Bruce began. "I'd imagine looking outside at that gorgeous sun would really get to you after awhile. I can remember in grade school, during spring I'd stare outside at the green grass and monkey bars, just waiting for recess."

"Wait...say that again," Nick exclaimed.

"I'd imagine looking outside at the gorgeous sun—"

"No, the last part," Nick interrupted.

"I'd stare outside waiting for recess," Bruce explained.

"Bruce you're brilliant!" Nick shouted.

"What?"

"Bruce go out to the office and tell everyone, 'finish the last things of whatever they are working on,'" Nick stated.

"Alright, are you feeling ok today Nick?"

"Like I said, I'm great, absolutely great."

Bruce gave his friend a peculiar look and left Nick's office.

"Mary, I need the number for a school bus company," Nick said, pressing a button on his intercom.

"What for Nick?"

"The company is going on a fieldtrip."

It was for another half-hour before Nick gathered everyone on his floor by the elevator. He went down first with Bruce and fifteen others. Forty others stayed behind until the next set of elevators arrived. Inside the elevator, Bruce gave Nick another doubtful look.

"So Nick...what exactly are we doing with our entire floor of your company?" Bruce asked.

"Well it's just our floor for now. I plan to do it with all the floors of the company," he explained.

"So what is it that you're doing?" Bruce began. "If I don't know I can't properly back you up."

"We are going out for a well deserved recess," Nick whispered.

Before Bruce could say anything the doors to the elevator opened with Mick and Curt standing in the doorway. There was a pause.

"Where are you headed Nicolas?" Mick questioned.

"I was wondering that myself," Bruce added.

"I'm taking the boys and girls here out to the park," Nick answered putting his hand in the way of the doors as they began to close.

"What are you talking about Nick?" Curt inquired. "These boys and girls have work to do."

"It will still be there when they get back," Bruce smiled.

"You're welcome to come along," Nick said.

"You can't just take the employees out to the park," Curt exclaimed.

"Why not?" Nick asked keeping the doors from closing.

"Because it's not policy," Mick said.

"Well, then I guess I'll just have to change the policy," Nick stated walking out of the elevator. "If you'd excuse me."

Nick walked outside the building with the group of employees. A yellow school bus waited at the curb with its motor running.

The Best Orgasms Come from the Universe

"Ok everyone, fill in from the back, everyone two to a seat, we have a lot of people," he said.

"You can't use company assets to fund your expeditions!" Curt exclaimed.

"That's good, because I'm not using the company funds, I'm using my own," Nick explained. "So go away or get inside. If you don't want to go this time, I'm making a second rotation in about an hour. When I'm finished there I plan to make another switch, and I plan to continue until everyone's had their chance."

"Chance for what?" Mick questioned.

"To attend recess," Nick said entering the bus.

Mick and Curt entered the bus, as the next crowd of people exited the building. They both stood in the aisle staring down at Nick.

"Nick you can't do this," Curt said.

"We can't pay these people for this recess time," Mick continued.

"Well, there is what...? Maybe four hundred people that work for my company a day," Nick started. "And according to our studies, each of them is paid an average of about fourteen dollars an hour. So that's about fifty six thousand dollars, for an hour's work, for each of them. So if it takes about ten minutes to drive to the park from here, and five minutes to get in and out of the building, then I'd say we have a half-hour to have recess. So if I take them all out for an hour each, then I owe the company about fifty six thousand dollars for the time they spend, well lets round it to seventy thousand in case traffic's bad. How's that sound?"

Mick and Curt didn't say anything.

"Could you two move, more people want to take the bus," Nick said.

CHAPTER TWENTY

The bus pulled up to the entrance of the park and Nick stood up.

"Ok everyone, you have a half-hour for recess," Nick started. "You may take a walk, play tag, or catch, whatever you want. Enjoy yourselves."

Everyone filtered off the bus into the outdoors. Nick looked around at the swaying trees, drowsy clouds, and the placid blue sky. The business men and women looked confused. Bruce looked around at his coworkers and then he glanced over to Nick who wandered over to a big tree. Bruce walked along side of him. Nick sat under the tree in the shade and Bruce sat next to him.

"What are you doing exactly?" Bruce asked.

"I'm soaking in the nice breeze, under the shade of this big tree," Nick said.

"That's not what I mean. What are you doing with your employees?" he inquired.

"I'm letting them soak in the fine offering of Mother Nature," Nick explained.

"Ok, Nick that's all good and well," Bruce started. "But look at them, they have no idea what's going on or what to do. They look like grazing cattle. Most adults don't think about recess anymore.

The Best Orgasms Come from the Universe

All these people are thinking about how to pay their bills and how to sell that deal they were working on."

"What are you saying?"

"These people have no order," Bruce said. "If you want them to have a good time, you have to give them something to do to forget about their work. If only for a half-hour, you need to help them along."

Nick stood up from his spot and glanced all around himself. He noticed a group of four boys tossing a big red ball.

"Gather everyone up at this tree," Nick said.

Bruce grinned and did as Nick told him.

"Hello," Nick said walking up to the four kids.

At first they didn't say anything.

"Not allowed to talk to strangers," Nick started. "Yeah I wouldn't talk to me either. But, I was wondering if you might sell me that ball."

"Maybe," one kid said.

"Shut up, it's my ball," said the one holding it.

"Why aren't you kids in school?" Nick asked.

"Extended weekend," answered the tallest of the kids.

"Oh, cool...well you see me and my friends...we are looking to have a good time. I was hoping you'd be willing to sell me that ball you have there."

"Fifty bucks," said the only kid who didn't speak.

"It's my ball," the one said again. "A hundred."

"Wow, the price of a kickball has gone up since my day. Alright, you drive a hard bargain," Nick started taking out his wallet. He removed five twenties and handed two of them to the one with the ball and one each to the others. "Don't spend it all in one place. See you later boys."

Nick walked back to the large tree and everyone stood waiting.

"What's the ball for?" Bruce asked.

"We're going to play kickball," he answered.

The mob of employees looked at each other in disbelief.

"Ah, Sir?" One man started. "Can you run that by me again?"

"Yeah, we're going to pick teams now," Nick answered. "In fact you can be a captain. What's your name?"

"Brad," he replied.

"Ok Brad...and you..." Nick said pointing to a redheaded man.

"Steve..."

"Steve and Brad are captains," Nick said. "Brad you stand to the left of the tree and Steve you go to the right. When you are picked, I want you to say your name."

The two men split off and started picking people they knew at first. Slowly the people being picked started helping the captains pick people they knew. Eventually everyone except Bruce and Nick were picked, because they both stood outside the group. The two gatherings began to look strikingly like the teams you'd have in grade school. Someone always knew someone else on the team.

"This is crazy," Mick said.

"Shut up," Nick stated.

"These men and women are in full work dress," Curt began. "You can't expect them to play a game in the hot sun."

"That's true," Nick began. "If any of you do not wish to participate, you are not required to."

Several people stepped outside the shade of the tree.

"As for the rest of you," Nick said. "Let's play some kickball!"

The Best Orgasms Come from the Universe

The sweat already began to show on the grown men's clothing. The wet spots began to form under the arms on their suits. A couple people loosened their ties as Steve's team took the outfield.

"Bruce will be the pitcher and I shall be the catcher," Nick said.

The game began and the thirty and forty year old men transformed in mere minutes into teenagers in gym class. The first kick was caught, although the second soared to the far outfield. The kicker ran for first in a rush, and his suit's buttons popped. He continued on to second as Steve's team retrieved the ball. Quickly the runner slid for the base as the soaring ball came to the catcher. The second base man caught the ball just before the runner slid to safety.

"We play to three outs," Nick started. "One more and it goes to Steve's team."

Brad's team got two more kickers onto bases before they got out. Nick began taunting Brad's team, as Steve's team took their kicking order. Brad's team quickly crushed Steve's, as kicker after kicker fell to Brad's superior catchers.

As the second and third round started many people not originally participating began to join teams. By the fourth round, everyone except Mick and Curt were playing on a team.

The game raged on for twenty-two minutes, and Nick could see the buses pulling up with a new crowd. The game was six to four, in favor of Brad's team. The bases were loaded with two outs already, and Herbert came up to kick.

Herbert was a forty eight year old engineer of Nick's company. He'd worked there longer than Nick was alive and he'd never been married. He was professionally alone. He'd worked everyday of his life and never had any siblings or children. His hair was turning gray and if one was to judge him by his hands, he'd look more like seventy. He was tired...tired of work, relationships, and life in general. He was out before he stepped to the plate to kick.

Herbert cracked his back and waited for Bruce's pitch. When the ball came within reach, Herbert's foot slammed the ball into the air. Not even twenty-eighty year old Brad could jump high enough to catch it. Everyone who wasn't designated to a base ran for the ball. Herbert charged down to first and continued to second. As Herbert reached third, Brad had gotten the ball and thrown it to Bruce. Herbert and his team had already won, but Herbert continued; he needed to win. The sweat flew in all directions as Bruce threw the ball at him. Out of the corner of his eye he noticed the ball, and with an uncanny flexibility which was hidden under his slightly overweight figure, Herbert skidded to a quick stop, bending his body back. In the last second as Herbert moved his head, the ball flew by him. He continued on his way, stepping on his triumph and the home base.

A wave of applause broke out among the workers. Everyone bombarded Herbert with claps on the back and high-fives. The excitement continued as they entered the bus. Nick saw them off. The people on the next bus watched, as the others left in high spirits. Bruce just grinned. And so went the day as Nick and Bruce led the employees back to childhood.

CHAPTER TWENTY-ONE

Nick came home with sunburn on his neck and arms. His eyes were already closing as he entered his foyer. He swayed past the end table, setting his keys and wallet on it. He pressed the play button on his answering machine as he slowly removed his shirt.

"You have four new messages...Monday...Ten thirty am..."

"Hi Nick, its Persephone. I was just calling to say that I'm feeling better, and I'll be coming back to the store on Tuesday. I know you only work a couple of hours on Tuesdays, so if you want to stop in to talk or something, that would be great. Ok Nick, bye. Oh wait, I just remembered, I'm helping to sponsor a writing magazine at a high school. I'm holding a writing contest, you enter an essay, and donate five dollars and you're entered into the contest. You get some kind of prize if you win; it's the kid's idea. Ok, I'm really going now."

"Monday...Eleven fifty-five am..."

"Hello...hello...hello, you home Nick? Nick? Hello? You home? Guess not...Nick! Ok, your not home, or you're ignoring me...ha-ha just kidding. Yeah well this is Griffon. Well I looked you up and now I'm calling. I have a thing going on...sometime this week; I wanted to know if you wanted to come. I'll call back later..."

"Monday...Four sixteen pm..."

k, it's Alfred..."

..."

...well anyway Nick," Alfred continued. "Remember when I said, I was an actor. Right, well, I have a part in a musical. I'm playing a tortured flower spirit. The opening is on Friday, so I thought you might want to come and take Leila. I have some extra tickets, being that I'm in the show. So give us a call. Bye-bye Nick."

"See you Nick."

"Monday...Five thirty-two pm..."

"Hi Nick, its Leila...I was just calling to say I had a great time last night. I look forward to seeing you again."

"End of messages..."

"She's thinking about me," Nick thought.

Nick deleted the messages and went off to his bedroom. After getting undressed, Nick bundled himself into his warm covers as he was apt to do when he set the air-conditioning on as high as it was. He curled himself into his pillow and shut his eyes. He tried not to think of anything. After five minutes, which seemed more like thirty, Nick's mind began to yammer to itself.

"I need to buy milk, I drank the last of it a day or so ago," Nick began. *"Milk is sure good for you...yeah; I should buy two percent or skim milk. That would definitely help in losing weight, since I drink so much milk. Oh no, I forgot to do my crunches. That's ok, I had a lot of exercise today...and sunburn. It kind of hurts now that I think about it...well, stop thinking about it. Yeah I exercised so much outside, I got sunburn. I don't have to do wannabe sit-ups. It's not even really helping...because I keep making up excuses not to do them. I should get up right now and do my two hundred half sit-ups. Then I might not get comfortable again with my sunburn, and then I won't be able*

The Best Orgasms Come from the Universe

to fall asleep. I'll end up doing my workout and then have to start writing, and lose a night of sleep. What would I write about...? (I wish I could fall asleep) I'd probably write that essay for that contest. I hate essays...I wonder if I could just give a five dollar donation. Sure I could, but it is for a contest. I wonder what I'd win, probably something dumb. But it is a challenge. I should show them what I've got; blow the doors off the other contestants. What am I going to write about?"

Nick sat and thought for over an hour about various ideas. The time went by rapidly without Nick realizing it. His mind worked itself faster than he could even think everything over. The anthology of Nick's entire being came to the brim of his psyche as he imagined writing an essay about life. What life should be, in fact what it was and no one realized it. All his ideas began to form, and all past inclinations of sleep vanished within the barricade of his imagination. His inspiration gathered itself into intelligible mental sentences.

"Life is what people are missing..." Nick thought and his eyes opened. *"Life...movies allude to it, books discuss it, art has it hidden somewhere within it, but human nature has made life into only a word, instead of letting Nature make it into a belief."*

"Yes!" Nick said aloud, jumping from his bed.

"What if life is more than just a word or an idea, as people believe it to be? Life should be big and bold...it should be written in caps lock..." Nick continued to think doing full sit ups with weights on his feet. *"This is good shit, I should be writing this down."*

Nick jumped from the ground and walked in his underwear to his living room where his laptop resided. Without turning on any lights Nick went to turn it on. It didn't turn on; he turned it over and noticed the bottom where the battery pack was stored. He opened the back, and found a dead batter to greet him. He must have left it on. He knew he had no spare battery pack, and he definitely didn't have the power cord. Nick ran to his walk in closet, which could no longer retain the title, for it was filled with junk making it so no one could 'walk in.' Nick riffled through everything and found his old typewriter. He heaved the heavy iron mass out of the closet. He couldn't close the double door again, for the contents of the it were scattered about the floor.

Nick put the monstrous thing on his floor in his room and retrieved some printer paper, from back in the day when he had a working printer. He began typing, thinking as he went.

"'Living Intentionally'…that's a good title. I hope this typewriter still has enough inked ribbon…good. Ok, 'Living Intentionally.'"

Nick continued writing on through the night. He'd type long sections, connecting his ideas, without really thinking. When a powerful point came up, he'd type with his full attention.

*"…life isn't a dirty word. Why do children enjoy life more than adults? It's not because they have less responsibilities. It's because they know life is simple, without ever thinking about it. They can love something like a stuffed-animal hippo more than most adults can love people. Love isn't something basic that can only be applied to some things; love like any emotion can be applied to anything and everything. A child begins to lose this love for everything when someone labels a reason to love things. There should be no reason for loving something. One should love only because they want to. To love is to be loved. To love life is to enjoy life. No matter how good or bad one believes the afterlife to be, one should enjoy life. Life is what you've experienced and what you're experiencing. You can't **know** what happens after you die, you can only believe. So why worry…so*

long as you are happy why even worry about your life. If you're not harming others and you're happy, you've won. Be happy with what you are doing and you will be living **LIFE** *intentionally."* Nick thought as he typed.

CHAPTER TWENTY-TWO

TUESDAY

"Living Intentionally" ended up being ten pages long. The essay took Nick until nearly four in the morning to write. While everything he said he believed, he found when writing straight from the heart, while still trying to form words from what he was thinking, takes a lot of time. He corrected it nine times and rewrote entire sections. Ten pages synopsized Nick's entire soul. The possible half-hour of reading it would take to finish the essay would only be like skimming the back of a movie jacket, if one truly wished to know Nick's entire soul.

Nick awoke at his desk at around ten thirty. He sat up to find a piece of scrap paper stuck to the side of his lip. After his shower, Nick gathered up his finished product and made his way for Persephone's.

When Nick came to the store, he noticed, through the windows, a large group of people. He stepped inside and was instantly greeted by an old woman wearing a kerchief. She held out her hands as if to grab Nick's face.

The Best Orgasms Come from the Universe

"Are you Chuck?" she questioned with wide eyes.

"No, I'm not Chuck?" Nick said. "I'm sorry..."

The lady turned away and hobbled into the crowd. It wasn't more than thirty seconds later, before Nick was confronted again, by another woman. This new lady was younger, had brown hair, and looked to be over two-hundred and thirty pounds. She put her hand out in front of her and asked:

"Are you Chuck?" she hoped.

"I'm sorry...no, I'm not Chuck..."

"Oh, well bless your soul, you look like him," she said.

"Ok...well I hope you find him."

She scurried off and assailed a middle-aged man. He shook his head and she proceeded to ask the man next to him, who presumably was the man's son. He too was not Chuck, or if he was he lied and shook his head.

"Their names are Laurence and Jack. They are two related poets, who are probably as perplexed as I am, about this Chuck guy. Both of them will probably write poems about the occurrence. Laurence will write what really happened from his personal point of view. While his son Jack will make a story about someone else being called Chuck. Both of them will consider their own piece better. Jack's mother will not take a side and Jack's older brother won't understand either poem." Nick began. *"And this Chuck guy must be some kind of movie star. Although then I would have heard of him. Well maybe he's a romance novelist. He's written thirty-seven novels, and women love his writing. They eat it up like bad rock candy, that all tastes the same; it just comes in different colors. He's probably ugly and still gets women because they think he's as passionate as the characters he writes. When they find out the truth they'll leave him for another non-writer type of guy...He creates a false image of himself. Laurence*

and Jack, write about themselves, and shall have many female friends. Yet because they write about real life they shall not get laid very often. Chuck will get laid, and never understand real life or people."

Nick didn't move as another woman approached him. Before she could ask, Nick shook his head.

"I'm not Chuck."

She turned away looking truly saddened.

"Who is this Chuck guy?"

Nick slipped into the crowd and looked for Persephone. He was asked three more times by various women if he was Chuck, before he spotted Persephone. He navigated the crowd, heading toward his friend. Just before reaching an open area where Persephone resided, he was tackled with the question once again, from the older woman *again*.

"I'm still not Chuck," he reassured.

Nick moved on passed the depressed woman and came to Persephone's side.

"I'm not Chuck," Nick said with a blank expression.

"I hadn't noticed," Persephone said.

"So who's Chuck?"

"He's a writer."

"And..."

"And he's written about three books; there self-help books for women. Apparently one of those teenagers from that magazine knows him, and to help sponsor, I called him to make an appearance at the store. It's good for business."

"Why do these women think I'm Chuck?"

"I don't know, I guess you look like him. I've never met the man."

It was then the doors to the store opened, and Chuck entered. He was tall and thin. He wore shorts, a t-shirt, and a baseball cap. His smile was simple and his teeth were all white. The brown facial hair made the man look older than he probably was. His big simple smile changed to a grin as he entered, and he gave everyone a thumbs-up.

"I am Chuck," he announced, before cocking his head to one side eyeing up the crowd.

"Congratulations," Nick said under his breath.

The ladies swarmed him with excited faces.

"Now ladies, you must calm down, I need to get into the door," Chuck insisted and then he turned to a man at his side. "Alphonse, get me some photos of me to sign for these lovely ladies."

"Could this guy be anymore full of himself?"

"Well, I'd best introduce myself," Persephone said, rolling her eyes. Nick followed her. "Ladies, please let Chuck in the door," Persephone continued. "There will be a chance for everyone to say hello to Chuck. Now please back up."

"Persephone, it's so great to finally meet you. You had such a nice voice over the phone, and I can see it matches you perfectly."

"Thank you," Persephone said plainly. "Now if you'll come with me, I'll get you a form for the essay contest. Nick, if you could find Andréa and tell her to set up a table for Chuck, I'd really appreciate it."

"Nick? Have we met?" Chuck asked.

"Not that I—" Nick started to say.

"Oh, yes, from Bermon University," Chuck started. "We were in the same college together."

Nick searched Chuck's face a moment. Then it hit him. Chuck the head assistant student of the drama department. Nick wrote a play which was performed at the college and Chuck played his leading character. Nick had wanted to play in it, but the drama department said he had no experience in acting. Chuck had pretended as if he knew nothing about the drama department decision, when, really, he probably made the choice of not letting him act in it.

"Ah yes, I remember you now," Nick started. "Chuck, you acted in my play."

"That's right," Chuck started. "That was one great play."

"I guess I'll get Andréa then," Persephone said.

"No Persephone," Nick started. "If you'll excuse me Chuck."

Nick walked off and flagged down Andréa.

Within an hour Chuck's little table was set up with pictures of himself, occupying every available inch of space and then some. All the women from ages thirteen to eighty three waited impatiently in line to get their very own personalized picture of Chuck. They all got the same identical picture of him with his squinting bat like eyes, half-grin, and trademark brown facial hair. Also on his table were his three self-help for women novels and his fourth book entitled, <u>Acting, You, and the New You</u>.

Nick and Persephone sat together at the small essay stand. After the women got their black and white picture of the great Chuck, they continued on and donated money to the high school magazine fundraiser. In the time it took Chuck to get settled, Nick had made a photo copy of his essay in Persephone's office, and submitted it to the contest. Persephone sat reading Nick's writing as the flocks of

The Best Orgasms Come from the Universe

women donated their money to the fund Chuck endorsed. When she finished the essay she looked up to Nick and handed it back to him.

"I like it," Persephone began. "It's very mentally pleasing."

"What does that mean exactly?" Nick asked.

"It makes you think and evaluate what you see in your own life. It's still steeping in my mind. I'll get back to you on my full report, but I think it's wonderful."

"Well thank you," Nick started. "It's me, the writing I mean, it's what I believe."

"This isn't you Nick," Persephone started. "It's only some of you. It's great as it is, but I'd expand it. If it's you, then make it all of you. Give it a life, show people something. Put yourself into it."

"What else should I add?"

"Everything...your hopes and dreams," Persephone said. "Write about cats and dogs, good and evil, black and white, or even the gray stuff in between. Make it your masterpiece. Conduct your soul into an opus. Give it everything. Make it your example of you."

"Well essays aren't exactly the best of ways to reach people these days."

"The heck with reaching people, reach yourself. When you reach someone with something else, they may come looking for everything, and when they find this, they'll find you. Do it for yourself."

Nick thought about it a moment.

"That's not such a bad idea."

"I know."

Nick looked up a moment from his conversation and noticed Chuck a few steps away from them. Chuck waved and Nick nodded.

"I'm going for a smoke break," Chuck said. "Nick, I was wondering if you wanted to step out with me, we could catch up."

Nick looked over to Persephone.

"Sure, I've got everything covered here," Persephone said.

Nick got up and walked with Chuck out the back door. They reached the back alley behind the store, and Chuck removed his pack of cigarettes.

"You want one Nick?" Chuck offered.

"I don't smoke," Nick replied.

"I've been saying that for thirteen years," Chuck laughed half-heartedly and removed his cap. "Media lately, damn...They make smoking out to be something evil. They say it's bad for your health, and all that. Well, so is eating too much, or drinking, or playing video games. Everything's so horrible these days. Everyone takes things to extremes. I mean they say cigarettes give you cancer, so does breathing in general. Everything gives you cancer. It's all about moderation, like them damn monks say out in them damn China mountains. I tell yah, extremes and over consumption are going to be the end of life itself."

Chuck took several hits of his cigarette and stared down one end of the alley, and then he paced back down to the other. He didn't go far and he could still hear Nick, when he replied.

"I guess..." Nick said. "I just don't smoke."

"You don't drink either as I recall."

"Not often," Nick said.

"It's so hard not writing in extremes. Playing up everyone's bad points and all. I mean how else can you show what someone's like? Readers are too lazy to search for things these days; you have to hand it to them on a silver platter, that's why I write self-help novels."

"Well, maybe you just write people as they are, and the people that care enough to look for it, find truth. The thing is there are no black and white people anymore. Extremes are just one aspect of an opinion. When you think about it, people take things to extremes when they can't deal with a minority. It's like believing that the word 'normal' actually holds any merit. No two people are alike entirely so there can never be a truly normal person in life. The closest you can get to normal is through a majority. And once a majority has an affirmative idea about something, they often take it to an extreme, which puts everyone else in the minority. Being in a minority is what makes you a real person. Anyone who only fits into majorities becomes just like everyone else. If you want to write real people, who are at least interesting, you have to give them their own ideas."

"Well, the hell with that, if you think I'm going to write about individual people. They all have their own thoughts and ideas yes, but the only way to make everyone happy is to write about them in groups."

"That's why you write about multiple people. So the reader can at least like someone."

"The hell with that, I'm going write about who I want, when I want. I'm not going to throw in characters for the reader."

"When you are writing real life you're going to have to write about people you don't like."

Chuck cursed uproariously, before looking at the sky.

"Writing isn't worth all that. I write about women and their lives as a whole. I'm not trying to help individuals, I'm helping a populace."

"I'm just worried they will all end up having the same ideas, and then they'll become a mob of single minded people."

"Writing is meant to lead others down one particular path or point of view."

"I guess you don't really enjoy writing..." Nick said grinning.

"Eh, you know it pays the bills," Chuck started. "I mean acting is great, but I have three houses, six cars, child support, and my girlfriends."

"Don't forget rehab you arrogant dick."

There was a long silence, and Chuck broke it after cursing.

"I'll tell you man, these women, they're so damn helpless. They weep about their men leaving them...and crap, and do nothing about it. You know if you've written one best selling self-help novel, you've written twenty. I'm serious..."

"No I thought you were joking."

"...I mean what the hell. I just want to grab these ugly women and say, what the hell!" Chuck exclaimed to Nick. "Yah know?"

Nick's expression didn't change, he just stared at Chuck.

"Ok listen; I'm not trying to be a prick. But they complain about not being beautiful and how they are fat, or short, or their hair sucks. They bitch constantly to their man, and when he cheats on them, they wonder why. I mean, if you beat the idea into their heads, what do you expect them to do. Then they read my book and think I'm telling them it's not their fault. When that's not what I'm saying, I'm saying if you want your man to stay, give them a reason. If you think you're fat, then do something about it."

"So if you're telling them to do something about it, then why aren't they? Your book is supposed to get them to help themselves," Nick said. "So maybe you should try it from another approach, if they aren't getting the idea."

"They get the idea, they're just too damn lazy," Chuck said.

"You make it sound like there is only one type of woman out there," Nick retorted.

The Best Orgasms Come from the Universe

"Hey, I know they're all different, but if you get inside their heads they are all the same. Once you learn what they want, then you've got it for all of them," Chuck continued.

"So what do they want?" Nick questioned.

"Your basic woman really just wants a strong, good looking man. Someone to do things for them, give them direction," Chuck explained, lighting another cigarette with his the last one. "If you're good looking, you can say or do anything. These women will do anything to stay with you. You threaten to leave, and they start feeling inadequate. They think you are everything."

"It sounds like you trap them with fear," Nick said, clenching his fist at his side.

"Well you know, you have to do what works. I remember you in college; you were a pretty nice guy. How far has that gotten you?"

"Far enough..."

"Really what have you accomplished?"

"Well I don't trick my women into thinking they love me."

"I'm not tricking them, they love me in there," Chuck said.

"Because you don't care about them..."

"Them who?"

"Your fans, your books, your girlfriends, maybe even your kids," Nick said.

"Hey, go to hell. I care about those things."

"You see, that's the thing, you should love them," Nick said.

"Where do you get off?" Chuck glared. "What makes you all high and mighty?"

"I get off on the fact," Nick paused. "That I'm not Chuck."

"What?"

"I'm not Chuck," Nick said. "And you're not the Chuck they're all looking for either."

Nick started walking back inside.

"Go to hell Nick, you damn underachiever!"

Nick stepped indoors into the back rooms of the store and noticed Leila walking down the same short hall.

"Persephone said you were back here," Leila began walking forward. "How are you?"

"Better now," Nick said coming to her.

He kissed her and all was well.

CHAPTER TWENTY-THREE

It turned out that Leila had made a big sale for her sister and she was given off for the rest of the day. She convinced Persephone and Nick to let her treat for lunch. So they gathered their things and headed out to a diner. On the corner of the book store's street was the diner which had been the scene of some of Persephone's greatest conversations with Nick. The sign outside read: The Corner Pocket.

Within the "L" shaped building where people of all types. Outside they were one collective, with the mob mentality of city dwellers, although inside everyone was completely different. All of them elaborated on everything in their lives. At Persephone's shop she and Nick basically knew everyone, or could easily meet them and strike up a conversation. Yet in the Corner Pocket, life was always fluctuating. People from Persephone's were always stationary, sedated by books and bagels. In the Pocket, everyone was moving to good music and singing praise to good food. Persephone's was home and the Pocket was adventure.

Nick held the door open for Persephone and Leila. Persephone was instantly greeted by Debra. Debra was a career diner waitress, and she loved her job. The locals all called her Deb, and they always had fresh coffee. Her true friends knew her stories, and knew that back in her hippie days she had been called Pearl. Nick and Persephone always called her by her hippy name and always were given fresh advice when they needed it. Pearl was a true Guru of real life.

"The usual table, Persephone?" Pearl said with her trademark grin which pushed her wrinkles to every end of her face.

"We have an extra guest with us today," Persephone answered.

Pearl eyed Leila up and down.

"She's a pretty one," Pearl pointed out.

"Certainly is," Nick said. "Leila this is Deb, but she's known to us as Pearl."

"I'll find you guys a table," Pearl began walking the group to a booth. "Leila you watch out for this one, he's a wild one. He had his first date here and his first kiss just outside as I recall."

"Really," Leila said looking at Nick.

"Who was that Persephone?" Pearl questioned.

"Cathy Michaels," Persephone answered.

"That's right, Cathy Michaels," Pearl continued. "She was a hot one, although not nearly as pretty as you are, dear."

"Thank you," Leila replied as they came to the booth.

Leila and Persephone sat across from Nick, as Pearl handed them their menus.

"I'll be right back with your usual drinks. What would you like, honey?"

"Just an orange juice please," Leila said.

"Coming right up."

"She seems nice," Leila said as Pearl walked off.

"She's great," Nick and Persephone agreed.

"How long have you two been coming here?"

"Since what...?" Nick started. "Since I was six, and Persephone, you were two years older than me. So about..."

"Well you've been coming nineteen years, which means I've been coming for over twenty," Persephone said.

"Nick, you're only twenty five?" Leila said looking up from her menu.

"Yup."

"So am I, when's your birthday?"

"January first, I'm a New Year's baby. So when's your birthday?"

"June eighth."

"That's this Friday."

"Yeah."

"Well what do you have planned, Leila?" Persephone asked.

Before Leila could answer Pearl came by with their drinks.

"Are you guys ready to order?"

"Just another minute please," Leila said.

"I'll be right back," Pearl said, she left and recharged several customers coffee cups.

"So what do you have planned?" Persephone asked again.

"Nothing really, my sister and I are going out on Saturday to Pennsylvania to see the folks, but I don't have any plans on Friday. I was just going to be getting ready for Saturday."

"Do you like theater?" Nick asked.

"I love acting; I used to want to be an actress."

"Me to," said Persephone.

"I think almost every girl secretly wants to be an actress. At least when they are younger," Leila said. "I love seeing plays and musicals, it's just movies are a lot more accessible."

"Well, my friend Alfred is in a play," Nick said. "He offered me some free tickets, would you like to go?"

"Who's Alfred?" Persephone asked.

"Oh, Boris' boyfriend..."

"Boris has a boyfriend?"

"I'll explain later," Nick said as Pearl came back.

"I've decided," Leila said. "Does everyone else know?"

"I'll have the usual Pearl," Persephone said.

"I'll have a bowl of tomato soup and some fries," Leila said.

"I'm just here for the company," Nick confessed.

"Oh isn't that sweet," Pearl grinned. "Now what the hell do you want to eat?"

"I'll just have some fries," Nick said.

"Good," Pearl said. "Do you all just want one big plate of fries to horde over?"

Nick shrugged his shoulders.

"Sure," Leila said.

"Did you want to come also Persephone?" Nick asked before taking a sip of his milk.

"I have plans this Friday. Jack and I are going to the shore."

"I'd love to go with you on Friday," Leila said. "I haven't seen a play since I moved here."

"Great," Nick said.

"So Boris finally admitted he is gay?" Persephone asked.

"That was abrupt," Nick said.

"Just trying to keep the conversation moving," Persephone said. "There was a slow pause after you said 'great.' So now you can answer my question."

"You knew Boris was gay?"

"Why do you say that?"

"Well the way you said, 'finally,' it sounds like you knew," Nick said.

"I guess I did know, I just never really thought about it. But when you think about it, he's definitely gay. Good for him. How is this Alfred guy?"

"He's a little strange," Nick started. "But he's nice."

"Will I get to meet Boris and Alfred?" Leila said. "I really want to meet your friends."

"Sure," Nick said.

"Actually you might have already met Boris," Persephone said.

"Really?"

"Yeah, remember about two years ago, when we were first becoming friends and we drove down to Jersey and the car broke down," Persephone said.

"The time we were going to meet that mysterious wine connoisseur," Leila added.

"Yeah you were uncomfortable going alone, and your sister was unavailable, so I came along."

"So what happened?" Nick asked.

"Oh well we headed down to meet this aficionado of fine wines, and everything in the universe didn't want us to go. We made a couple wrong turns," Persephone began.

"We...you were driving."

"Yeah, but it was your directions. So we made a couple wrong turns and ended up on this scary dark road in the middle of the woods. That was when the car broke down. Apparently the car was leaking fluids for the entire drive."

"I didn't think there were any woods in New Jersey," Nick grinned.

"Well I don't know if there are or there aren't, because we were no longer in New Jersey. We ended up in Pennsylvania somewhere," Leila said.

"So when the car broke down, we didn't want to leave."

"Why exactly?" Nick asked.

"Silly girl stuff, we were both too nervous to leave the car in the dark woods," Persephone explained. "The last gas station we came by was more then twenty miles off. So we stayed put for the entire night. That's when we became friends. We were too hyper on soda, fear, and excitement, so we stayed up all night. We kept each other up by talking. It was great."

"Where does Boris fit in?" Nick asked.

"The next morning we hitched a ride with some nice college guys and went back to the gas station. Jack was out on business and Jonathan was conveniently occupied..."

"Jonathan?"

"That was my old boyfriend," Leila said.

"The guy from the art gallery?"

"That's him..."

It was then Pearl came back with their orders.

"Wow, that was fast," Leila mentioned.

"Yeah, well, we had the soup already brewing, and Persephone's burgers take like a half-minute to cook..."

"The foods always good here," Nick added.

"Stop sucking up in front of the ladies...Here is your soup dear, and your bloody bacon cheese burger Persephone, and the fries. Is there anything else I can get you guys?"

"Just a refill on my milk please with a side of sarcasm," Nick said.

"You sure you don't want anything stronger?" Pearl said smiling.

Nick just stared at her. She smiled back, before walking off with Nick's glass.

"So anyway, we ended up calling my old friend Rich and he was hanging out with Boris at the time."

"I remember Rich; he went off to Hollywood right?"

"Yeah, so anyway Rich and Boris came and picked us up," Persephone said.

"Oh I remember him now," Leila said.

"Why didn't you call me?" Nick said just as Pearl came back with the milk.

There was a long silence where Persephone just looked at Nick. Pearl noticed Persephone's look and just put the milk at the table and walked off. Nick nodded to Pearl, ate a couple fries, and then looked up after she didn't say anything. He noticed Persephone looking at him with one of **those** looks. A look he knew very little of, though he knew enough about it to know it wasn't good. He wasn't sure why she looked angry. He hit a conversation mine, and didn't know what it was.

"You know why."

"Do I?"

"It was two years ago, don't make me say it," Persephone said.

"Oh I'm sorry..." Nick said.

"Am I being left in the dark about something?" Leila asked.

"We just weren't talking then," Persephone said. She took another bite of her hamburger. The juices of the flame kissed meat were soaked up by the hefty wheat bun.

Everything came rushing back to Nick, and he felt horrible.

CHAPTER TWENTY-FOUR

The rest of the lunch went by quietly. Leila talked about other stories to cheer up Persephone. Persephone threw on her unmatched, fake smile, which was flawless to everyone except Nick. He could tell she was uncomfortable. She continued the conversation, but he knew she'd be thinking about what plagued her memory. The demonic, lethargic memory would not leave her until she forced herself to muse over it. She'd reconcile with her past for a time, and would be her normal self again soon. When everyone had finished the meal, Persephone stood up and said:

"I have to get back to the store."

Nick got up and hugged her and whispered, "I'm sorry. I'll call you later."

She shook her head and he could see her holding back tears.

"Tell her about it," Persephone whispered back. "She's worried."

Leila couldn't see the sadness, but she could feel it. Persephone was like an emotion amplifier. If she was happy, you couldn't help but be happy yourself, but on the rare occasions when she was sad, everyone around her could mentally feel themselves breaking down. Leila stood and kissed Persephone on the cheek. They hugged and Nick could tell they said something to one another, but he wasn't sure what it was. Before Persephone left Pearl hugged her also. Leila sat back down and there was a long pause.

"Is Persephone ok?" Leila asked.

"She'll be ok," Nick said. "She told me to tell you about it if you are interested."

"Yeah, definitely, please."

"I don't know if you know that Persephone and I dated for over a year and a half. She says a year, but really it was closer to two. The reason she says one is because she broke it off with me, because she only loved me as a friend. I went through a bit of a destructive period. I didn't know it then, but eventually I would have realized I only really loved her as a friend also. Being together just felt really good. And when it ended, I thought our friendship would also. Then she called me up one day. We got together and she said she was pregnant."

"Persephone said she couldn't have children," Leila interjected.

"Right well, at the time I believed it would save our relationship if we had the child. I didn't say that, I just said I wanted to help raise the kid. So we got back together, well, we were back together, but there was no passion. I admit now it was the wrong reason to want a child, but as time passed I got into the idea of having a son or daughter that I could call my own. I noticed something was missing from our relationship. We didn't love each other as lovers anymore. She weaseled that out of me, at a really bad time. She kicked me out and went on to have the baby without me. Well obviously Persephone doesn't have any kids...she had a miscarriage. Really the baby died in her womb. They had to cut the baby out..." Nick's eyes filled with water. "They told her she could never have any children after that. She blamed me. She was angry and didn't really mean what she said. It's still a really hard subject for her. Persephone's dream was to have a family, two girls and a boy."

"I'm sorry Nick..."

"It's not your fault," Nick said, clearing his eyes.

"I'm just sorry for you and Persephone."

"Well, about a year ago, we became friends again. Jack convinced her. For a long time I hated that bastard. I used to think he took her from me. He's a good man; it was his dream to have a family also, but he married her anyway, he really loves her. He's still a bastard," Nick laughed. "It just hurts, knowing she wouldn't let me help her though the experience. It was my kid to," Nick paused. "I can't believe how stupid I was saying that earlier. I just wasn't thinking."

Leila leaned across the table and kissed him on the lips.

"You're a good man, Nick," Leila said. "It's not your fault. Persephone isn't angry at you."

"I know," Nick said. "Hey, do you want to get out of here, and go take a walk or something?"

"I'd like that," Leila said picking up the check.

"You know this is the first time I've went out with a woman who pays for my meal," Nick said.

"Well you didn't exactly eat very much," Leila said.

"Still it's nice," Nick said. "You're not like anyone I've ever met."

"Because, I treat you to lunch?"

"No," Nick said. "It's something in your eyes. I just told you a series of the stupidest things I've ever done, and you still kissed me."

"Listen, if those things about your relationship with Persephone are the worst things that have happened to you in your life...then I'd say you're quite a find," Leila declared.

The Best Orgasms Come from the Universe

"Well they are the worst things that have happened to my spirit," Nick said. "It was the time I was most ashamed of being me."

"You see that's the time you should be most proud of yourself," Leila began. "The times you get through by the skin of your teeth. Because if you can get through the bad times and still be yourself, then you are a true man, and a true human being."

"She's right you know," Pearl said.

While Nick and Leila were talking, he hadn't realized it, but they were also heading toward the register.

"The meal was wonderful Pearl," Leila said.

Leila paid and Nick held the door open for her. Before Nick left Pearl whispered something.

"What?" Nick inquired.

"I like her," Pearl said. "Don't screw things up Nick, she's a keeper. Don't worry, just enjoy the time you have, women like that are hard to come by."

"Thanks Pearl," Nick said.

Nick and Leila left the diner. They walked along the side walk holding hands. On the outside, Leila's air was like that of a young girl. She was short enough to rest her head comfortably on Nick shoulder or upper chest. Her voice was soft, and it changed almost entirely when she was smiling. During their walk Nick was struck with the thought that he had only known her for five days, six if you count the Thursday he first saw her. She knew about his childhood and his failed relationship with his soul mate friend. He had already told Leila the run-through of two of his most significant life experiences, yet the only thing he knew about her past was that she moved to the city from Pennsylvania, because she liked people.

"What about you?" Nick said. "I want to know more about you."

"Like I've said, your stories make mine seem so boring," she repeated.

"A story can never be boring, if the person listening wants to hear it."

"Good point," Leila paused. "I don't really have any stories. I'm just a middle child in a family of five daughters. My second oldest sister is Ray, she owns the winery. The wine is made back home in PA. I'm the shortest of all my sisters. My two younger sisters both play on girl soccer teams, because of their long legs. My oldest sister died two years ago, which is the real reason I moved out here. She was more of a mom than my real mom was. My mom and dad aren't rich enough to qualify for the title rich snobs, although that doesn't mean they don't try. My father is quieter about it, but when he was younger he was worse then my mother. I can't stand going to see them."

"I'll come with you this weekend if you'd like," Nick offered. "I don't have any plans."

"I'm not really ready for you to meet my parents yet."

"As you wish."

"Do you ever actually work?" Leila started. "I mean, I know you write, but you said something about being in business?"

"Yeah, I own a company. Well I own sixty percent of the decisions. Everything has to go by me. There is also a board of about ten people who make up the other forty percent. My father left it to me after he died. He also left me two shadows who watch over everything I do. I can't fire them either; it's part of the contract."

"You never talk about it."

"It's not something I'm proud of."

"What are you proud of?"

"I'm proud of Boris for coming out with the fact that he's gay. I'm proud of Persephone and how she's dealt with her life, after she lost her dream."

"I mean, what you are proud of in your own life."

"I don't know...I've never really thought about it." he said. "I'm just proud to be alive."

"Aren't you proud of your writing?"

"Not really," Nick said. "I love it, don't get me wrong, but I can write anytime I want. I don't consider it an accomplishment to finish something. I want to reach people, and I haven't."

"You've reached me and Persephone."

"Yes, but I could have done that without my writing."

"Well maybe once you stop worrying about reaching people, you'll rediscover something in yourself. Maybe you should just be proud of what you're doing, because people recognize that. You put a lot into your writing, you should be proud of it."

"What are you proud of?"

"I'm proud of where I am in life."

"I guess that's a good way to be," Nick said.

"It's worked for me," Leila paused. "How would you like to have dinner tomorrow night?"

"I'd love to," Nick said.

Leila looked into her purse, and pulled out a piece of paper and a pen.

"Turn around," she said.

When Nick turned around she began writing on the piece of paper, using his back as a hard surface.

"Be careful of my sunburn please," Nick said.

"Sunburn?"

"Yeah, I'll tell you later."

"Oh, well, here is my address," Leila said. "Come by around eight and we'll have dinner."

"Alright," Nick said. "Are we saying goodbye?"

"For now," Leila said. "I'll see you tomorrow."

"Tomorrow..."

"Tomorrow," she said putting her hands on his chest. She came closer to him and went onto her tiptoes to kiss him. The kiss was soft and light. She went back down to her heels.

"You don't close your eyes when you kiss me," she said smiling.

"I'm worried you'll disappear," Nick said. He leaned in and kissed her again, slowly closing his eyes. "You're still here."

"I'm still here," she said turning around. "I'll see you tomorrow."

"Leila," Nick said.

"Yes?"

"Say I'll see you tomorrow again," Nick said.

"I'll see you tomorrow..."

"I'd be happy to hear that everyday."

She smiled, and walked off.

CHAPTER TWENTY-FIVE

Curt and Mick had a devious grin over their faces when Nick entered the office. Mick rubbed each hand five times with the opposite hand; this was his usual indication of being excited about something. Usually this meant Nick was in trouble and Mick and Curt thought they could do something to keep it that way. Curt played with his glasses.

"You decided to come by," Curt began. "How nice of you."

"Good morning, Curt," Nick said.

"Oh I don't think being pleasant is going to get you out of this one, Nicolas," Mick winced.

"You two seem different," Nick said. "Let me guess, it's the hair, you both used twice the amount of hair products to give your hair that professionally disheveled look."

"Actually Nick..." Curt said.

"Oh wait, I got it, you switched ties for the day," Nick continued. "Or maybe you forgot to polish your shoes. Or did one of you have sex last night? Gasp, egads, and a bit of whoopee. Let me guess, it was you Mick, the girls just love it when you howl their full names in bed, and Curt, you are still feeling the recoil of imaging how Mick feels by using your wild creative intellect. Was she crazy? I bet she was crazy, a down right animal. You probably really cut loose on her didn't you."

"I really don't appreciate your humor, Nicolas," Mick said.

"Listen, I know what you guys are going to say," Nick said. "You are going to tell me how stupid my kickball idea was, and then you're going to say the board wants to see me. After that you'll say, 'you're in real trouble this time;' as opposed to the other times which were fake trouble. You two don't do any work around here, if I wasn't here, what would you do?"

Curt and Mick didn't say anything for quite some time. Nick didn't move, he expected one of them to come up with a crappy, half-witted answer. Neither of them did, and the pregnant silence continued, for over a minute and a half. Nick refused to speak first, he wanted them to either answer the question, or concede.

"They know I'm right," Nick thought. *"I won't let up; they need to answer this question."*

"The board wants to see you," Curt finally said looking down at the floor.

Mick glared at Curt, and Nick just grinned.

"So, what do they want to talk to me about?"

"What do you think Nick?" Mick said.

"Nick! He called me Nick! What's going on?"

"I'm sorry what?"

"What?" Mick said.

"What did you call me?"

"He said Nick, ok!" Curt said.

"I'm your life support aren't I?" Nick questioned. "And you just realized it, or maybe you just now accepted it. If by some chance the board does find a way to get rid of me, you two are gone, too. That's why you are always so worried about me screwing up."

Curt and Mick looked away.

"You're going to have to speak up," Nick said.

Curt shook his head, yes.

"It's true Nick," Mick said. "Your father knew you didn't like us. He knew, or thought you'd fire us. We were his advisers, but you don't need an adviser do you, let alone two."

"He thought, if we watched out for you, we'd still have a job," Curt continued.

"I see," Nick said. "You two are a pain in the ass."

"Sorry Nick," both of them said.

"Listen, the best way we can get through this is if you support my decisions," Nick said. "That way if the board isn't pissed, I don't have to worry, and neither do you. You have to give me a free reign."

"Ok Nick," Curt said.

"Good," Nick began. "To start, you have to convince the board that this kickball thing wasn't as bad as it appears."

"Actually Nick, the worker's productivity has increased," Curt said.

"The board just doesn't like your methods," Mick said. "They were going to take the job out from under you."

"Well they never much liked me," Nick said. "You two have done good work. Keep the board off my back, and you'll still have a job. I'll see you gentlemen later."

"Bye Nick," the both said, at once.

When Nick exited the elevator to his floor, everyone in the office just looked at him. Then someone stood up from their cubicle, and started clapping. All his employees bellowed out words of praise. They were only applauding because of the recess from the day earlier, nevertheless Nick took it to mean all his recent triumphs.

ything seemed right in his life as he bowed extravagantly and continued to his office. In his moment of appreciation Nick took himself into his office and immediately called Persephone. He called her at the store, figuring she would stay and work throughout the rest of the day. His inclination was correct, and Persephone answered the phone her office.

"Hello?" Persephone said.

"Yeah Persephone, it's me."

"Nick, hi," she started. "Did you tell her?"

"Yes..." he began. "Listen Persephone I'm really sorry, I just wasn't thinking straight, I was just enjoying the moment so much I wasn't keeping track to timelines."

"It's ok Nick, you are a dumb ass, but I forgive you," Persephone said. "Life's not fair. You know that. Life evenly divides things for people; we all get an equal hand of cards. It's just some people have the cards you want, and they lie and tell you to go fish. That's what life is, it's one big go fish game, were no one plays by the rules. I'd trade almost anything to have kids, Nick. It's not the game that's unfair, it's the other players."

"I know Persephone."

"Do something for me Nick."

"What's that?"

"You make Leila a happy woman."

"I can't make anyone happy Persephone."

"I know, I know...I mean, just do what you do best. She's had it rough, be careful. Be happy with her; don't let her throw you away like I did. You're a good man Nick, and it wasn't your fault."

"I know Persephone. Are you going to be ok?"

"Yeah I'm fine."

"Ok and I'll try," Nick said.

"Good, you try. Never stop trying."

"Alright...do you want me to come by later?"

"No, I'm going to be alright...I'm going to let you go," Persephone said.

"Bye, Persephone."

Nick hung up the phone and leaned in his chair, as he was apt to do. He just smiled and continued leaning. When Mary entered, Nick shifted his weight wrong and the computer chair tipped over, sending him to the ground.

"Are you ok Nick," Mark exclaimed running over.

"I'm great Mary," Nick laughed sitting on the ground. "I'm great, how are you?"

"I'm...tired," Mary said kneeling on the floor with Nick. "My husband Jerry is such a bum. I mean we both get home at the same time; he plops down at the television and watches it for hours. He doesn't give me any attention. I'm just tired, I need something."

"You're a beautiful woman, Mary," Nick said. "You should go out tomorrow, get your hair and nails done. Then you should go get some nice black lacy lingerie, and get a killer outfit. Put on the lingerie under the hot outfit. When you go home, seduce the hell out of him, he'll give you some attention. In bed afterwards eat ice cream together and watch a movie. Stay up really late, and talk to him about your feelings, believe me if he'll ever listen to you, that would be the best time. If you have a good time together, it's easier for the man to know you're not all business."

"I don't know Nick."

"Listen, sleep in the next day, and convince him to do the same. A job is just a job, it's not more important than your relationship with your husband. Make sure he understands that one day is not going to ruin his career. Spend the day together. Paid vacation time, I'm making it a holiday, just for you. We will call it International Mary Needs a Good Orgasm from Her Husband Day."

"It's a little long of a name," Mary laughed.

"Ok, Mary Needs Off from Work Day."

"I'll take it," Mary said. "Why the sudden interest in my life Nick?"

"What do you mean?"

"Well you've always been a great boss," Mary began. "But beyond a pleasant attitude and a lasting platonic relationship, you've never really asked about me before."

"Well, that's true Mary, to a point...but then you've never offered much, like you just did either. Now have you?"

"I guess not, but you still seem different. You seem...more colorful. I mean you've always been very exuberant person. But usually you're a little overpowering of a personality. Now you seem...I don't know, different."

"Well I guess I'm just happy to be alive Mary," Nick said. "I'm having several good days, which is starting to add up to a good week. I guess I was just hoping others felt the same way. I've learned something Mary."

"What's that?"

"Little things in life feel good," he explained. "No one notices that anymore, normally I'd just grin and bear unhappiness in other people, but now...Now I know that maybe I can show it to them...or maybe I can't, but I can try. So one day, someone might fall off their wheelie chair at work and say...'Wow.' There are a lot worse things in life, then falling off your wheelie chair."

"Wow?"

The Best Orgasms Come from the Universe

"Wow...no explanation point. Plain and simple...kiss...kiss........ ...Keep It Simple Stupid. Just wow...the word is self-explanatory. People need to say 'wow' more often."

"Wow..."

"Wow is right."

"You're a good man Nick."

"Women keep saying that to me," Nick said. "What exactly does that mean?'

"It means...you're good," she said, just before kissing Nick on the cheek. "And I am going to leave you with your thoughts."

"Thanks Mary...you're the best. Is Bruce around?"

"No, he didn't come in today. I think he called in sick."

"Thanks again Mary."

Mary left Nick's office and he sat back atop his wheelie chair.

CHAPTER TWENTY-SIX

Nick came to Bruce's apartment building after getting off from work. Nick forged up the six flights of steps to Bruce's room. Nick knew where Bruce lived, but he had never been there. He walked down the un-soundproofed hallway. He could hear teenagers playing videogames, a mother yelling at her children, and the out of place new-age music. Nick glanced at the letters and numbers on the doors. This was the "F" floor, and all the overhanging lights were cracked, totally ruined, or flickering in an indecisive fashion. The sounds and darkness could not be uprooted from his mind. Fear was something Nick had in check. He believed that any real fear could be broken down into five basic cores: fear of death/being forgotten, fear of helplessness, fear of being alone, fear of the unknown, and the worst fear, the fear of yourself. Any other fear can be broken down into one or a combination of those five categories.

Nick was not afraid of the darkness or the noises. Nevertheless he walked with caution. From past experiences he knew disregarding your surrounds, so as not to admit fear, was the worst possible thing to do. Overcoming fear can be hazardous as well, for many people become overconfident. He accepted the fact that something biological in his body, felt the need to put his senses on guard while walking in the area. He accepted fear as something he would have to live with.

Nick walked along the row of apartments looking for F12, Bruce's apartment. He walked along the left wall looking at the numbers. The lights made him a bit dizzy as they continued to flicker as if they were meant for a disco. He passed F2, and F4, and he presumed the next door was F6, although it had no metal ID. The next door had caution tape around it. As Nick walked around the next corner he came, eye to chin with the Devil himself. Or at least he thought he was the Devil, as Nick lifted his eyes to meet the face of this tall man.

The shadows and darkness of the hallway accentuated the man's chiseled face. Every part of the his face ended with a sharp edge, including the man's glaring eyelids. The black man's muscles were picture perfect, excluding the scars that decorated his arms. Nick noticed the man's broad shoulders before meeting his eyes. Fear didn't ever enter Nick's body, for if it were the Devil, Nick wouldn't much mind. He had a few questions he definitely didn't mind having answered. Besides, evil is in every man, and Nick was happy with what he had, and wouldn't have been tempted into action. Although temptation is undeniably healthy for without it everyone would be either all evil or all good, and what fun would that be? If life was black and white, we'd all be colorblind.

Unfortunately, the man was not the Devil. He was also not nearly as angry as his air would've indicated. He moved all his dreadlocks to behind his head, and smiled a smile which would reveal that of the most blissful poets.

"We all need to find our own way 'man," said the Jamaican behemoth.

"I couldn't agree more," Nick said going around him to continue looking at the doors.

"Find yours, and tell the world!" the dark man said still standing by an apartment door. "Joy is making a comeback!"

When Nick came to Bruce's door, he found it open a crack.

"Bruce?" Nick said into the door. He knocked and repeated Bruce's name again quietly.

When there was no answer, Nick entered into the pitch black room. As the creaking front door opened, the living room and part of the hallway leading to Bruce's kitchen became illuminated. The coat rack was snapped in two on the ground and just next to it, resided a smashed lamp. Nick tried the light switch anyway, to no avail. His eyes grew wide as he came into the living room. The windows were open wide and the night air was complimented by the sounds of rain. Nick could only hear a light drizzle of rain and by the window he saw a turned over picture.

Light from the kitchen trickled into partially lit corridor, as Nick reached the hallway. He continued on, noticing the refrigerator was open and a heap of food products were scattered on the ground. The tiles were covered in a red liquid which leaked from an open tomato juice container lying on its side. Nick continued down the hall. He peeked into the unaltered bathroom and den area. Nick reached the bedroom, and an unforgettable smell fell across him. Although it was not the smell of a rotting body, as Nick's nerves had played him up to think, it was still an undesirable odor. It was the undeniable smell of stale liquor.

Nick checked the light switch, with filled the room with bright light. As the light went on, he could hear a familiar grunt. Nick could saw two bottles of Jack Daniels on the ground. One of the two bottles was attached to loose open hand. Nick circled the bed, and found Bruce sprawled across the floor. Nick could tell Bruce was making a conscious effort to open his eyelids.

"Drunken bastard, you had me scared half to death," Nick said kicking Bruce's leg.

"Hey...hey...man who sent for the light brigade," Bruce said. "Ha, get it, light brigade."

"I should let you drown in your own vomit," Nick said, lifting Bruce up and putting him on his bed. "So what, you thought you'd skip work, and have a party with Jack and his twin...Jack."

"Actually, Jack's a triplet," Bruce chuckled. "There's a third in the kitchen with Bloody Mary, but she doesn't taste good with Jack in her."

"Yeah, funny," Nick said picking up the two bottles, and that's when he saw another bottle. This bottle wasn't glass, it was plastic, orange plastic, and it had a doctor prescribed label. All the pills from it were gone. "Bruce, did you take these pills?"

"Wow," Bruce said.

"Did you take these fucking pills?" Nick questioned at the top of his lungs. All the fear rushed him at once.

"He's being adopted..." Bruce said getting incoherent.

"Ok Bruce, stay with me," Nick said. "Bruce!"

Nick picked Bruce up and shook him. Nick picked up the phone, which was dead.

"She didn't want to talk," Bruce said. "So I broke it."

"Bruce, do you have another phone?"

"We are all telephones...philosophically speaking," Bruce said. "After thirteen years, I thought we'd have gone head first into deeper shit."

Bruce's eyes began to shut, and Nick slapped him.

"Help!" Nick bellowed. Quickly, Nick maneuvered his way through the small apartment dragging Bruce under the arms. Nick came out into the hallway, and looked in both directions. He saw the dark skinned man still in the doorway of one apartment. "Do you have a phone?"

The man shook his head.

"Call an ambulance!" Nick said. "My friend...he's taken many pills, please!"

"Quick, bring him inside," the man said.

"I don't think he's going to move much farther," Nick exclaimed.

"Alright, I'll be right back. Keep him talking! Keep him awake."

The man rushed into the room and Nick jostled his friend in his arms again.

"Come on Bruce, talk to me," Nick said aloud, and his eyes filled with water. "Come on, don't BS your way through a conversation, by making me ask, talk to me."

"He's his boy now," Bruce said. "I'm just some bum in the big city, living in a dump to support him. Well good, good go, to hell with him. Now I can get a nice house in a nice place."

"Where do you want to go? Tell me Bruce," Nick said.

"Up-town, I'm going to meet a nice fine refined lady, like that girl we saw at the bagel place," Bruce said. "A real beauty."

Bruce started fading again, and Nick shook him vigorously.

"Hey Bruce, come on now, that can't be it," Nick said.

"You're a good man Nick...a true friend..." Bruce went on. "Maybe I'm not your best friend...but I'm up there, right..."

"Yeah...Bruce, yeah you are...great friend," Nick said, very flustered. "You just keep talking."

Bruce didn't say anything, even after Nick shook him.

The Best Orgasms Come from the Universe

"Bruce! Bruce!" Nick screamed, and then he buried his head into his friend's shirt. "No! Come on Bruce."

Then the Jamaican man stormed out of his home and barreled down the hallway.

"I can smell him from here," he began and Nick looked up with a glare at first. "He's been drinking. We have to get him to throw up."

"Will that work?" Nick questioned, lifting Bruce up.

"Do you have a suction tube," the man said. "Because, if you don't, this is our only alternative. What's his name?"

"Bruce."

"Ok, help me put him up against the wall," he started. "I'll hold him up, you need to stick your finger into the back of his throat, and make him cough up. Make him gag."

The Jamaican man held Bruce steady as Nick touched his friend's uvula. In less than a second Bruce's entire body arched. The bile and vomit shot out of him like water overflowing from a gorge. He hurled up twice, and fell to his knees. The hallway was filled with a brown shadow, and the disgusting contents of Bruce's stomach were splashed across the floor. Everything seemed silent to Nick, save the tapping of the rain against the rafters. Nick's mind throbbed in agony, and only properly registered the information of the events in slow motion. He just preformed as the dark man told him to help Bruce gag yet again.

CHAPTER TWENTY-SEVEN

WEDNESDAY

The night cried for its entire duration, into the morning of the next day. It was still dark, and Nick's expression was emotionless as he stared outside from the hospital. Beyond the massive, waiting room windows, Nick watched hustling ambulance crews. His headache still remained, and would likely not leave him for hours to come. In the interim of saving Bruce's life and getting him to the hospital, Nick found out the kind Jamaican man was named Duncan. Duncan sat next to Nick, on his right side, with a similar expression. Both of them stared off into space, just waiting...in the *waiting* room. On Nick's left sat Life in his normal, ruffled, penniless clothing. Or at least, it comforted Nick to think the person next to him was Life. Really, it was just an old homeless black man. The man's curly gray hair cascaded around his beat up brown hat.

"*Where am I?*" Nick thought. "*Who am I...? I'm a good man...am I? I hope Bruce is ok. He's good...a very good friend. I don't want him to die. Damn bastard. How can he be doing this to me? What the hell am I saying to myself? He didn't do this to me; he's not putting me through this grief. I'm putting myself through this grief, because I care about him. I'd miss him. I hate that. I hate just now realizing that I'm going to miss him if he dies. What if Persephone dies? What if Leila dies? Am I going to break down? You're damn right I am. What the hell is this? It could all fall apart...and I don't even think about it. I've never even contemplated what I would do. I'm afraid! I'm afraid of being alone...I'm afraid of dying and being forgotten."*

"I'm fucking afraid!" Nick said, grabbing the homeless man. Everyone got startled and shuddered a moment. "Is that what you want to hear?"

The poor man looked back at him with wide, confused eyes. The man who Nick obliviously associated with life, glanced back with fear as Nick looked into his eyes for an answer. Duncan put a hand on Nick's shoulder. The happiness in Nick's day had all been washed away with the trauma he had not expected. If one gets too used to the gray, then red seems more beautiful or possibly more aggravating. Although, equally, if someone sees all red and revels in its beauty, when gray comes it strikes like a bullet. The pain fell out of Nick's eyes. The homeless man could see the pain, yet had no words to help. Nick only found himself in the man's deep brown eyes. The sorrow in him turned to remorse, as he recoiled from the man's space.

"I'm sorry..." Nick said. "I'm sorry..."

Nick looked away and stared at the ground.

"It's ok," the man said back.

Duncan leaned forward in his seat.

"We all can lose our way," Duncan said. "You should be happy, 'man. You're not dead. Neither is your friend Bruce. Joy is making a come back."

Nick looked up and turned to his new friend.

"But it'll only come back…if you let it," Duncan continued.

Nick smiled, and Duncan was almost always smiling when he spoke.

"Thanks…"

"I think I'm going to head home. So, you keep at it, I see a lot of joy in your life. Then again…I see a lot of sadness too."

"I don't believe in predetermination…"

"Well…joy is what you make it be, like everything in life. When you're speaking from a human point of view, anything and everything is what you make it be. It's not predetermination 'man, its human nature. You'll have joy and sadness; it's what you do with them. Like fear…you don't control these things, but you do have control on how much you let them effect you."

Duncan removed a rectangular card from his pants pocket.

"If you ever lose your way," Duncan began, and then he tapped Nick's temple and his chest, over where his heart would be. "Here… or here, read this card, and it might help put things into perspective. You're doing a good job. And no matter what people say to you or about you, stick with it…and…remember…"

"Remember what?" Nick asked as Duncan headed toward the open sliding doors.

"Just remember…"

Nick couldn't help but contemplate what Duncan meant by 'just remember.' He ran over ideas in his head for the remainder of the night until he fell into a pleasant sleep.

CHAPTER TWENTY-EIGHT

Nick was awakened by a nurse at around six thirty in the morning. Everything in sight was white, including the morning light from outside. He was led to Bruce's hospital room. Nick stood in the doorway. Bruce was lying still in his bed. His eyelids were half open.

"Hey Nick," he said.

"Hey Bruce."

"Look at my feet, Nick," Bruce replied. "I've never really looked at them until now. It's strange, I've made all this money, I have a good life, it's not a great life, but it's good."

"Really good…" Nick said.

"But not once have I just looked at my feet. I've overlooked them for so long, I never really expected anyone to take them away."

"Are we still talking about feet," Nick said still standing in the doorway.

"I don't know."

There was a long pause, which Nick wanted to fill with his angry feelings towards Bruce's stupidity.

"I've been such a one dimensional person for so long, Nick. Can I stop? Can I go home now?" Bruce asked blinking his eyes numerous times. "Can I go home now?"

Nick sighed out his grief before answering.

"Yeah..." Nick said entering the room. "Yeah, you can go home."

"I don't have a home, Nick. No one will have me, I'm homeless... do you know how that feels Nick!" Bruce exclaimed. "Do you know what it's like to be married to a woman for three years because you got her pregnant? Loving a woman that doesn't love you for three damn years...Do you know what it's like to be sixteen, and have a little boy Nick?"

"I don't know how it feels to be married, or what it's like to have a little boy, or how it feels to have those things and not be loved. But I do know how it feels to be dead inside everyday, and not having a home. I know what it's like to live in a house with your parents...yet still not be in a home and not having a family. Yes I know what that's like Bruce. And I know that when a friend of mine tries to kill himself, it makes me think about my own life. I think about what the fuck I'm doing. When my friend is hurting inside so much, and I can't see it...Do you know how that feels you selfish bastard? So don't act like you're the only one that has problems. I go by people everyday with problems. What do I do about it? Nothing...what do you about it? Nothing...no one does anything about it. And then you think you have the right to take your own life."

"My son is gone; my wife left me for a man that works at a gas station!"

"At least you can have kids!"

"What do you know about it?" Bruce bellowed.

A nurse walked by the room and stepped inside.

"Get out of here!" Bruce yelled.

The nurse stumbled back in fright and left.

"What do you know about losing a kid to another man? She moved away with him, and went to Arizona. He's adopting my son!"

"So do something about it!"

"I've been supporting him since I was sixteen," Bruce said. "I live in a dump because of it!"

"So what, you give up?" Nick exclaimed. "You throw it away... drowned your fear in a bottle of JD with a side of antidepressants... smart!"

"What would you have me do...?" Bruce said, wiping away his tears.

"Talk to her, tell your wife that your son means something to you," Nick said.

"She knows."

"Does he?"

"I don't know..."

"I suggest you find out."

"No...I can't."

"You'd rather be dead, then see if your son cares for you the same way you feel. My father was dead to me at the age of six on. On my sixteenth birthday he bought me a car, but he didn't have the time to teach me how to drive. So yeah, you're right, I don't really know about being a father, but I can remember what it's like to be a fatherless kid. Do you want this new guy to be his father? Cause if you do, then to hell with it. Don't worry about it, your son's in good hands. Or at least a pair of hands, as opposed to a paycheck every week. But I have a feeling you don't want that."

"No..." Bruce said, and then he cleared his throat. "No."

"Right, no," Nick said.

"So what do I do?"

"That's for you to decide, but what I would do, is as soon as I got out of this hospital, I would ask my boss for my paid vacation time, and head to Arizona."

"Can I have my paid vacation time?"

"No."

"What?"

"If you leave today..." Nick said.

"That's bribery..."

"Damn right...'it's better to be at the right hand of the devil than in his path.' I believe you said that," Nick quoted.

"Thanks Nick."

"I don't want to see you at work tomorrow. In fact if I do see you, I'm going to kick your ass, and force feed those pills down your throat."

"I'm lucky to have a friend like you," Bruce said.

"You're lucky you were chasing those pills with JD, and not water. I don't know if your body would have stalled long enough, if it didn't want to get rid of those toxins," Nick explained.

"I love you Nick," Bruce replied as Nick began to leave.

"I know." Nick said with a grin.

"I'll see you later."

"You're an asshole," Nick said still smiling. "I can't stand the fact that you're my best friend."

Nick left his friend, went home, fell onto his pillow, and didn't wake up until one o'clock pm.

CHAPTER TWENTY-NINE

Before Nick's eyes opened, the light from outside fell across his face. All Nick could see was the red glow from outside his eyes. When he got himself out of bed, all the events which previously transpired came rushing back to him all at once. After showering, his mind became all the more clear. The proceedings, adding up to this particular Wednesday, filled Nick with the magic of creativity. Emotions flowed in his mind like a sewage pipeline. He gathered his thoughts and sat down at his typewriter. For another three hours Nick let loose, adding to his essay.

"...*Fear, hate, hope, and even love, are chemical imbalances of the human spirit. When you take any such emotion, it may imbalance your overall life, tipping the scales in one of many directions. Believe it or not, hate is not the opposite of love. For hate has one or many reasons behind it. You hate someone or something, because of direct impressions that it's left on you. True love has no reason behind it. True love is unconditional, yet an opposite needs to have similarities; it sounds like a contradiction, but it's true. The opposite of bad is good. Both of them are controlled groups of spiritual pathways. For hate and love to be true opposites, they have to be in the same category of thinking, although be totally different ways of thought. It's like saying the opposite of an elephant is a raisin. Yes, both of these things are nouns, and tangible, but an elephant is an animal and a raisin is a dried fruit. Yes, both hate and love are emotions, but they are different types of emotions.*

Extremes in life make living easier. It's a more pleasing idea to believe if you don't love something, then you should hate it. Really the opposite of love is always rooted in fear. Fear and love are both undeniable forces. Both of them are unalterable basic emotions caused by similar basic chemical imbalances in the human body, putting them in similar categories. Although these two thought patterns take you in completely opposite directions of your desired balanced state of living..."

It was than the phone rang.

"I'm trying to prove a point here!" Nick yelled at the loud interruption.

"Fear and love..."

It rang again.

"Fear makes you..."

Obviously, it rang again. He got up from his chair and walked to the phone, cursing and mumbling under his breath like an old man.

"Hello," Nick answered.

"Nick, it's me," said the voice.

"Me who?"

"Griffon."

"Oh, hi Griffon...listen this isn't such a good—"

"Yeah, well, I called you a couple of times the past few days."

"Yeah..."

"My thing is taking place on Thursday."

"Alright, I'm free, where should I meet you?"

"Meet me at that old bar we used to go to."

"I don't drink."

"I know, but I do."

"Oh...ok, the Dripping Bucket, right, wasn't that it?"

"That's the one, see you then."

"Yeah bye, oh wait, what time?"

"Six-ish...do you remember where it is?" Griffon answered.

"Yup, bye." Nick said, although it didn't strike him till he hung up, just how far that bar was.

"Dam it," Nick thought. *"That's pretty far...I guess I'll need to drive down. I hate driving...damn...oh well, back to my writing."*

Before leaving Nick looked down at his answering machine, which had four messages on it.

"Hell no," he said to himself.

Nick sat back at his desk and continued writing.

"Both fear and love give you sweaty palms. Fear cannot be controlled; it can only be coped with. It's the same way with love. Your fears never go away, you just learn to live with them, and work with, or around them. Love never goes away either, it just changes; you learn to live with it, or work around it. These emotions cannot be controlled, yet they are both completely different feelings. If you incubate love or fear in fertile soil, such as varying life experiences, these two emotions can turn to hate or hope. Hope comes when you are willing to love life freely and faith is blind hope. Hate comes when you are willing to fear life overly, and revenge is blinding hate. If any of these emotions are overindulged you destroy yourself. Running on one thought pattern leaves you undefended against life. Don't try to control your emotions, once you start telling yourself when to, and not to, feel something, is the day you die inside. Acknowledge your

feelings, and work with them as peers. Try not to rule your own emotions, and don't let them rule you either, work with them."

Nick continued to refine his ideas until they were structured and coherent. When he finished he gathered his three new pages, and added them logically to his base essay of ten pages.

As Nick continued cleaning up his work area, he began listening to his messages from the previous night.

"You have four new messages...Tuesday...One thirty-two pm..."

"Hi Nick its Alfred. I'm sorry to call again so soon, it's just I need to know if you want those tickets. Please give me a call at Boris' if you do, I need to know by tomorrow around six. Me and Boris are getting together with a friend, and I want to be able to offer it to him if you don't want them. Ok...well you have the number, give us a call."

"Tuesday...One fifty-one pm..."

There was a long pause, and then someone came on.

"Yeah, hey Nick. It's Griffon...I hate answering machines. Yeah well I'll call back."

"Tuesday...Two thirty pm..."

"Nick, hey it's Bruce. I just wanted to say you're a really good friend. I ah...oh shit I don't know. I'm going out drinking later, I know you don't drink, I was...well if you want to come by later, that's cool, bye."

"Tuesday...Five thirty-eight pm..."

"Nick hi, it's Persephone, I just wanted to say thanks for calling. I was just calling to talk, but you are not around so, I'll see you later, bye Nick."

The Best Orgasms Come from the Universe

Nick deleted the messages and called Alfred. He laid his claim to the two free tickets, and then got ready for his date. At seven he left his apartment, got a taxi, and headed to Leila's address.

CHAPTER THIRTY

The door opened, and there stood Leila. Her hair was tied back in a ponytail.

"Hi," he said.

She smiled, threw her arms around him, kissing him suddenly. The kiss was a shock at first as she held on. When she pulled away, her smile was brighter than before, and she held Nick's wrist, walking him inside. Leila's dog came scurrying around Nick's legs. The cast on the dog's leg scraped against the ground, making a very annoying noise.

"This is Ralph, and this is my apartment," she explained excitedly. "I'm not exactly ready to go yet."

Leila brought Nick to the living room and continued on to her bathroom.

"Where do you want to go to dinner?" she asked.

Nick didn't answer at first. Since the occurrences of the previous day, all Nick thought of, with any sort of comfort, was his date. He couldn't help but relish in his well deserved, long awaited moment of happiness. He tried not to speculate about how long the joy was going to last. Leila was just so full of life. She turned back to him, peeking around the doorframe of the bathroom.

The Best Orgasms Come from the Universe

"Hey, did you hear me?"

"Yeah..." Nick grinned, petting her small terrier.

"Are you ok?"

"Things are looking up."

"Good."

Nick looked around at her large living room. The walls were filled with pictures. Even her glass table had framed pictures standing up.

"You sure do have a lot of pictures."

"Well the way I see it is: white wall space means that you don't know anyone, and you haven't been anywhere, or seen anything. I would like to believe that I've had a good life, that's worth showing off. Everything in my life isn't perfect, and there are plenty of things I could redo, but then I might not be right here right now."

"I'm not much of a photographer."

"Neither am I. I just like surrounding myself in good memories. I don't dwell in the past, but it is important to keep your experiences close at hand. That way you know what you've done, you know what not to do again, and you know ways to help others."

"I thought you said you don't have any stories."

"What I said was, 'stories like yours make mine look boring.'"

"Oh, well, based on these pictures, I'd say some of them look pretty interesting."

Leila walked out from the bathroom. She even looked gorgeous when she was dressing plainly. Her clothing accentuated nothing. She wore her hair back and only had on a little makeup. She was undeniably beautiful; it was something in her smile, and her eyes. Every part of her face complimented everything else. Nick sat on her couch, stricken with contentment. Nevertheless he stood up as she came in.

"So, where should we go?" She said smiling as she met him in the middle of the living room.

"You have the most beautiful smile I have ever seen," Nick said. "None of these pictures do it justice."

She couldn't help but blush.

"Thanks...but that's not what I asked."

"I want to go anywhere!" he exclaimed excitedly throwing up his arms.

"So you wouldn't be apposed to pizza...I guess?"

"I would love to go eat pizza with you," he answered.

"Then let's go," she started. "Be good Ralph."

They traveled to a small Italian pizzeria one block from Leila's apartment. Nick had never eaten there before, although he had passed it numerous times in the past. The inside was filled with cool air. The light was dim, and as you entered you could hear the sound of two arcade games, and a pinball machine.

"Hey Leila," said a heavy set man. "Long time no see."

"Hey Teddy," Leila exclaimed.

"And who's this handsome chap?"

"Oh, Teddy this is Nick,"

"Ah, Nick, it's a pleasure to meet a friend of Leila's," Teddy started. "He's taller than the last one. He looks Italian to...Are you Italian Nick?"

"Partially..."

"Well, we can't all be perfect."

"Yeah, I'm a regular mutt."

"We have the customary *Lady and the Tramp*," Teddy exclaimed, and his laugh was a hefty one. "Should I get the meatballs?" He clapped Nick on the shoulder. Nick grinned in response. "Let me get you a table," Teddy said as he led the way. "I'll be right back, here are your menus."

"He's charming," Nick smiled.

In the background they could here yelling, "Stony, Leila's here."

"Ah Leila!" Stony bellowed with a thick accent.

"Stony doesn't speak any English," Leila said. "He understands it though."

"I'll keep that in mind."

"I love it here."

"How did you come to be so well known here?"

"Once you taste their pizza, you'll know why I keep coming back. So what kind of pizza do you like?"

"Anything except mushrooms."

"Do you like Hawaiian?"

"I've never tried it; there is something odd about fruit on pizza."

"Tomatoes are fruit," Leila retorted.

"True...but I wouldn't want chopped up tomatoes on my pizza either. You see if there was pineapple in the sauce, than it might be ok. There are rules for these things. Well...actually pineapple sauce ...might be rather nasty..."

Leila laughed and then asked, "Does that mean you aren't going to try it?"

"I guess I'll try anything once; twice even, if it doesn't kill me."

Teddy returned with two glasses of water.

"So what can I get for you two today?"

"We are going to have a Hawaiian pizza."

"What would you like to drink?"

"I'll have a root beer," Leila answered.

"Make that two."

"Two root beers and a Hawaiian pizza. I'll come back with some breadsticks."

"Thanks Teddy."

"Thanks," Nick said, with a melancholy look about him.

"Is something wrong today?"

"Ever since I left you yesterday, my day kind of went to hell. My secretary isn't coming to work tomorrow. Actually that's not that bad. In fact it's not bad at all. In all honesty I was having a good day up until after work. My friend had some problems."

"What happened?"

"He tried to kill himself. He took a lot of pills. I got there just in time. Me and a man name Duncan saved him, but it got me thinking."

"About what?"

"Lot's of things…"

Teddy came back with the bread sticks, a pitcher of root beer, and two glasses. He filled their cups, smiled, and was off back to work.

"He's not as loquacious as I thought."

"Well, he's pretty good about not interrupting a conversation. Please continue with what you were saying."

"Well I was just wondering how I didn't notice his unhappiness. I mean I've known him for thirteen years. He had a kid when he was sixteen, and I didn't even know. He was married at eighteen, and was with his wife for three years. She moved to Arizona with their kid, and he continued supporting him," he said eating a bread stick. "She's getting remarried, and the man is going to adopt my friend's son. I've known him through all of this, and I didn't know any of it. I couldn't help him. He was right under my nose for thirteen years, and I didn't help him."

The Best Orgasms Come from the Universe

"If he didn't tell you, it's not your fault."

"It just kind of made me wonder who else I've never noticed. I've always been a fairly observant person. I just don't want that to happen with anyone else I know. My friends don't seem to understand that I'm here to talk to. I know more about some acquaintances than I know about my best friends."

"What do you want to know?"

"These are good bread sticks," Nick started. "What do you mean?"

"What do you want to know about me? You've been subtly hinting towards wanting to hear about me. So, what do you want to know?"

"I haven't really given it much thought. I ah, just wanted to know about you. You told me you moved down here after your older sister died. What happened when you got here?"

"I started working with Ray at the Winery. That's when I met Jonathan. He was a successful sports agent. The relationship was really over before it began. John was always so distant. Whenever he kissed me before work, it always seemed like something he'd forget to do. I don't mind if I don't get kissed before my boyfriend leaves for work. I just don't want to feel like I'm something on someone's checklist. Like, ok pack suitcase, put on tie, brush teeth, kiss girlfriend before work, get a cab, and get to work at nine. Do you have any idea what I mean?"

"I know what you mean. My father was like that. How long were you two together?"

"About a year and a half, but I was unhappy for a while."

"Did you tell him you were unhappy?"

"I tried, but he didn't really listen."

"Ok, I want you to promise me something. I want you to promise to tell me if you're ever unhappy with me. Force it down my throat if you have to, just make sure I know. To many times I've been dumped, without really knowing what I did. Please let me know, and give me a chance to rectify the situation."

"I promise...do you promise to do the same with me?"

"I promise."

"Good."

Teddy came back with the pizza. Leila's and Nick's conversation continued, talking about more interesting topics, like books and movies. The discussions were fulfilling, and the pizza wasn't bad either, even with the fruit on top.

Nick and Leila walked back down to her house, after a two hour date. When they got to her building, Leila stopped and looked at Nick.

"That was a great dinner," he said. "The pizza was fantastic."

"I'm glad you enjoyed it. It doesn't have to be over you know... the date I mean. Do you want to come up?"

"Yes..."

"I want to, but I don't want to rush things."

"We are adults Nick, we can have sex. We aren't in high school; we don't have to worry about the next day at school, and everyone talking about it."

"I know, and I want to have sex with you. I really want to. I just don't want to screw things up."

"What, are you bad in bed?" she said jokingly.

"It's not that at all," Nick said. "Although if I was...would I really admit it?"

"Probably not."

"It's just, I really like you, and I want to enjoy all the stages. You are the most beautiful woman I've ever been with," Nick said inching closer. "When I make love to you, I want that to be a bonus. I don't want it to be the reason I'm here. Everything about you is worth relishing in. I could kiss you everyday, and be happy."

He moved in and kissed her. His lips stayed on hers, and they stood under the doorway of her apartment building.

"You are unlike any guy I've ever met. And that's a good thing," Leila said. "But I'll tell you this much, it gets a whole lot better than just kissing."

They kissed again.

"You are so beautiful," Nick whispered. "And I'll see you soon."

"Tomorrow?"

"If you'd like..."

"When?"

"We'll have lunch..."

"I can't, I'm having lunch with a regular tomorrow. They are buying a lot of wine. What about dinner?"

"I'm seeing an old friend at six, I have to leave at five; it's pretty far."

"Do you have a car?"

"Yeah, I just don't really like driving."

"Well, I guess us seeing each other tomorrow isn't in the cards."

"I guess not."

"But...Friday, we'll go to the theatre, for my birthday."

"That's true..."

"Will I see you on Saturday?"

"You're leaving for your parent's house."

She just looked at him, still holding on to him.

"Yes, if that's what you want," he continued. "And I'll see you when you come back on Monday. And I want to see you, again, on Tuesday. And I want to see you the next day, and the next, and the next, if you're not sick of me."

She kissed him again. "I'll see you on Friday, and we'll see... about next week."

"Till then..." he blew her a kiss before bowing dramatically, as he had at his office, just the other day. He smiled and walked backward to the sidewalk. She waved from the doorway.

CHAPTER THIRTY-ONE

THURSDAY

And so another Thursday rolled around. Seven days passed since Nick first told Boris about his idea for his book. Nick got up at eight o'clock, as he tried to do everyday, unsuccessfully. He groomed himself, like any other day. After his shower, he put a dime sized glob of hair gel, which helped to give his hair that controlled, scruffy look, without the frizz. He looked at himself in the mirror, and reflected on what and who he was. When eight thirty moved into nine am, Nick changed into his normal clothes. He gathered his essay, "Living Intentionally," and left his apartment.

Nick headed confidently and joyously down the street, heading to his Thursday coffee shop, where he would meet Boris. The sun was indecisively covering itself behind puffy clouds. The blue sky stretched itself out languidly behind the city scene. Today Nick could see more than just the rushed business folk. His eyes were open to everyone who walked down the street. A smile was branded on his face like an endangered species in the jungle. Not a stupid smile, or even an obnoxious smile, but a simple smile, the kind where, if you use it correctly, it seems natural and almost eable. Nick's expression was complimented by his slightly raised eyebrows. He was the stunning opposite to the slant-browed, straight-lipped, furrow-foreheaded, average street prowler.

Nick just walked the streets. He didn't need to meet Boris until ten. The city hallways, known as sidewalks, were air-conditioned by a clever breeze. Nick moved like a seasoned dancer. He side stepped, snapped his fingers, and moved his body in unusual directions. These actions of course perplexed the other hallway inhabitants. They looked at Nick with one single expression that could only be compared to that of a weatherworn hag. They stared like suspicious hall monitors, back in high school, as if Nick's half prancing movements were harming anyone. Then he stopped dead in his tracks. He stood up very erect like a bronze statue.

"I call for a dance," Nick exclaimed, and then he clapped his hands above his head. He envisioned a group of hoboes removing medieval instruments. "Let the minstrels play us a tune!" he cried jokingly.

"Shut up," one city man yelled.

"Joy is making a comeback!" Nick bellowed, and then he laughed uproariously. "I'm in the mood for some warm soup!"

"Good for you!" someone else shouted.

"How would you like a free bowl of soup?" Nick said asking a random person.

"Do I look like a bum to you?" said the disgruntled man.

"Well, a good day to you anyway," Nick smiled. "Would you like a free bowl of soup?" he asked an older man. "I know this great coffee shop, which makes great New England clam chowder."

"Get out of here you crazy, whipper snapper."

"Ok, have a nice life," Nick jumped straight up in the air, laughed, and moved on to the next possible soup devourer.

The Best Orgasms Come from the Universe

Boris glanced at his watch seventeen times, before Nick finally wandered in twenty minutes late. Nick entered with a trail of three people. Boris looked up from his cup of coffee, noticing his friend's new company. He made his way hesitantly towards Nick, just as he started ordering the soup.

"What are you doing?" Boris asked.

"Buying soup," he answered.

"And who are these people?"

"Oh, well, this is Clarence, he's an accountant, this is Bernie, he's a furniture salesman, and this is Emily she writes a comic strip for the newspaper."

"Hello..." Boris said. Then he pulled Nick aside a moment and whispered to him. "I understand...but, why are they here?"

"I invited them to a bowl of soup," he answered.

"So what, you walked up to complete strangers and offered to buy them soup?"

"Yeah."

"Oh, ok..." Boris said, finally understanding. "Well, you do realize that Bernie is wearing a monocle, right?"

"Yeah, that's actually a pretty interesting story," Nick said. "Hey, Bernie, tell Boris why you're wearing a monocle."

Bernie was a big man, bigger than Nick in all dimensions, and while neither of them were exactly fat, this man could be misconstrued as being so. His hair went down to his shoulders in thick frizzy strands. He had a big round face and a hidden grin somewhere past his big lips. He introduced his pleasant nature with a massive smile to Boris.

"Hullo, I'm Bernie, I am from France, although my mother was Danish and my father was English. When I was six I was hit in my left eye with a baseball, and now I am blind in that eye. So instead of being politically correct, by wearing glasses, I wear a monocle. I'm trying to bring it back into fashion."

"Oh, very good..." Boris said, with an unsure grin.

"And Clarence is an accountant. Apparently I know him, he's been my accountant since I was eighteen, and I have never met him. Imagine the chances of that happening."

"How many people did you talk to?" Boris whispered.

"I lost count after sixty-ish," Nick replied.

"Hi, I'm Emily," she said. "Did you know that the average clitoris is only this deep?"

She held her hand out, putting her fingers apart. Boris stared off into nothingness for a good thirty seconds before answering.

"No, I did not...know that," Boris said, trying to continue smiling.

"Aren't they great?" Nick said.

Boris just nodded, "Wonderful..."

So there they sat. Nick and his four members of his company sat eating New England clam chowder, in silence. The coffee counter was much like that of a bar, and they sat in a line on the swivel stools. After about a minute of pure unaltered silence, a conversation arose. The discussion lasted until everyone had finished their soup. They talked about the uprising of bohemian poetry, in coffee shops like the one they were in. Clarence discussed how he would love to bring his bongos down to the shop sometime, and play one of his "ditties" as he called them. Emily continued her idea that people are too worried about discussing the female sexual organs. And Bernie elaborated on his desire to be a folksinger. When they left, Nick turned to Boris.

"Wasn't that great?"

The Best Orgasms Come from the Universe

"Ah, no."

"You didn't like them?"

"I don't see the point in buying people soup."

"We learned something about people we didn't even know, unusual people with real lives and dreams and ideas. You're a writer Boris, didn't that experience fill you with ideas and creativity."

"It fills me with something, but it isn't creativity."

"Just think Boris, I asked over sixty people if they wanted a bowl of free soup from a coffee shop, and all but those three people said no."

"Because it's crazy to just ask someone if they want soup. It's unnatural...it's not nor..."

"It's not what? You were going to say normal."

"No I wasn't."

"Well your right, it's not 'normal.' It's something better, it's different. What if people accepted soup from a total stranger? It's not like I'm giving them my soup. Then I could see being suspicious. But it wasn't suspicion in their eyes...it was disgust. It was ignorance; it was down right looking down on someone. Why is that Boris?"

"Because you were offering soup to total strangers!"

"Look past the soup...think of something else, any simple not harmful statement. Why should something as simple as that, make someone look down at someone else. I'll put it into something you may understand. Imagine what would happen if Jesus were reborn in modern days."

"Oh, Christ, Nick...let it go..."

"No Boris, I have a point, and I need to see in your eyes that you're at least listening."

Boris glared at Nick a moment, and realized he was serious.

"Ok, ok, tell what would happen if Jesus were reborn today."

"Would he be well received? The son of God, which so many people say they believe in. One thought pattern that so many people blindly follow. If Jesus were born the same time I was, and he started walking the streets of the city offering people help...they'd laugh at him. They would look down upon him. The people that believe in him would cast him aside in disbelief. Their faith which they hold on to so readily would be all but useless, because they wouldn't take into their hearts the man which supposedly loves them the most. He would have to prove it to them time and time again to remove their skepticism. He shouldn't need to prove it. It should be in their hearts. And yet a man like me, a man more Pagan than not, would open my arms to him. I'd give him soup, and embrace him in a hug. Not because I believe in him, but because he's a good man, and is trying to help people. If Jesus were alive today, he'd be a Pagan."

At this Boris became very flustered.

"Listen Nick, I love you as a friend, but you can't insult my beliefs so blatantly."

"I'm not; I'm not saying Jesus wouldn't believe in God. I'm not even saying he wouldn't preach the word of the Lord, but when you get down to the root of things, he's only talking about being a good person. He's spreading the good in the best way he knows how, through the word of God. But good Pagans were saying be a good person long before Christ. Sure there are bad Pagans, just like there are bad Christians, and Jews, and Muslims, and Buddhists. So why can't Jesus be a Pagan, as long as he's spreading a good word. What would he see walking the streets, when looking into peoples hearts? He'd see a bunch of people saying they believe in God and his word, but not following it. He would cry...he would cry a long time. When he spoke the Word, he'd sound just like a Pagan who believed in God. Pagan's can still believe in God if they'd like. He would speak the ideals and no one would listen...and that's sad, even to a man like me."

"I don't agree Nick," Boris said.

"Well give me your opinion."

"No."

"Ok, why not?"

"Because I'm getting insulted by your talk, and I don't want to get angry."

"Why? Get angry, we're friends its not going to kill us. Why can't we have a heated disagreement? I mean if you need to get angry over an opinion, that's fine, but the Boris I know would at least be decent enough to share his opinion."

"Listen Nick, I need to go."

"But Boris?"

"I need to contemplate my feelings towards this Nick. You've changed...over the years and I need to think about how I feel about that."

"Wait a second Boris, just last week I was helping you through you decision about being gay. I gave you my opinion and I said some pretty strange things about God then to. You didn't get all offensive then, what gives now. We used to have fun debating over people's beliefs."

"I said I don't want to talk about," Boris said getting up. "I'll call you later."

"Alright, bye Boris."

CHAPTER THIRTY-TWO

Before picking up his car from a rented garage space, Nick sent a flower to Leila's office. One yellow carnation, with a note saying:

Because it's Thursday...all day long...

Nick rifled through his pocket retrieving his keys. He opened his garage space, and removed a cover from his green-algae colored, wannabe-turquoise *Dodge Neon*. He unlocked the car door and pulled out of the space. He locked up his space, and went to put a sticker on his car bumper. Already on it were two others which read: **More Pagan than Not** and **Harm None Have Fun**. Then Nick added Duncan's saying, **Joy is Making a Comeback**. He got back into his car, and headed out to his job.

Traffic and road rage were the two major reasons for Nick's limited driving. It wasn't that Nick was a poor driver; it was that he felt he was the only good driver on the road. Other vehicles cut him off, and eighteen-wheelers nearly pushed him off the road. It wasn't often that Nick felt the need for profanity, but when he was behind the wheel of a car, everything changed. To someone who didn't know Nick, it would have appeared that his vocabulary was only made up of curse words and normal words used out of context.

After repeated growls, sneers, and grunts he reached his building. The anger passed almost as quickly as it had appeared. He entered his job at around two thirty and went straight to his office. Mick and Curt nodded with plain grins, as he passed them by. On his floor Nick looked for Bruce and Mary. Both of them were nowhere to be seen. This helped to put a grin on Nick's face. There was no replacement for Mary, or Bruce.

Nick sat in his office, and looked over new paperwork for the Emerald Deal, which appeared to all be in order. He was finished with his work within a half-hour. He was just cleaning up his desk when he heard a knock at the door.

"Come in."

The stocky man entered; it was Herbert.

"Do you have a minute Nick?" he asked.

"Yeah sure, take a seat. What can I do for you?"

"Well, I just wanted to thank you for Monday. It felt really good to win at something, so simple. It put things into view."

"Your welcome Herbert, I wish I could do it more often."

"Once was enough," Herbert laughed.

"Was there anything else?"

"Yes Sir..."

"It's still Nick."

"Ah right, Nick, I've been working here for about thirty years. And...I was hoping that I could give you this statement I have here. It's just some ideas on how the company could conserve money and expand productivity. I was wondering if you could read it. Would you?"

"Sure," he answered.

"Thank you Sir..."

"Nick..."

"Right, sorry Nick. When I talk business I tend to get formal."

"It's alright Herbert; I'll take it right now."

"Ok, here you are," he said handing over a folder full of paperwork.

"I'll try to read it soon."

"No rush, take your time."

"I'll see you later Herbert."

"Bye Nick."

After Herbert left, Nick finished gathering his things and headed back outside. In the street, by Nick's car stood a man. Nick approached him and the man turned.

"Hi, is this your car?"

"Yes."

"I was wondering if I might comment about your bumper stickers."

"Sure," Nick replied. "Which ones?"

"Just the first one."

"Ok."

"What do you mean by, 'More Pagan than Not?'"

"It means that I have no religion, but I'm closest to being a Pagan. Basically I believe in what I believe, and my thoughts just so happen to correspond with many Pagan beliefs."

"You don't believe in God?"

"Nope."

"How can you not believe in God? Jesus died for our sins, and he is the son of the Lord."

The Best Orgasms Come from the Universe

"Well, what if a Pagan sacrificed his life for our sins, would you worship and praise his name. Technically we are all the children of God, based on the classic belief systems that go along with believing in God. So basically anyone could be like Jesus."

"Jesus made miracles happen."

"Yes, Jesus was a great man..."

"You believe in Jesus?"

"Yes, he was pretty awesome; I just don't need pictures of him on my wall. I mean I've never met the man. Besides true life miracles are what impress me, not the superhuman ones. He was just a wonderful man with many amazing gifts."

"Jesus was more than just a great man...how can you believe in Jesus and not God?" the man questioned harshly.

"Well I don't believe in God because I don't believe a benevolent supreme being would want us wasting our precious lives praising his name. And I believe in Jesus, because he found a beautiful way to look at life. Really all he was saying when you get right down to it; it was love life and love others, without reservation. He just believed the key for life was God. I simply disagree. People are allowed to disagree with one another; it's what makes us unique. The biggest message really is...what's the key to life?"

"The word of God."

"Well you're right about that, but there's a bigger picture than that."

"There is no bigger picture than God."

"Ah, not to be contrary, but that's where I believe your wrong. You see, it's a trick question. There is no key to life, because life is an open door, and there is lots of ways inside," Nick began. "I'm glad you found your way inside. I've found a way as well, and I'd appreciate it if you'd respect that, or at least not care enough to leave me with my right to believe in my own thoughts, without being chastised. I simply believe differently than you do, it doesn't make either of us wrong. The only time someone can be wrong in a situation like this, is when one person says to the other: 'you are totally wrong.'"

"You are wrong. God is the only way to get to heaven."

"I'm already in heaven."

"I'm not going to argue it any further."

"I didn't realize we were arguing."

"God is the only way to save your soul!" the witness proclaimed. "And it's never too late to be saved."

"I'll keep that in mind," Nick paused as the car sped away. "It was nice talking to you. Joy is making a comeback!"

Nick got into his car and drove off with a grin.

"*Its fun being happy,*" he thought. "*It's strange that he didn't comment on Joy is making a comeback. Maybe he needs some happiness.*"

"Joy is making a comeback," he said aloud. "I love that."

CHAPTER THIRTY-THREE

Nick had forgotten just how far his old stomping grounds were. He drove for the better part of an hour to get to his old college. The Dripping Bucket was a shabby place, were Nick used to go to woo away his problems. He had a bittersweet association with college. During that time, Nick was often the life of the party. He attracted people of all types with his ideas and opinions. The Dripping Bucket was a place where creative college students went to drink and chat with other people of their disposition. It was truly a time to shine, for someone like Nick. Nevertheless all the people he had discussions with, or slept with, or fought with, or "drank" (drank meaning...they drank beer...and Nick watched the stupid things they did) with, were all searching for who they really were.

Nick already knew what he was, and who he was becoming. None of the people he met were anything more than an image to him. His life seemed to be a series of images which would be collected in a photo album for the future. All his experiences led to nothing. They didn't bring him enlightenment or future friendships. The passage of time seemed to be only that, one pointless step for him to get to his future. Since nothing transpired from Nick's time in college, it seemed insignificant. His many interesting conversations furthered nothing, and the great stories which he uncovered, fueled nothing except his ever growing void of creativity.

So when Nick parked his car at the Dripping Bucket, he was filled with a contemptuous lethargy. It was a strangely comforting feeling to know he had the correct viewpoint on his college experience. When, others in the opposite position of Nick probably learned the most about life during college. For a moment he felt better than the other people, and then he only felt pity for himself. Pity because he learned his life lessons too quickly in life, and never really got to enjoy the experience of studying the process at the same rate as his peers. Nevertheless, one cannot choose when Life is going to share its lessons with you. The only thing that individuals control is how much they accept the truth in their own lives, and how they deal with it. Since Nick was never one to put himself in denial, he quickly accepted his life for the way it was. This in turn put him in his hidden, undesired, state of living, during his college days.

The Dripping Bucket was **exactly** how Nick remembered it. Well everything, save for the youthful faces that filled the room. Although after reminiscing, everyone probably had a similar life-ready face when they were that age. Each spoke as if they knew what they were talking about, and everyone was willing to defend their opinions with anything...blood even, on some occasions. Barbarosa, the bar owner, was still standing behind the counter, eating peanuts and potato chips. He was a fat, balding, older man with sweaty armpits. He made a fortune selling liquor to college students. He had three simple rules, and Nick presumed they were still the same. The rules were as follows:

The Best Orgasms Come from the Universe

1. All fights and people going to vomit are taken outside.
2. Drink as much as you like, but you "ain't leavin'" (as he said) "in a car...and that's countin' trucks...and jeeps and shit..."
3. Don't tell anyone about my bar, unless you can trust 'um.

Barbarosa used to be on the police force. He was good friends with everyone in the jurisdiction, and they didn't bother him. He been running the Dripping Bucket for twenty three years and no one was ever injured or killed because of Barbarosa's willingness to serve his best customers; his best customers being the college students of course. When saying no one was ever *injured*...this means no one ever was injured without prior consent. Fights happened all the time outside the Dripping Bucket, just like any good bar. These fights were between two people, with a mutual desire to pummel each other's brain cells into nonexistence. Griffon was often involved in these fights, including one which involved Nick. Nick was the only one to ever beat Griffon in a fair fight.

Griffon was inside the bar speaking to Barbarosa. When Nick entered, Griffon turned to notice him.
"Nick, you made it," he said.
"Nick...it's been a while," Barbarosa said. "I was upset when I heard you dropped out of college."
"Bar and I were just talking about you Nick."
"It's a pleasure to see the two of you."
"Neither of you ever come to visit me anymore."
"Yeah, well I don't know about Nick, but I'm a pretty busy man," Griffon chuckled.
"In fact the last time I saw the two of you...you were fighting. That was the last time I saw you Nick."

"That's why we are here Nick," Griffon began. "I want a rematch."

"What...?"

"I'm just kidding," Griffon grinned. "You always were gullible, Nick."

"Ha-ha...yeah funny," Nick said sarcastically, sitting on a stool at the bar. "But really, what did you call me for exactly?"

"You want something to drink, Nick," Bar asked.

"No thank you."

"Can't a friend just call up another friend and want to rehash old times?"

"You were never that type of friend, Griffon."

"True...true...well Nick," he began moving to a closer stool. "I need a job."

"What?"

"You heard me; the art isn't doing as well as I had hoped."

"What are you talking about; you just had an entire section of the Stillwater Art Gallery devoted to you work."

"Yeah well...it's not enough..."

"Griffon, are you in some kind of trouble?"

"Not exactly..."

"The last time you said that to me, I found you the next day with a black eye, split lip, and a two thousand dollar debt on **our** credit card."

"Yeah...yeah...well it's along the same lines."

"What's along the same lines?"

"Well, I owe some people some money..."

"Ok..."

"A lot of money."

"How much is a lot?"

The Best Orgasms Come from the Universe

"About thirty thousand dollars..."

"Damn Griffon, that's not along the same lines. That's not even in the same vicinity of the same lines."

"I know...I know..."

"How the hell did this happen? Wait, do I really want to know."

"Probably not."

"Then never mind. Damn it, Griffon, I don't want to know, but I need to know. Tell me."

"I got into a fight with someone."

"Ok."

"And it turns out he has some friends..." Griffon started. "Ok a lot of friends. They said if I don't pay them fifty thousand dollars by the end of the month..."

"Yeah..."

"They are going to kill me. I already got twenty thousand saved up."

"Wait, wait go back...kill you? Who the hell did you beat up?"

"Ricky Marson, apparently he's part of a pretty big gang. He was a prick, Nick...ha that rhymes, prick Nick..."

"Very funny Griffon. So, you expected good, old Nick to bail you out? Is that it?"

"I just thought you could give me a job."

"A job is not going to pay you thirty thousand dollars by the end of the week. You wanted me to give you the money."

"No, it's not that."

"Griffon, I know you better than that."

"Yeah, I was hoping..."

"Well I'm not giving you the money."

"What do you mean you're not giving me the money? Nick this isn't a joke."

"Am I laughing? I know it's not a joke, but you made your bed, now lie in it," Nick paused. "I'm not going to give you the money. You are going to earn every penny of it."

"What? How?"

"I'm going to buy some art from you. Your good paintings...only the good stuff."

"You'd do that for me?"

"Assuming your as good of an artist as I remember."

"How can I thank you, Nick?"

"You can give me good deals on your art. This isn't a charity, Griffon, this is a purchase. I plan to finagle the price down as far as possible."

"You're a good friend Nick."

"Not today. Today I'm a preferred customer."

CHAPTER THIRTY-FOUR

Griffon's massive loft apartment was filled with paintings of all types. The apartment was an hour drive from the Dripping Bucket, which put Nick close to Leila's home. After an hour and a half of perusing Griffon's work, Nick found several pieces which interested him. Many of the paintings were made by the use of uncommon colors displayed on various parts of the canvas. Many of the paintings were abstract. It wasn't until Nick reached a large canvas with mostly sky blue paint, that he was truly intrigued. The greens and yellows reminded Nick of Leila. If the painting was her, he kind of hoped that the bits of red in the assembly were him. The painting truly looked like a woodland scene from a summer home Nick had spent time at during his childhood.

"How much do you have marked on this one?"

"I'm not selling this one."

"I must have it...well it's not for me, it's for my girlfriend. It's her birthday tomorrow."

"Nick I can't sell you this painting."

"Listen Griffon, I love lots of your paintings. But not selling me this could be a deal breaker," Nick paused and could see Griffon's indecisive expression. "Listen...I'll give you forty five thousand dollars for this painting. That's almost all the money you owe left, including the money you've already collected. Then I'll give you five thousand for the other three I saw. That's your entire debt."

"Nick, you said you were going to give me the money. If you're only buying one painting, it's almost the same thing."

"That's how much this painting means to me Griffon. You should take it as a compliment; it's the greatest painting I've ever seen."

"Deal."

"Ok..."

"Ok...I'll wrap it up for you."

"Thanks Griffon. Do you have phone I could use?"

"Yeah, in the area that resembles a kitchen."

"Thanks."

"It's only seven, maybe Leila's still at the office."

Nick removed his small booklet of phone numbers and called her office, with no answer. Next he called her house and Ray picked up.

"Hello?"

"Hi, this is Nick."

"Hi, Nick, it's Ray."

"Is Leila in?"

"Not yet, she's out shopping right now."

"Oh."

"Why?"

"I just wanted to talk to her."

"Well she just left, and he's shopping for the week and for the trip."

"I could surprise her at the store, and keep her company."

"What store."

The Best Orgasms Come from the Universe

"The T-Mart down the street from her house."

"You two didn't have plans tonight did you?"

"No I'm going to be leaving, I'm just making sure Leila's packed; you know big sister stuff."

"Right, ok Ray, thanks a lot. Have fun at your parents if I don't see you."

"Bye Nick."

"Hey Griffon, I'm going to be heading out, where do you want the check?"

"Oh, the stool out there," Griffon began. "I've got your paintings right here."

"Thanks Griffon I'll be heading out now."

"Ok, see you later Nick."

Nick gathered the paintings and headed to his car. He packed up his car and headed to the T-Mart. The sky was black and the moon was hardly noticeable behind a mist-like gathering of clouds. Nick entered the grocery store and walked down the aisles looking for Leila. It wasn't until he came across the double row of frozen foods, that he found her. Leila rolled her cart along looking at the things in the freezer as she went. Nick watched her a moment and then ran down to her. He could hear her humming to the song on the radio as he approached.

"Excuse me Miss...have you misplaced a scruffy looking, brown-haired male?"

She looked up to see him and her face lit up with an open mouthed smile.

"What are you doing here?"

"I called your house, and Ray said you were here," Nick replied. "I thought I'd surprise you."

"Surprise me...and come with me shopping?"

"If you'd like, I thought we could have dinner together, if you haven't eaten."

"I haven't, I got out of work late."

"It happens."

"So what would you like for dinner? I was just going to have a little bit of ice-cream and curl up with a movie."

"Do you want some company?"

"It's pretty late."

"That's true...but I'm a big boy, I can drive home in the dark."

"Ok, sure, what type of ice-cream do you want...?" Leila started, and before Nick could answer, she continued. "Wait...wait, listen...I used to love this song, when I was in high school."

"It's a good song," he paused as she started moving behind the cart. "Well I like tin roof, ah, and...wait, what are you doing?"

"Dance with me," Leila said, moving her body.

Nick watched a moment.

"I'm sorry, what?"

"Dance with me."

"I'm not much of a dancer," Nick said.

"You don't need to know music to love dancing," she said. "Move with me."

Leila started swaying her hips, and bending her knees. He moved closer to her and started moving to her lead. His statement was true; he wasn't much of a dancer. It didn't matter though, while he moved with her next to the shopping cart. Other customers looked at them; many of the shoppers couldn't help but smile.

The Best Orgasms Come from the Universe

Leila looked deeply into his eyes as she lifted his arms into the air. All of Leila's being fell onto his arms like paper. Past Leila's utopian grin and Nick's own reflection in her eyes, he could see her. She was a little girl holding her hair over her eyes to see the world in gold. He could see her spinning around in a circle as fast as she could, with her arms held up, as she held his, as if to hug the world. Eventually the world would let go, and she would fall; eventually the song would end, and Nick would take her to *her* home. The best thing about hugging the world is you can do it as often as you'd like. And they could always dance through the next song. And they did…

CHAPTER THIRTY-FIVE

When Nick and Leila came to her apartment, the lights were on, and Ralph came running to their feet. The small dog did laps around Nick's legs as he brought the bags of groceries to the kitchen counter. He started taking things out of the paper bags as Leila listened to her messages. When all the groceries were put away, and all the messages were heard, they made their way to the couch. Both of them sat down to watch the movie. They both sat watching the film in all its duration. When it ended, the two of them continued sitting there together, with Leila lying against Nick.

"I love that movie."

"It's a fine film, thank you for sharing it with me."

"I first saw that movie when I was fifteen, with one of my girlfriends," Leila explained.

"Did you see a lot of movies?"

"Yeah, I'd go to the movies all the time."

"I bet a lot of guys paid for you at the movie theaters."

"During high school? No, only one really. His name was Arnold; I really loved him."

"What happened?"

"Well, we dated during high school and the beginning of college. We were engaged to be married when I was twenty. I had this beautiful dress from my older sister. I looked like a princess. He was going to give me his grandmother's wedding ring. He died in a car accident, two months before the wedding date," Leila paused and Nick took her hand. "I thought I'd never find someone again. I dropped out of college for a while. When I went back, a year later, I started dating again. It was really hard. I kept comparing everyone to Arnold. A lot of guys didn't want to take the time to get to know me; they just wanted to have sex. Well, I finished college and went into my family business."

"I'm sorry..." Nick said. "I don't know what Arnold was like, but I really care about you. I don't want to just have sex with you."

"I know Nick...how about we watch another movie? A comedy, maybe..."

"Sure..."

The two of them started watching another movie together. They didn't get more than half way through, before both of them fell asleep on the couch.

FRIDAY

Nick awoke with Leila under his arm. The television was still on from the night before, which filled the room with a bluish tint. It was still very early and the sun was just coming up, leaking only slightly through and around the blinds. He slipped himself out from under Leila's head and upper chest. He moved some of her hair away from her face before kissing her cheek. She stirred, but did not awake.

Nick found paper and a pen to write a note, which read:

Leila-
    I'll be right back; I'm just getting something from my car. Happy Birthday...

                                        Nick

He ran to his car outside, which was parked just next to Leila's. After opening the trunk, he removed the painting he bought for her. When he returned upstairs he knocked lightly before coming in. She was already up, and brushing her hair in the bathroom.

"Morning birthday girl."

"I got your note."

"Oh, good."

She walked out from her bathroom and came to the living room. As she entered the living room she saw the covered painting.

"What's that?" she said just before kissing him.

"Aw, minty," Nick said with a smile.

"I just brushed my teeth."

"Ah, well this is your birthday present, along with the theater tonight."

"Can I open it?"

"Wait, wait one second," Nick said looking at the painting leaning up against the TV. "Come sit on the couch."

Nick slowly rolled his fingers over her eyelids.

"What are you doing?"

"Close your eyes."

Nick got up and removed the leather covering.

"Before you see it, I want to tell you something."

"What's that?"

"This painting makes me think of you."

"Really..."

"Now open your eyes slowly."

She did so, and as she did, she saw the sky blue painting, with the mesh of greens and yellows...and the bits of reds.

"It's beautiful," she said. "I don't see why it makes you think of me though?"

"Well there's a story behind it. Do you want to hear it?"

"Absolutely."

"When I was eight I remember hearing a series of bird calls, and I heard them answered. I had never heard these types of birds before. I was with my friend Anthony, and his family had a summer home in the woods some place, I don't remember where. And I'd go there with him every year from the age of eight to eleven. Anthony died when I was twelve. He had leukemia. But anyway, I heard these birds and everyone else was asleep, and I crept outside. The sky was all blue, and the sun leaked through the mesh of freshly reborn Spring leaves. It was windy, and the light flashed on and off my face as I closed my eyes. I could hear the wind calling through the leaves...it sounded like rain. It was the most beautiful thing I've ever seen...and I had my eyes closed. When I saw this painting, I didn't think of it, I thought of you. That's what you are to me, the sunlight falling on my face in the morning."

She didn't say anything, she looked sad. Nick touched her cheek. Her eyes were slightly filled with water as she moved her finger across Nick's face; the tips slowly slid down his eyelids. She sniffled a bit and waved her hand in front of his face. The light fell on and off his face like a sonorous tide. Leila took his right hand in both of hers, and brought it to her lips. All of his fingers gradually caressed the indentation above her bottom lip, and moved his fingers across her cheek. She moved in closer and put her lips to his, as if it were the first time they had kissed. As they parted, Nick continued his middle finger up the line of her nose and up to her hair.

"Open your eyes," she whispered.

He opened his eyes to see only Leila. Nick moved her hair behind her ears, with his fingers, continuing the movement back down her cheek and neck. Leila inched forward, still kneeling on the couch. He moved his other hand to her right side and slid the thin strap of her shirt and bra down her shoulder, as he kissed her neck. He put his hands on her back and moved her forward into his space. Leila put her legs around his sides, and the morning draped itself on both of them for all its duration.

CHAPTER THIRTY-SIX

The universe allowed Nick to get his orgasm from someone else... three times that morning. Making love with Leila was as close to a life orgasm as a mere mortal could get. In fact, after making love to Leila, he felt as if he just had another life orgasm. He was unrestrictedly and incomparably happy. He had a threesome with the universe, and everyone came out feeling content. It's a good thing the universe is bisexual, or else someone would have been left holding in the...enlightenment. Actually when Nick really contemplated it...did the universe pull its weight in the sack? Leila seemed pleased with Nick's performance, or else there would have been no encores. But what about the universe...or really when talking out of code...did she feel the same way as Nick did, beyond the sex. Did Leila exact from the universe a life orgasm? When she woke up, did she think to herself "Could this be it?" Or did she at least ask herself "Is Nick it...the one?"

He couldn't stop thinking about it. Did she see their morning together as sex...or love?

Nick brought his car back to the garage and took a taxi home with the topic still on his mind. Inside his house, he continued letting the thought rinse over his mind. He sat down at the typewriter and power wrote. His ideas flowed so quickly, he nearly forgot each line as he wrote it. His feelings were like nothing he had ever imagined. Nick just emptied his mind onto each page. He let the first stages of love open his being. The first rush was like magic.

"...Magic, an unexplainable force, an energy which is in every human being, if only we would let it be what it is. Your emotions, your ideas, your movements, your ideals and morals...these are all energies which can be harnessed...harnessed for any means, good or ill. We, as a people, take these things individually. While instead if we envelope them into our own lives as a whole, then we can truly be the best in and of ourselves. Although if harnessed for ill, we could easily also become the worst of ourselves. The path between is a wide one, and should be accepted as life. An extreme is simply that, in any form. If one is all-evil, that person will destroy himself; if one is all-good one will be destroyed by something else. Accepting evil in one's self makes you free. Living by the good is what makes you divine. If you except that everyone is not perfect, or pure, or one hundred percent correct, than you shall truly be one with every given power of the universe. Do not search for only balance, and do not worry about a power greater then yourself all your life. Balance allows for no indulgence of the beautiful life around you and seeking only a power greater then yourself diminishes your infinite potential. Do not only live for the moment, for the next moment may turn out worse because of the previous one. Don't overly plan for the future, and miss out on the day you are in. These are all extremes, and there can never be a truly one hundred percent correct fundamental idea. Maybe there is a heaven, maybe the afterlife is all just darkness, and maybe we'll all come back as platypuses, don't worry yourself, you'll find out eventually. Believe in what you like, but live because you

want to, die because you have to, and be proud and grateful for the time you have, because it always runs out."

"Damn," Nick said aloud. "This is good...I might really help people with this."

Nick continued spilling his avalanche of thoughts onto the pages. Then he casually glanced at the clock, which read: 5:35. He took no notice of it, and continued typing away. When six thirty came about, Nick was unprepared for his departure. The plan was, Nick was supposed to leave and pick up Leila at seven, and then they were to take a taxi to the theatre. The play started at eight, and the drive alone to the theatre was about thirty minutes. Nick glanced once again to the clock noticing the late hour. The time still did not register on his mind for about three minutes. After the several minutes, he looked up at the clock once again and realized the time. Jumping out of his seat, he dashed for his bathroom. He showered, changed, and groomed himself in less than fifteen minutes.

Nick arrived at Leila's apartment, and tapped on the door, at around four after seven. When the door opened, Nick gasped in shock. It was a very rare occasion when he couldn't contain his composure around women, although this was one of those times. Leila stood before him, in a long, tight black dress. The slits going up either side revealed black heels and stockings. The "dress"...a religious experience would be a better title for it, was low cut and had thin straps going over her shoulders. Leila had her hair down and just enough makeup to accentuate anything and everything that may have needed...accentuating.

"Hi," she grinned. When he didn't say anything, she grabbed him by his suit jacket and pulled him in for a kiss.

Nick couldn't mentally, emotionally, or psychologically formulate any words. He just stood there a moment contemplating the basic necessities of life. In that short time, he almost lost memories of his childhood. His facial appearance changed about seven times before he settled his bearings. To Leila, Nick looked ponderous, and his looks were at least "cute."

"That good?" She asked.

"There should be people worshipping you."

"Aren't there?" Leila inquired jokingly.

"There certainly are now..."

"You're lucky you're cute. Shall we get going?"

"Sure..."

A shiver went up Nick's spine as Leila turned to lock her door after closing it. He looked in utter bliss to see just how far down an open back could go. He smiled to himself, before moving toward her. As she finished locking the two locks on her door, Nick kissed her shoulder blade.

"Happy birthday, again," Nick whispered.

Leila turned around and fixed his sleeve, which was unbuttoned.

"You forgot a button of your shirt," Leila said.

"I lost track of time."

"I believe you once said, that I was worth waiting for, well the feeling is mutual," she paused. "I love this shirt on you, and thank you for this morning."

"It was my pleasure."

"Really?" She asked, as she finished buttoning his shirt under his suit jacket. She continued holding onto his lower arm as she moved in closer.

"I love making love to you."

"More than everything-bagels?"

"Well, not everything...has everything."

"Oh, thanks," she said smacking him lightly, humorously annoyed.

"No, no...I've never been happier," he said putting his arms around her.

"That's dangerous, Nick..." Leila said.

"What do you mean?"

"I might disappoint you..."

"What are you talking about?"

"Nothing...I'm just saying anything could happen."

"Whoa...whoa, listen, nothing about you is disappointing. I wouldn't change anything about you. You know why?"

"Why?"

"Because then, you might not be...you. I'll never **wish** for you to change. If you change, you're still you. The only way I'd want you to change, is if you choose to change."

There was a short silence, which neither of them wished to fill.

"Maybe we should get going."

"Yeah...maybe we should get going."

Neither of them let go.

"One of us is going to need to let go..." Nick continued. "It might be hard getting into the cab, holding each other like this."

Leila took Nick's hand in hers and they walked outside.

CHAPTER THIRTY-SEVEN

When Nick and Leila arrived at the theatre, and entered through a series of three double doors, they were instantly greeted by Alfred.

"Oh...my...God," Alfred started dramatically. "You two look so precious together. And Leila, that dress is amazing. I swear only someone as beautiful as you could wear something so wonderful."

"Alfred, from Persephone's store," Leila said. "It's very nice to see you again."

"Hi Alfred."

"Nick I'm just going to steal your woman for about two minutes. She must meet someone. Here are the two tickets Nick."

"You're the best Alfred."

Alfred took Leila by the hand and walked her down the hall. Nick glanced around for someone he might recognize. Then he noticed a very tall, fit black man dressed in a brown suit.

"Taran Aaron," Nick began. "Taran is a retired military man. His buddies in the service called him Rhymes, because of his skills with lyrical poetry and because his first and last name rhymed. Taran killed seventeen men in Bosnia with a knife in the space of two days, while he was in the Special Forces. He was planning to retire three days prior to the incident. He lost his taste for combat and left the

The Best Orgasms Come from the Universe

military. He moved out west and became a cattle rancher. His business failed when the competition muscled him out of the market. He took what money he had saved and went back to college, and after ten years of hard study, without a real career goal, he decided to become an astronaut, just like his little sister was, before she died of food poisoning. Now he has just taken his paid vacation time and Taran...good old Rhymes...decided to take his family out to see his little sister's favorite play..."

As Nick was about to continue, his thoughts were interrupted by someone tugging on his clothing. He turned around to see Bernie and his monocle.

"Bernie," Nick began. "You were the last person I expected to see."

"Hey Nick," Bernie started. "Yeah, I'm here on a date."

"Really that's great."

"Yeah it's Emily," he said nervously. "I'm here with Emily."

"Really? You're here with Emily, from the coffee shop."

"This is what I'm saying."

"That's really fantastic."

"Really?"

"I'm saying really. You just asked her out?"

"Yeah, after the soup, she and I went out to get some real brunch. After brunch we went to the movies, and then had dinner. To whit, we decided to start going out. Where are you sitting? Maybe we are close by."

Nick removed the two tickets from his pocket and looked at them, they read:

Seat No. 1782 Balcony One & Seat No. 1900 Balcony Five

Nick's face turned from happy, to confused, to distressed, and ended at determined.

"What's wrong Nick?"

"My seats...they aren't together."

"What?"

"Bernie, would you excuse me. I'm really glad I ran into you, I'm happy for you and Emily and I wish you two the best of...the best of...well the best..." Nick said turning toward where Alfred went.

Nick rushed down the hallway. He noticed Alfred, Leila, and two older gentlemen. When he approached, Leila turned to see him.

"Mr. Master and Mr. Stewart, this is my boyfriend, Nick," Leila said.

"Ah, Alfred has told us so much about you," Mr. Stewart said.

"It's a pleasure," Nick said. "Alfred, could I talk to you a moment."

"Sure, Nick."

"I'll be right back," Nick said to Leila.

"Excuse us," Alfred said.

Alfred and Nick stepped away a moment, and they turned to one another.

"Leila is really great Nick," Alfred said.

"Thanks."

"Alfred, there's a problem with the tickets."

"What's the matter with them, don't you like balcony seats."

"Oh, no...no that's not it. It's that, they aren't seated together."

"What?"

"There not seated together."

The Best Orgasms Come from the Universe

"What? I mean how?"

"I don't know."

"Oh, Nick, I'm so sorry. I didn't...oh...no," Alfred started. "I'm such a screw up. I can't even get you the right tickets."

"No, that's—"

"No I am," Alfred said crying. "I can't do anything right. Don't look at me, I'm a failure."

"It's not that big of a deal, don't cry."

"Now the show's sold-out and..." Alfred continued. "And I have to go to the dressing room, and I'm going to be a mess, and the shows going to be ruined. I can't do anything right."

"Listen Alfred, its ok."

"I've ruined Leila's birthday, I've ruined our friendship, and Boris hates me, and now...I have to play the tortured flower spirit, who loves everything."

"You didn't ruin anything, and Boris doesn't hate you."

"Yes he does, he said so."

"Did you two breakup?"

"I called you yesterday, and left a message."

"I wasn't home, I've been with Leila. I'm sorry...you guys broke up?"

"Yeah."

"When?"

"Wednesday."

"Listen, Alfred, you are not a screw up, and you're not a horrible person. I'm sure Boris was just angry. I've known him a long time; I don't think he meant what he said."

"Do you think so?"

"Yes I do...listen I'll talk to him tomorrow, I'll see what happened. Maybe the two of you can work it out."

"Ok, Nick, I'm really sorry about the tickets, I should have looked at them more carefully."

"It's ok; maybe I can switch them with someone."

"Alright."

"Now, go on into that dressing room, get ready, and come out ready to be the best damn flower spirit you've ever been."

"Thanks Nick."

"Sure."

Alfred went off to Leila, said "see you later," and continued to his dressing room. Nick just stood where he was a moment, and then noticed Leila walking toward him.

"Hey," she said.

"Hey."

"You ok?"

"Yeah I'm alright, it's just Alfred's having some problems, and at the moment our tickets don't sit together."

"Oh."

"Yeah, exactly."

"Do you want to leave?"

"No, you got all dressed up, and Alfred went through a lot to get the tickets...that is unless you want to leave, it is your birthday."

"You're sweet," she said kissing him.

"Why don't we go inside, maybe I can buy the seat off of someone."

"Alright."

Nick and Leila arrived first at seat number one-thousand-nine-hundred. The seat was at the end of the row, and Leila walked up to the man sitting in the seat next to it.

"Excuse me," Leila began.

"Yes," the man answered.

"We've had a bit of a mix-up with our tickets, and we aren't seated together. The show is sold-out now, and we can't get new seats, even way in the back. I don't suppose you'd be willing to switch seats?"

"I'm sorry, I'm here with my family."

"We could pay you," Nick added.

"Ah, no, no amount of money is worth loosing time with my family."

"Thank you anyway," Leila said.

"Hope everything works out."

"Thank you."

"Well that's one down...I'll go over to the other balcony, I guess it's over there," Nick began pointing to a diagonal wall. "You stay here, if I get him to switch seats, I'll come back for you."

"Ok."

Nick kissed Leila and went off to the other balcony. When he arrived to the other seat, the man there looked up.

"Yes."

"Hi," Nick greeted. "I was just wondering if you'd be willing to switch seats with my girlfriend over on balcony five. We were given these tickets by someone in the play, and they aren't seated together."

"But, balcony five is farther away."

"Yes I realize that. But I would really be grateful."

"Sorry no, I like my seat."

"I'll pay you a thousand dollars for that seat."

"No, you can live with your mistake. You're not going to buy me."

"Please sir. You don't understand, she is looking really fine right now. She has on this great black dress that emphasizes everything holy in the world. Please...I beg you, take the money, and go over to the other side."

"I get it...you know...Jesus loves me this I know, he created women to tell me so."

"Exactly..." Nick said.

"I guess..."

"No."

"What do you mean no...Please sir..." Nick said very anxious, and then he pulled himself together acting normally. "I'll give you ten thousand dollars..."

CHAPTER THIRTY-EIGHT

Nick sat next to the man, who was unable to be bribed. The play started fifteen minutes behind schedule. Nick glanced between the actors on the stage and Leila sitting on the opposite side of the theatre. The man who would not leave his seat was incorrect, when saying Leila's seat was further from the stage. She sat watching the play in complete silence, every now and again she too would glance toward Nick. So for the duration of the three hour play (with no intermissions), Nick and Leila glanced back and forth at one another. At one point they caught each other's eye and proceeded to make several inappropriate facial expressions. At another point, Leila slid the strap of her dress off her shoulder, down to the bend of her elbow. Nick in turn contemplated two things very vigorously. One: how to kill the man who wouldn't switch seats, and two: what would be the fastest way to get to Leila. He acted on neither impulse, and continued "watching" the stage.

The only portion of the play Nick or Leila watched completely was Alfred's scenes, where he primarily took part in the witty banter and pointless whining. When the final curtain fell, Nick jumped out of his seat and ran to Leila's balcony side. He arrived to find her standing and clapping. She turned around to see him, and they embraced, kissing and otherwise groping one another, though only for a short time.

"Be careful, there may be children watching," Nick said moving his head in the direction of two young kids.

She moved him behind the curtain of the balcony and wrapped her arms around him.

"Composure is a dirty word," she whispered.

"Happy birthday," Nick said when they split.

"It's not over yet."

"For you or me?" he added smiling.

"Let's get out of here," she said taking Nick by the hand.

Leila led him off the balcony, through the main hall and out the series of doors.

"It's nice outside," she said.

"That it is..."

"I'm kind of hungry."

"Really?"

"Yeah, I haven't eaten anything all day."

"Me neither. I know somewhere we can go."

"Where?"

"It's a surprise, it's not too far."

The two of them got a cab, from down the block. Neither of them spoke much in the ten-minute long drive.

"Ok, it's just outside," Nick explained.

Leila stepped out of the taxi and Nick paid the driver. She looked at a series of three buildings.

"Which one?" she asked.

"That one."

The Best Orgasms Come from the Universe

Nick pointed the center building. It was an old red brick building. The sign outside was red and flashed on and off.

"Warm Bagels?" she questioned.

"Warm bagels..."

"Nick its eleven thirty at night."

"That's true," Nick said. "But I know the owner, he lives above the store."

"And...it's still eleven thirty at night, he's probably in bed."

"Biff? No never. He doesn't sleep. He's Zimbabwean or Scandinavian...or maybe he's Mexican...I can never remember, but whatever his nationality is...has one serious work mentality. He'd always say, 'In my country sleeping is for people who don't work for a living.' Besides he owes me a favor or two."

"Oh, well don't waste your favor."

"No, no, these bagels are...oh...words don't describe his bagels. Don't tell Persephone, but this guy, he makes bagels like no other. When Boris used to live down here, we'd come to Biff's bagel shop every Thursday. I miss these bagels..."

"Are you sure he won't mind?"

"Like I said, he owes me some favors. Here, help me out, grab a handful of stones and throw them at that window."

"This is by far one of the oddest things I've ever done on my birthday."

So there they stood at the curb throwing stones at Biff's upper apartment building. Neither of them had very good aim, so they made a bit of a game out of the challenge. He would throw one, and then she would throw one.

"So what kind of name is Biff?" she asked.

"I don't know…he really liked *Death of a Salesman* by ah…Arthur Miller. I think he named himself after a character from that when he moved to America."

"Oh…that's a good play. Oh! I got it!"

Leila had just hit the window when the police car pulled up.

"Excuse me," said the officer.

Nick turned around quickly, and Leila did the same.

"Hello officer," Nick said.

"What do you think you two are doing?"

"We are trying to throw these stones and hit that window," Leila said.

Then the policeman stopped his car and stepped outside.

"You're trying to break a window?"

"Oh no, not at all, we're just trying to hit it," Nick explained.

"Oh, well, Sir I hope you know destruction of private property is no joke."

"Well—" Nick began.

"You see officer, it's my birthday," Leila said.

Nick threw another stone trying to hit the window while the cop wasn't paying attention. And of course, he missed, nevertheless he kept trying.

"And we were hoping to get some bagels from this bagel shop," she continued.

"At nearly midnight? Do you know what kinds of criminals prowl the streets at night, Miss? And with you all dressed up, you're like a slab of meat waiting for the flies."

"That image will flatter my thoughts for weeks," Leila began trying to act pleasant. "But truly the streets can't' be that bad with you watching them, officer…"

"Malcolm."

"Officer Malcolm," Leila said, and it was then Nick hit window, which made a loud clacking sound. Malcolm turned to him, but Leila stepped to one side and continued. "I'm sure you have a reputation around these parts Officer Michael."

"Malcolm."

"Right, Malcolm."

"Yes well, you two should still call a cab, and head on home before the bad guys come out."

"But I really wanted some warm bagels, before my birthday ended. It's almost midnight like you said," Leila touched Malcolm's arm.

"Well I've been known to have a craving for warm bagels, myself."

"Who the hell is hitting my window," yelled Biff from his window.

"I'm sorry for the trouble Sir, but we are in the need of some bagels," said Malcolm.

"What?" Both Nick and Biff said. Nick continued, "Biff, it's me Nick."

"Nick? How the hell are you? I'll be right down."

"Thank you so much, Malcolm," Leila said.

"Ah, it's no trouble Miss."

"Thanks Officer Malcolm, for all your help," Nick said.

"We still have to talk," he began. "About disturbing the peace."

"Oh it's not his fault," Leila said. "I put him up to it."

Malcolm sighed and was about to say something just before Biff came down the stairs and out the door.

"Hello, hello, hello," Biff exclaimed.

"Good evening Sir," Malcolm said.

"I was hoping you'd make me and Leila...I mean the three of us, some bagels," Nick corrected.

"For you Nick?" Biff began. "Of course."

239

ed the front door and slipped inside, the three others

ou three sit right here," Biff said.

Nick, Leila, and Malcolm sat at a small table, on chairs attached to the floor. Biff scurried off behind the counter into the back kitchen, flicking light switches as he went. No one said anything for quite some time. Nick and Malcolm sat across from Leila, which of course put the two gentlemen next to one another. Leila smiled at Nick. He held in a grin, and shook his head up and down a bit. Malcolm cracked his neck.

"Long night ahead of you?" Nick asked.

"Actually, I'm off duty," Malcolm said. "Do you really think I'd be sitting in a bagel shop at eleven thirty, if I had things to do at work?"

"Is that a rhetorical question?"

"I'm sure not, no," Nick replied.

"Right, I was just passing through when I saw you two. It's never too late at night to right a few wrongs, I always say."

"Oh, that's so sweet," Leila said.

"That is..." Nick began with both Leila and Malcolm staring at him. "Sweet... It's just right up there...with...sweet. Right, so...what kind of bagel do you enjoy, Malcolm?"

"I'm a plain man myself," he said.

"I couldn't have guessed," Nick started. "And you like cream cheese?"

"No, I eat it plain."

"Good, good...that is sweet as well..."

"What are you talking about?" Malcolm questioned.

"I haven't the first clue."

The Best Orgasms Come from the Universe

It was then Biff came back.

"So, what kind of bagels can I get you?"

"A dozen plain bagels," Malcolm said. "I'm going to bring them back to station for night shift."

"That is so nice," Leila said.

"And for you young lady?"

"One everything-bagel."

"Ah, and the same for you right Nick? Only butter on the bottom half, isn't that it?"

"That's the one."

"Alright then, I'll be right back," Biff said.

"How long do the bagels normally take?" Malcolm asked.

"For so few? Only about an hour," Biff said and then walked off.

CHAPTER THIRTY-NINE

SATURDAY

Midnight arrived. The conversations around the table were dull at best. Leila got Malcolm talking, and he didn't seem to have a noticeable off-button. He explained the ins and outs of his job, and how he never had anytime for his family; which is why his wife divorced him.

"She looked like a ripe summer flower," he said.

At one point he went into great detail into the fact that she didn't love him. To this, Leila responded by saying:

"Maybe she loved you too much. Maybe if she stayed with you, she'd have hurt you more. I mean, speaking from a woman's point of view, being neglected, as you said you did towards her, could drive me into another man's arms. It could be that she divorced you because she knew she'd hurt you more, and herself more, and her kids more, by staying with you. I mean if you really loved her and she really loved you, it must have ripped her apart when she couldn't spend time with you. How long has it been since the two of you broke up?"

"A year," he answered.

"Is she seeing someone?"

"Yeah, a guy from her job."

"Well, if she still loves you, then she's only dating him to replace you. So, if you give a reason for her not to replace you, then you'll find she'll want to get back together. That's if she still loves you, and if you try to get her back, you're going to have to show a change."

"What do I do?"

"Well you'd know what she likes better then I would, but I'd start by trying to get less time at work. Then I'd turn on the charm, I mean you're a good looking guy, show her everything she's missing, but be careful not to let your ego show. Just throw yourself at her, not literally, but really be the man she fell in love with, or the man that she wants or needs today. Show her the man that loves her."

"Are you sure it will work?"

"No, but isn't it worth a try if you care about her so much?"

Malcolm didn't answer. Nick listened almost as intently as Malcolm did. He reflected on his past relationship mishaps. He thought about just how far he went to keep his girlfriends after they left. He always believed that if they leave, it's already over, and if he were to pursue them, he'd only make the problem worse.

"How could you make the problem worse, so long as you don't stalk them," he thought. *"I mean...if I care about them...and if they really cared about me. Have I cared about them that much? Excluding Persephone, but I think I knew inside that she was more like a sister than a girlfriend."*

"I guess you are right," Malcolm said.

"I think Biff is coming back," Leila said, since she was the only one not deep in thought at that moment.

"Here is your bag of bagels, officer," Biff said.

"Great. How much do I owe yah?"

"Oh, no charge."

"Oh, thank you."

"Don't thank me, thank Nick," Biff began. "He kept this store open long after I thought it was going to fail. He cosigned for me to keep this place, and never has he asked for anything in return. The least I could do for him, is give him and his friends some free bagels from time to time."

"Well, thank you both," Malcolm said standing up. "I've got to be going. And thank you Leila."

"Oh please, it's my pleasure. You just hang in there," Leila said kissing his cheek. "Don't give up on her; it took her a long time to work up the courage to split away from you. Give her time, a lot if need be."

"Alright Leila, thanks again."

"Bye Malcolm."

Malcolm waved and exited the store.

"And for you two, two warm everything-bagels, with enough everything to last both your lives," Biff said with a smile. "And Nick your glass of milk. I'm sorry Miss did you want something to drink."

"No thank you I'm fine," Leila said.

"This is Leila, by the way Biff," Nick added.

"Pleased to meet you."

"Thank you Biff."

Biff bowed his head, walked off behind the counter, and continued into the kitchen.

"You guys take all the time you need," Biff yelled from the kitchen.

"Ok Biff!" Nick yelled. "He's the Bagel Guru."

"Bagel Guru," Leila repeated.

"Yeah, and Persephone's the Tea Guru."

"Is that so?"

"Yeah it is, and happy birthday, one last time."

"It's twelve-eighteen," Leila said looking at the clock on the wall.

"Hey, birthdays with me— it's hot," Nick said taking a bite of his bagel. He quickly sipped his glass of milk. "Sorry, the bagel is kind of hot, the butters melted already. Anyway, birthdays with me last until you go to sleep."

"You really have a thing about birthdays don't you?"

"It's the remembrance of the most important day of your life. That's a big deal; it's an annual reminder, that you're still alive on this earth. I say enjoy every minute of it, and since you slept through the first couple of hours, I say have fun afterwards to make up for the lost time."

"This is the greatest birthday I've ever had. In fact it's one of the best day's I've ever had."

"Since I met you, I've been having the best week of my life."

Just then, Biff came rushing out.

"We must have picture," Biff said.

"A picture?" she inquired.

"I'm sorry, sometimes my English grammar is mistaken...yes a picture. To commemorate the day that Nick came back to the store."

"It's Leila's birthday as well."

"Then to commemorate Leila's birthday as well," Biff said with a massive grin. "You two smile together, and I take picture."

Various pictures were taken of the company, and the night went on.

Nick and Leila arrived back at her home at around one-thirty in the morning. She stepped inside, set her purse on the couch, and continued walking into the room. The entire apartment was dim as Nick stepped inside. Leila looked over her shoulder and let the strap of her dress slip down her arm. Nick walked forward slowly and removed his suit jacket. He stepped up behind her, starting to massage her shoulders, until he moved down her back. Crouching behind her, he moved his hand up the side of her leg until reaching her hip. He started to stand, blowing a light stream of air along the line of her back. After moving her hair to one side, he kissed the back of her neck, and she turned around. Leila looked up at him, unbuttoning his shirt.

The heathen buttons found there way out of the loop, the divine dress fell to floor, and the night enjoyed its religious experience.

CHAPTER FORTY

Nick awoke almost at noon, feeling refreshed and laid back. For the first time in his entire life, he did not need a shower to remember who and where he was. He knew he was in Leila's home, and he knew his name was Nick. He looked around at the bed he was in and realized it was Leila's, although she was not in it. He started to walk out of the bedroom and found a note on the door, which read:

Nick-

I had a great time last night. Thank you for making my birthday, worth remembering. I left for my parent's house, with Ray. Stay as long as you like, but please lock the door on your way out. I'll talk to you soon.

Leila

Nick walked out of the bedroom after getting dressed and made his way out of the apartment just as quickly. He took a cab home and was greeted by eight messages. He sat down in his wheelie chair and played the messages.

"You have eight new messages...Thursday...three twelve pm...

"Nick, you home? Nick, you home?" began Griffon's message. "Just calling to make sure you're getting ready to meet me later today. You're not there or ignoring me...so I'll talk to you later."

"Thursday...six-o'-seven pm...

"Hey Nick, it's Persephone, I'm just calling to tell you that the essay contest has picked the semi finalists, and you made the cut, congratulations. Well give me a call sometime this weekend, maybe we can do something."

"Thursday...eight pm..."

"Hey Nick its Leila, I got the flower and the note. Thanks for thinking of me, I look forward to seeing you tomorrow, ok I'll see you then."

"Thursday...eight ten pm..."

"Nick hi, sorry for calling so late, it's Alfred. I just really needed to talk to someone, but you're not around so, I'll see you tomorrow."

"Friday...eleven thirty am..."

"Hello, this is Curt from Sermon Enterprises calling in regards to the absence of a one Nick Sermon. Please contact us as soon as possible."

"Friday...seven fifteen pm..."

"Hey Nick its Bruce, I made it to Arizona alright. I'll be talking to Burt tomorrow so send up a prayer for me, or do what ever you almost Pagans do. Right well, I'll call you on Sunday and tell you all about it. Ok, bye Nick."

"Friday...eight eighteen..."

"Nick, yeah it's Boris. I know you're at Alfred's play thing, which is why I'm calling now. You'll notice when you get there that I'm not there. I'm sorry about yesterday, and how I treated you for your opinion. Alfred and I are having some troubles and I'm sorry about taking it out on you. Well, I hope the show goes alright."

"Saturday…eleven forty-four am…"

"Hey Nick its Boris again. I was hoping I could catch you so we could talk. Give me a call back anytime. Yeah bye."

"End of messages…"

Nick showered and changed his clothes before calling Boris back. Boris answered after the first ring.

"Hello?"

"Boris?"

"Yeah, hi Nick."

"So do you want to talk on the phone, or go to the coffee shop, or something?"

"We can talk over the phone if you don't mind."

"Sure what's going on?"

"Alfred and I are having problems."

"I caught that."

"Well it all started because I was making a deal for my new book, and my agent read it and he had a lot of changes. You know how it is Nick, when they think everything is horrible, and they are just missing the point."

"Yeah you're usually the one with the changes."

"Oh…"

"But yes, I know how it can get annoying when someone only has criticism," Nick said. "But what does that have to do with Alfred."

"Well we were expecting to celebrate, and I forgot to pick up milk on my way home, so Alfred went to get it."

"Right."

"And he got two percent instead of whole milk, and you know how I hate two percent. Well you like milk...you drink it all the time...two percent is like water mixed with a little flour."

"Yeah I know."

"So I got angry. I hadn't told him about the agent thing, I just exploded on him. I have a lot of built up anger and...well Alfred is the first...he's the first guy I've ever been with. Well, he's the first guy I've been in a relationship with. In fact he is the first person I've been with in a relationship since the end of high school. I've been a bachelor for a long time. Relationships are like cattle, and I'm used to raising chickens...and Alfred he's like a buffalo, as far as relationships go, even some cattle don't understand him. Do you know what I mean Nick?"

"Absolutely...no, not really...you lost me when you started talking about the chickens."

"I was making an analogy...oh never mind...Anyway, I yelled a bit, and Alfred is very sensitive, he took everything the wrong way. So then, I got angrier and said the things he was saying I was trying to say. But I didn't mean them Nick, I didn't."

"I know Boris."

"He really thinks I hate him, doesn't he?"

"Yeah, yeah, he really does."

"Damn it...I was just angry, I'm just so damn angry. I don't know what to do Nick. It's like everything in my life is going in the opposite direction that I am. I'm like one of those Japanese fish, the ones that go against the tide. But I don't want to go against the current Nick; I've been doing that all my life. What do I do?"

"I don't know...but I'll tell you this much, you've been alone for a long time. Alfred is good for you, and you're good for Alfred. I don't know if it will be a relationship that will last forever, but it's definitely something that will make you a better person, and isn't that one of the things a relationship is all about."

"Yeah you're right."

"If you don't try to make it work, then you're going to revert back to what you were before. Don't force a relationship out of it, but at least work for it if it means something to you. Once it stops meaning something to you, you'll have to address that with Alfred, and see how he feels about it."

"I don't know Nick."

"You always say that Boris, I'm not saying you need to know, I'm saying you need to try."

"We'll see Nick."

"Are we ok, as friends I mean?"

"Yeah Nick, we're ok."

"Good, because you're an asshole."

"I'm sorry Nick. I've always considered you kind of...well I haven't considered you the way I should have. You're not beneath me, you're my equal Nick. I just want you to know that."

"I do know that Boris, but it's nice of you to say it. You are at least a likeable asshole."

"Thanks again Nick. I better get going, so I'll talk to you soon. I'm flying down to Los Angles on Thursday; I was hoping maybe we could get together on Wednesday this week. Is that alright?"

"Yeah."

"Right, well I'll see you then."

"Get back to me about Alfred. He considers me a friend. If he asks for advice I'm going to give it to him, you know that right?"

"Yeah I know you Nick; whatever you think is best. Maybe you'll see him on Wednesday too. Usual time, usual place...unusual day... I guess I'll see you then Nick."

"Bye Boris."

Nick stepped away from the phone, and walked to his typewriter. He started typing even before he sat down.

"What's a relationship? Is it two people who are in a romantic gathering? Truly, a relationship is any contact between two people. It could be bad, and then again, it could be good. If a relationship is worth keeping, we, as a race, fight to keep it. Our emotions denote whether a relationship is a positive or negative one. The reason why love relationships are so hard to keep is because when you honestly and completely love someone you know and accept their flaws. It's hard to work through people's blemishes and still love them. Nevertheless, as you see someone, you see through them. You sometimes see the real them. Hopefully this experience is a good one, because you can love them more. Unfortunately, other times you see the real human being and become bored or disappointed. If you can accept the flaws, or help (not force) to show how to change them, then you have found a believable relationship."

"It needs more..." Nick said.

"These examples are of learned love. True love is beyond that. True love is like a light breeze, it cools you even when you don't know it's there. True love empowers you and inspires you. True love is like a thunderstorm that can strike down any obstacle. True love is a walking contradiction; it's different for everyone. No one can tell you what true love is, because it's always different, and it's in a constant state of change. When two people are in love, they can do the greatest things, and enjoy life as freely as possible. Then again, true love can crush you; it can make the two people push each other so far from one another. True love is a plague that can peel away your flesh and soul. People can be so afraid of this love that they'll run away or hide *themselves from all of life. The only thing about true love that is true for everyone is this: In some way, or many ways, when it leaves or is taken away, you can't get it back, and it will always feel horrible. When it is gone, you can lose yourself in it's memory, or you can go into denial so much that you disappear, or worst of all you search for it and never find it, and harm everyone in your path in some way or another. Nevertheless, if it doesn't leave and isn't taken away, and it is still there somewhere, then it will live forever. When love comes, take it in full. Maybe you'll know it, and maybe you won't. Or maybe you'll be standing in a grocery store, on the seventh day of knowing the person, and you'll never want anything else. The only thing I can say for knowing love is this: Before you have it, be content with life, when you have it, the contentment doesn't leave, and when you know it's there, don't push it away."*

Nick fell asleep at the typewriter and didn't wake up until nine thirty when the phone rang. He rolled his chair to the phone, bumping into the end table, slamming into his groin. The pain was excruciating, and it wasn't until the answering machine picked up the message, that he even remembered the phone had rung. Every once and a while in a man's life, his groin is hit by something undesirable, although never in Nick's life did it hurt quite this much afterwards. The pain blocked out the sound of his answering machine message, and then he heard a voice.

"Nick! It's Bruce," he said excitedly on the machine.

He struggled to get to the phone. His hand couldn't quite reach it as he crouched on the ground.

"I guess you're not around. I know my message said I'd call tomorrow, I'm just really needed to tell someone..."

As quickly as possible Nick brought himself to his knees and grasped the phone in his hand.

"Hello..." Nick said still in pain.

"Nick?"

"Yeah."

"You ok?"

"I've been better. What about you?"

"I'm great! I'm great, I mean...wow, I am...Nick you are such a good friend."

"It went well then, I'm guessing," Nick forced himself up into a chair.

"Oh Nick, if it wasn't for you I'd be dead. Now I had lunch and diner with my son."

"Well what happened?" he asked half listening. He tried desperately to listen, but the pain continued.

"Well I got there a little late. When I got off the plane, I saw my wife and her new husband. He's not that bad, I mean he's not me, but you know. He's a decent man; he's got the goatee thing going on."

"Are you going to tell me the story?"

"Hey you're a writer, can't you appreciate a little character development. So anyway I stepped off the plane, and my ex whispered something to my son. Probably something like, 'go to your father.' Something like that, right? 'Cause he was probably pretty nervous, which made me feel a little better, 'cause we were in the same boat and all. So he comes up to me...just him and me. And he says, 'I have a picture of you,' and he continues to say, 'but it doesn't really look like you.' I got all choked up, worried and stuff, I thought...well I don't really know what I thought. So I knelt down and said, 'I've got a picture of you for every year you've been alive.'

He had really good hands; he's going to be strong. He reached to my face and touched my cheek. He moved my face around, and wiped away my tears. Then you know what he said?"

"What did he say?"

"He said, 'don't cry Daddy, there you are,'" Bruce said, and then he repeated it, and Nick could tell Bruce was crying a bit. "'Don't cry Daddy there you are.' Then he took my hand after hugging me, and we walked to my wife. He's gotten so big Nick. I wish you could have been behind me there, like my ex-wife was for my son. You've been a really good friend."

"Thanks Bruce."

"No, thank you Nick. I have to get going; I need to put Burt to bed. I snuck to the kitchen to call you. So I'll be back on Monday."

"I'll see you then Bruce."

"Bye Nick."

Nick smiled to himself and got ready for bed.

CHAPTER FORTY-ONE

SUNDAY

Nick slept well that night and awoke at six in the morning. Many ideas competed in his mind that morning. He showered and ate a small breakfast. When he sat down to write his thoughts were uncooperative. Instead of writing he turned and watched an hour of television. Although whenever he wasn't doing something creative, with his spare time, he felt unproductive. Nevertheless he searched for a good movie. Even with the seven hundred satellite channels, he could not find any good programs on at nearly seven am on a Sunday morning.

He sat in a half daze, flipping channels for an hour before he became disgusted with himself and the lack of entertainment. He searched his desk for something undone, which is when he found Herbert's documents. He spent just over an hour reading every line of the writing. Every inch was filled with interesting and important observations about the business. There were nearly thirty theories of how to cut down on pointless costs, and how to expand the range of the business, and how to advertise more for the company while not paying anything extra. All around, the writing was filled with

The Best Orgasms Come from the Universe

information that would save millions. After finishing the entire body of work, Nick jumped from his seat and grabbed his phone book, which is when he realized he didn't know Herbert's last name.

In a stretch of desperation, Nick called his job. A secretary he didn't know answered the phone.

"Hello?"

"Hi this is Nick," he began. "I was wondering if Herbert was working today."

"What's the last name?"

"Of him or me?"

"His last name."

"I don't know."

"Well I'm sorry Sir."

"Well, I know what floor he works on. He works on the twentieth floor and he works in engineering."

"Alright let me check, give me one moment." There was a short pause filled with the lady's humming. "Yes, there is a Herbert in.

"Great could you connect me with him please?"

"What's your name Sir?"

"Nick, I own the building."

"Oh, Nick, sorry for the wait, one moment please."

After a half a minute Herbert came on the other line.

"Speak to me."

"Yeah Herbert, its Nick."

"Nick!"

"Yeah I read the documents you gave me. They are very...well they are really damn good. How long have you had this Herbert?"

"About sixteen years, I update it almost every month."

"Why didn't you put it forth sooner?"

"Well Nick...to be honest...I didn't really trust you. I didn't know you, and I thought you'd be like your father. After the kickball game, I realized something...your not like him...so I decided to entrust it with you. Call it a thank you, if you will."

"It's great work. I'm going to look into putting these things into effect. I need to run it by the board, just to let them know. Maybe I could get you seat on it."

"Not interested."

"Why not?"

"Too political...I know my own faults Nick, and one of them is, if I am given power, and I don't have control, I'm useless. I'd need to work my way up to the very top, and I'm too old to work that hard to get there, besides I'd never try. You are a good leader. The best guidance is the kind that is given only when needed, and that's what you do. You give to your employees what they need when they need it."

"Is that how they think of me?"

"Every last one. You do as little work as possible, yet don't push the work off to other people, they respect that. And the kickball, it was crazy as shit, and the most surreal thing I've ever experienced, but it showed who you were Nick. You're a boss any man would want."

"Well thank you Herbert, you are a very fine kiss-ass," Nick said jokingly.

"I try, I'll see you tomorrow."

"Yeah."

Nick hung up the phone and called Persephone. Persephone's husband Jack picked up.

"Good morning."

"Yeah Jack, this is Nick, is Persephone in?"

"It's kind of early Nick."

"Yeah I know, I'm sorry, I knew you'd all be up. So is she in?"

"Yeah she just got up."

"Thanks Jack."

"Sure Nick," he began. "Persephone!"

Nick heard someone, he presumed was Persephone, say "Yeah," in the background.

"It's Nick."

"Oh," she started. "Hello, Nick?"

"Hey."

"I got it!" she bellowed.

Jack hung up the phone and there was a quick silence.

"Jack seems chipper this morning."

"Yeah well his business deal didn't go to well."

"Give him a great big kiss for me."

"What are you calling about?" she asked, sounding tired.

"Well, I was calling to see if you were coming into the store today."

"Would I be up this early if I didn't need to be?"

"Probably not."

"Right, so yes I'm going to be in later."

"Great, what time, I was hoping I could talk to you."

"You could talk to me now."

"I've been on the phone constantly since yesterday. I've haven't seen a familiar face since Friday at like two o'clock in the morning. I have so much to tell you."

"Great, I'll be in the store at around ten."

"You're the best, I'll see you then."

"Yeah, bye Nick."

Nick hung up the phone and cleaned his apartment before leaving for Persephone's store with his essay. He arrived a half-hour early and went inside. He walked himself to a comfortable chair, and sat down. He looked over his essay, which was now over twenty pages, after being beefed up. When Persephone entered he looked up and waved. She waved back and walked over.

"Hey Nick."

"Good morning."

"So what did you need to tell me?"

"I don't even remember, so much has happened since I saw you last."

"Well just give me the basic drift, I can't really talk today."

"What's going on?"

"I have to go out of town for a couple of days."

"Why what's going on?"

"Jack's mother is sick; we don't know if she's going to make."

"Oh, shit, Persephone I'm sorry."

"No it's just; it was really hard for Jack. He got the news while on his business trip, which is why he didn't get the deal. His mind was sidetracked."

"I would imagine, wait I thought you were going to the shore."

"It was cancelled because of business."

"Oh, I'm sorry."

"Yeah well, what can you do?"

"So, when are you coming back?"

"Tuesday, hopefully," she answered. "But I may end up there a little longer. If something comes up, I'll give you a call."

"Yeah, well tell Jack I'm really sorry. The closest thing to a mother I ever had was your mom. She was a great woman."

"Yeah she was. Anyway, I have about thirty minutes, but after that, I have to make arrangements for the store, you know what it's like without me."

"Ok, well...where to start. I don't know; I don't want to keep you from your work. There's so many things...most of the highlights are from other people's lives. But I think I'm falling in love."

"With Leila?"

"No, Boris. Yes of course with Leila."

"I don't know Nick; you've only known her a little over a week."

"Don't you believe in love at first sight?"

"I believe in lust at first sight."

"No it's not lust..."

"I know Nick; you were never really like that. But do you really love her? I mean have you two slept together?"

"What does that have to do with it?"

"I don't know...maybe you're just enjoying the experience of something new."

"That's not it."

"Then what is it? You're a writer, describe it."

"I don't know."

"You don't know? Since when do you not know how to describe something? Haven't you ever been in love before?"

"No..."

"Never...?"

"Not romantically."

"Really?"

"I'm only twenty five."

"How than do you write it so well? In the past I mean?"

"I can feel it. I get vibes."

"Vibes?"

"Yeah, haven't you ever been sitting at a restaurant and felt someone's pain from another table."

"Sure, I see it all the time."

"No, I mean can you feel it. It's like watching a movie with a really good actor in it. You can feel the emotions they're emoting, before you see it. That's it, life is like a movie to me, and I know what people are going to say, before they say it. I don't mean psychically, but emotionally, like they have lines and it all depends on how they want to say it. Then, before they speak, I can feel it coming out of their faces, and I can read it in their eyes. And I guess when someone is in love, they actually emote less emotion, because it becomes them. When they speak they are kind of...free. It's the closest anyone ever gets to being in touch with life. I mean I guess it can make you sloppy if you don't pay attention, I mean what can't. That's what I feel. I feel free, and when I'm around her everything inside of me works itself out, and then I can be there for her, or you, or Boris, or Bruce...or whoever else needs me."

"I was really only looking for a one liner, but that was very inspiring."

"Oh, thanks for the encouragement."

"No, I'm proud to be your friend Nick, and proud to have you as a friend. I just hope it will always be like this for you."

"I want to be with her."

"Good, now, do you want a bagel or something? You know before I have to boot you out of my store so I can get some work done."

"I've already had breakfast actually, so I'll let you go back to your work."

"It was good talking to you Nick, and I'll see you later in the week."

"Yeah I'll see you then."

CHAPTER FORTY-TWO

Nick left the book store and continued on to his home. When he walked inside he was struck by a pain comparable only to some of his worst headaches. He felt as if his kidneys were hit with a flaming baseball bat...repeatedly. He staggered to the bathroom, meanwhile hoping the agony would pass. He was confused beyond belief. He had no idea what was happening. The situation seemed like his kidneys were rebelling, and wanted to commit suicide, taking the rest of the body with it. In the bathroom he relieved his urinary track without any extra added pain. The pain struck again harder, it felt as if something was tumbling through his body.

Nick's thoughts weren't flowing as well as his urine. He couldn't remember any number for a taxi service, even though he used them almost every week. He flipped through his numbers and came upon Boris' number. He called it, while breathing in through the nose and out through the mouth. Someone picked up after the sixth ring, just before Nick was going to hang up.

"Hello?"

"Hi is Boris there?"

"No, he's out right now, can I take a message."

"Alfred is that you?"

"Yeah, who is this?"

"It's Nick, do you have a car?"

"Yeah Nick."

"Can you get here as quickly as possible?"

"What's wrong?"

"I don't know. I need to get to a hospital."

"Ok, Nick, I'll be right over."

Nick hung up the phone and left his apartment. He went down the elevator to the bottom floor and braced himself against the wall. After about ten minutes of constant pain, a car screeched to a stop and out of the passenger door came Boris.

"Nick! Are you alright? What's wrong?" Boris questioned, running over to his friend.

Boris walked Nick to the car and put him in the back. Alfred began talking as Nick slid into the backseat.

"Nick what's going on? I can't take this...what's wrong? Is your appendix going to burst or something? Oh, no Nick hold on, don't die."

"Alfred shut up!" Boris yelled.

Alfred sped off down the road and the charade inside continued.

"Don't try to bully me, Boris; this is my car I'm driving."

"If it's your car than drive it right! Run the damn red lights."

"I have to agree with Boris on that one..." Nick said as loud as possible, which wasn't much at the time. And of course neither Boris nor Alfred heard him.

"The only reason your even in my car is because I didn't know where Nick lives," Alfred clamored.

"Well he called me!"

The Best Orgasms Come from the Universe

"You see, that's it! That's the thing about you Boris. You want control of everything! Why couldn't he have been calling for either of us? He's my friend too."

"Yeah well he was my friend first! You can't take over someone's life. And let me remind you, you didn't have to come to my house after church!"

"You invited me!"

"Shut up!" Nick screamed. "Both of you! I'm already in pain, and I'm starting to get a headache from the two of you, and that is pissing me off. Boris you're a stuck up cry baby without any regard of other people's feelings. And Alfred you have to stop putting words in people's mouths, because you think they hate you. The both of you need to grow up, or remain childish on your own time, because I am God damn sick of it! Both of you just shut the hell up!"

No one said anything after that. They all got to the hospital with glares. Boris helped Nick out of the car and Alfred ran to the person at the front desk.

Everything seemed to fly by, and suddenly Nick found himself in a hospital room with a doctor standing next to him. Somewhere along the line he was given morphine for the pain, and an IV had been inserted on the top of his hand between his left index and middle fingers. He was staring off into space when the doctor began the pleasantries. He answered but wasn't really paying attention to either end of the conversation. He started listening when the doctor told him what was wrong.

"Nick we found kidney stones in your system. I don't know if you know what they are."

Nick shook his head, "no."

The doctor continued to say: "They are caused by many things. We believe yours were created by a calcium build up in your body. Do you eat a lot of cheese or drink a lot of milk?"

"Yeah I love milk; it's just about my favorite drink. I don't really drink much else."

"Well, we believe you have two significant kidney stones. One is on the move, and that is what you felt. We are going to have you try to pass it."

"We who?"

"Well you."

"What do you mean by pass it?"

"Well, the stone is going to go through your urinary track and discharge from you penis."

"Say again…It's going to discharge…what like an orgasm?"

"Well no…not nearly so pleasant, I'm afraid. Discharge, as in it's going to come out in your urine. By my estimates, it should be arriving on Tuesday. So don't make plans."

"Wonderful. So how big is this thing?"

"It's about a forth of your pinky nail."

"Oh that's not that bad," Nick said confidently.

"Yes, well, it's going to feel like a beach ball."

"A beach ball! I'm not even that big, Doc."

"Well that's not the worst of it."

"Bring it on Doc."

"There is a larger consolidation of calcium in your system, which is far too large to pass. We need to operate. By operate I mean, we need to perform an operation called lithotripsy. Basically what that is, is we send several shock waves into the cluster and brake it apart. If done correcting we can completely destroy the "stone." We would like to perform this sometime next week. The good news is it's not going to bother you for quite some time. If we get to it soon, it won't bother you at all."

"So what do I need to do?"

"All you need to do is concentrate on passing this stone."

"What do you want me to do, Zen meditation for six hours a day, and use my chi to command the stone to leave?"

"No Nick," the doctor chuckled. "I want you to drink a lot of fluids. Water is good, cranberry juice is better."

"I hate cranberry juice."

"Well you can stick with water, but I strongly recommend the cranberry juice. Unfortunately we didn't find out about this sooner, you could have been preparing for it. The water and cranberry juice may not even help, although if it does, it's going to smooth out the stone."

"And you said it was coming Tuesday."

"Approximately, optimistically and probably," the doctor said jokingly. "Yes, that's correct. And remember stay away from the milk. The nurse will give you a list of things to stay away from until the surgery. Come back and make an appointment to come see me, unless something goes wrong. I'll have the nurse come and remove the IV and you should be good to go. I'll write you a script for any pain and/or discomfort...and remember drink, drink, drink."

Nick shook the doctor's hand and laid back down awaiting the nurse's arrival. When he was freed and dressed, he moved a bit more gingerly than earlier and headed towards the waiting room. He noticed Alfred and Boris asleep on the gray heavy plastic chair, holding hands. He woke them up and they took him home.

CHAPTER FORTY-THREE

MONDAY

When Nick got up that morning, no light shined through the window. At first he thought it was still night. He glanced at the clock, which proved him incorrect. It was just shy of nine o'clock. He walked to his window and looked outside to see another gray sky. He opened his window and breathed in the sent of the pre-storm breeze. Oddly enough it smelled like freshly blooming flowers. The smell just before a rain storm was just what he needed to remind himself he had a new day ahead. It was a Monday, the day everyone hates, although if it didn't exist, people would hate Tuesday.

Nick gathered up his essay once again. He showered and fixed his hair. He opened his empty refrigerator and closed it just as quickly. He drank about a gallon of water in many refills from his faded *Thundercats* collector cup, which normally would have been used for milk. At last, he put on his brightest red shirt and walked out of his apartment, ready to forge through the Monday streets. With all the confidence in the world, Nick headed to Leila's apartment. He knocked at her door and Ray answered.

"Hi Nick," she said solemnly.

The Best Orgasms Come from the Universe

"Is Leila in?"

"Yeah," she said similarly, and then she bellowed as normal. "I'm going to take the dog for a walk!"

"Bye Nick."

"See you later Ray."

Nick stepped inside and wandered through the house to the bedroom. He found her packing suitcases as opposed to unpacking them.

"How was your trip?" he asked, a bit confused.

"It was ok," she answered plainly and she didn't look up.

"What's wrong?"

"My mother's sick," she said stepping past him with the suitcase.

"So is Persephone's mother-in-law."

"I don't have any brother's if that's what you mean," she said, and it was the first time she looked at him.

"Jack, your brother? No I wasn't implying that. I was just making...well I was just saying. So is there anything I can do to help?"

"No, I going to be going there on Friday," she headed back to the bedroom.

"Oh, do you want me to come with you to see your mom?"

"No."

"Listen; are you angry at me about something?"

"No," her voice wasn't convincing.

"When are you coming back?"

"Actually Nick, I don't know if I am coming back."

There was a pause, and she stopped packing a moment. After about fifteen seconds passed she looked up at him.

"What do you mean?"

"I have to take care of her," she looked back down and zipped up the big suitcase. "My other sisters have more important things to do, and my father is too old."

"So when am I going to see you again?"

"I'll call some time."

"You'll call some time...I see. What does that mean exactly?"

"It means maybe when I get back from Pennsylvania, I'll call."

"Maybe you'll call."

"Yeah maybe," she said looking up again, although now she looking annoyed.

"What am I missing here? Maybe you'll call? Well I'm sorry that's not good enough for me. I thought we had something going here."

"Well, obviously we don't!"

"Why are you doing this?"

"Because my mother's sick."

"No, why are you doing this to us?"

"Because I don't want to fall in love with you Nick," she answered stepping away from her bed. "I want to end it now before I do. I can't go through this again."

"What are you talking about?"

"You're too good to me Nick. I'm not good for you."

"Let me be the judge of that.

"That's such a common answer...'Let me be the judge of that.' You sound like a drug addict."

"Well try this then. All I want is you."

"Well I don't want you!"

"What the hell is this? It's like a complete turn around. I mean last week..."

"Last week was all we had, and I'm trying to keep it that way."

"So, what I mean nothing to you?"

"No you mean too much to me, which is the problem. I can't live like that; I can't have someone in my life like that. It's not healthy. I'm simply ending it before anyone gets really hurt. You're a good man Nick, and I'd change you. I'd change you into something you don't want."

"I haven't the first clue about what you are talking about. You don't spring this on people, like it's nothing!"

"I have to keep it like it's nothing. Why can't you be like other guys Nick, get over it," she moved out of the bedroom and into the living room.

"What the fuck are you talking about?" Nick cried loudly getting adamant. "I really love you, but you are fucking insane. Haven't you noticed I'm not like other guys? I don't know what these other guys were like, because you don't tell me."

"I don't want you to give up your dream for me," she said reaching the kitchen.

"Where did that come from? Now you're just making it up as you go along."

"I can't let you come to Pennsylvania with me. We'll end up like my parents. Then one day you'll look at me and say, 'you kept me from what I really loved,'" Leila progressively worked her way back into the living room. "And then I'll lie and say 'I didn't want you in the first place.' It's a big mess and I don't want it. We are only one year apart in age; you are only twenty-five. You'll find love again."

"Don't change the subject! Why can't you let me in Leila? Why?"

"Because I don't want to talk about how guys have liked me ever since I was thirteen," she said crying her eyes out. "I don't want to tell you how my older sister, used to take me to high school parties, when I wasn't even sure what sex was. I don't feel the need to tell you that every guy I've been with has either only wanted me for sex or wanted to show me off, and get extra claps on the back from his buddies. No man has ever fought for me Nick. Never! I've never been important enough to chase. And you want to hear something really fucked up? I lied, Jonathan, he didn't do anything wrong, he loved me and I pushed him away, until he couldn't take it anymore. He was going to quit his job for me, and I wouldn't let him. So we broke it off. What about Arnold? Oh, he did die," she said still crying. "But we weren't getting married anymore. I was cheating on him, and I told him. He got mad and went out that night to drive away his anger. He was speeding and he went head first into an eighteen wheeler. How is the woman you love, seem now?"

"She seems sad," Nick began, with tears in his eyes. "She seems lost, but I want to find her. And I still love her...and she seems too good for me. You want to know why? Because when I feel lost...or dead inside, I can think about her smile, or her laugh, and that gets me through it. But I don't think my smile does that for you, and that makes me not good enough, all because I can't do that for you."

"Just go Nick," she said squatting on the ground, leaning against the couch.

"No, it's my turn now."

"I thought that maybe I could take it slow with you. I thought maybe we'd slowly fall in love and I'd get to be with you. But I couldn't do that; I couldn't hold back what I felt for you. I couldn't be one of those guys who gradually makes a relationship work. I don't know the tricks...and yeah I'm young enough to learn them, but I don't want to. I don't want to learn to hide my feelings. So I'm going to leave, and I'm going to remember you and love you for the rest of my life. If that's alright with you, I'm going to hold on to that. I can't leave that at the door when I leave...and slowly but surely I'm going to become like everyone else. Maybe I'll meet someone someday and have some kids, and buy a home. I'll be small inside, and I'll disappear, but that's better than being with you and knowing you are dying inside. Especially if I know I can't do anything or, worse yet, if I know and you won't let me help you. So I guess this is goodbye then..."

She didn't say anything.

"Yeah," he said. "Goodbye."

When Nick stepped outside, rain was falling. Big fat raindrops descended from the sky and saturated him. He held his essay under his shirt, desperately trying to keep it dry. He didn't go to work that morning. Instead he continued on home. He hailed no taxi, and took no breaks under shelter. When he reached his home, he stepped into the elevator and removed his manuscript. The pieces of paper were soaked, and the ink on every page was smeared. The pages literally started tearing apart in his hands. The only copy of his complete essay, destroyed in his hands. He didn't care.

CHAPTER FORTY-FOUR

TUESDAY

The remainder of Nick's night was spent with him curled up on the floor in agony. Leila was gone, or as good as gone, the stone was on the move, a headache had decided to drop in for good luck, due to his stress over losing Leila, and his essay which took so much of his spirit to write was ripped to shreds on the ground. The next morning began and Nick hoped it was all a dream. He was reminded instantly of the truth, by the curling pieces of paper on the ground. He left his house for his job in the same rain-dried cloths.

Nick looked at his black and white world. The simple fact that he was the only thing colorful in his own life, made him colorblind. Not even the peach skin of the universe held any tone. The tint of the world disappeared. All was gone. Nick looked at the people on the street, and became one of them. He could feel all the reds and pinks in his nature turn gray. The tears that rolled down his face were not seen by anyone walking passed, for they matched his skin. Nick's song ended, his symphony was as good as over. He was in the climax of a story written by a bad writer. The writer he was and the writer inside of him lost their edge, trapping his story in the paradox with no logic in its making.

Nick's hours passed by and the world around him bloomed with thunderstorms. The reverberation of cars driving over puddles sounded much different from the gutter. To him the universe revealed its true guile. The cosmos was a tease. It's constant and inevitably pointless foreplay finally left him impudent and flaccid. Leila had vanished, and he was in no spirit to retrieve her. He could have found her if he tried, but he didn't. He could have called or visited Persephone's café, but he didn't. The book store was no longer a sanctuary to him, yet instead it had become a dungeon.

For once in Nick's life, he was out of words. He was left in the dead end corner of his life, waiting for the *stones of history to pass...*

Nick did not absorb anything anyone said that morning. Mary told him about her quest for romance from her husband. She smiled outrageously over her conquest. Nick faked a grin, without truly hearing anything. Unbeknownst to Nick, the last words out of her mouth were:

"All thanks to you Nick."

Nick stared outside his office at the storm clouds. The rain had stopped, after raining for all that morning and previous day. The overcast showed no signs of passing. Bruce stepped inside and told his long tale about his reunion with his son. He too smiled uproariously. His ending remarks were similar to Mary's. Bruce was still in the office when Nick got a call from the board. Nick didn't answer it. They called again, and Bruce went over to his friend. He put his hand on Nick's shoulder, which brought him back into reality.

"Nick you have a call."

"Do I?"

Nick walked over to his phone and hit speaker.

"Hello?" he said.

"Nick, this is your board."

"All of you can speak at once?"

"Well this is Gary."

"Hi Gary."

"We'd like you to come up to the board room."

"No, I'm good."

"What?"

"I don't feel like moving…"

"Then we'll be forced to do this over the phone…Nick there is no easy way to say this."

"Okay…"

"Nick, we're firing you."

Bruce eyes lit up with anguish.

"How?" Bruce bellowed.

"Well, you see Nick; you've been doing a lot of things behind the company's back. For one, that recess stunt you pulled cost the company its full working potential, because of it we lost some very important opportunities. Second, we have been informed that you've been giving out vacation time…paid vacation time, to your secretary and a, one Bruce Dodge. Is that correct?"

"Hey they can't do this Nick!" Bruce shouted.

"Sounds about right yeah," Nick said.

"We wouldn't have even known about this if it weren't for two very loyal members of our business. Basically, even though you are the head of this company, we, as your board, can terminate you if you are performing illegal activities against the corporation. You will still get your shares of any profits until the end of the year."

The Best Orgasms Come from the Universe

"Nice birthday present," Nick retorted.

"Although, from this point on you will have no say in any decisions made for this company. Your percentage shall be split up for the members of the board."

"Ok," Nick said. "Bye."

He turned off the speaker and Bruce looked back at him in shock.

"You aren't just going to take that, are you Nick?" Bruce asked.

"It's life, Bruce."

With that, Nick walked out of his office, smiled to Mary, and walked to his elevator. Bruce came toward the elevator just as it closed. Nick could feel the stones on the move once again. When he got back home another headache introduced itself. His new mind-guest was rooted into his entire body. His headache pounded worse than ever in his entire life. His heart psychologically bled from loneliness, and just for kicks the stones decided to move. He had consumed no extra fluids, making the stone very rough. The pain dropped him to his knees in the middle of his living room, and then...the phone rang, and rang, and rang, and rang. He stood up with any energy he could muster, and made his way to the phone. The answering machine kicked in and Mick came onto the line.

"Hello Nicolas? I guess you're not home. Well you need to come in to pick up your stuff by the end of the week, or it's being dumped, just thought..."

Before Mick could finish, Nick grabbed the machine, ripped it from the wall and threw it through his window.

"You have no more messages," Nick said to himself.

The pain from the stones let up, leaving him with only his excruciating headache, and his own self torment. Nick undressed himself down to his underwear and dropped into bed. The chance of sleeping was minimal to none, but he didn't care. He laid there for hours thinking about everything and nothing. Then out of nowhere, Nick became very aware of his penis. He rolled out of bed, and waddled like a pregnant goat to the bathroom. His groin felt like it was filled with liquid magma. The classic term *pissing razorblades*, didn't do this pain justice. The feeling of a knife tearing through his flesh, wasn't correct, it felt more like a blow torch. The combination of a flamethrower firing from his genitals and the trash compacter over his head brought him to his knees once again, this time only inches from the toilet. He felt like he couldn't breathe out of his mouth, and seemingly nothing productive was occurring at the other end. The pain became so much Nick cried out. Tears rolled down the sides of his face, and then came the dizziness. He inched himself across the floor to the almighty toilet. Surprising little blood left him as he felt the stone move down its track. Then it was gone. He saw what seemed to be a gathering of ten grains of sand, just before the relief hit him like a thunderclap. He fell to the ground and passed out.

CHAPTER FORTY-FIVE

WEDNESDAY

Nick awoke from sleeping in the fetal position as his doorbell rang. Gradually he composed his strength and brought himself to his knees. Using the wall as a brace, he lifted himself off his cold bathroom floor. The air freshener, plugged into the outlet, spritzed out a liquid which had the fragrance of pine trees. Pine trees which were wrapped in plastic and burnt in a fire made from bad alcohol. The sound of the doorbell rang again and Nick stumbled to his foyer in his underwear. Without realizing his lack of attire, he opened the door.

In Nick's doorway stood three teenagers. The two guys grinned at his grungy appearance. The young lady couldn't help but stare at his bare chest a moment. No one said anything for about fifteen seconds. Nick couldn't help but notice their expressions. Upon comprehending the nature of his appearance, he went from ignorance to apathy.

"Can I help you?" Nick said scratching his head.

"Umm...do you know Persephone?" the young lady asked, trying to hide her obscure attraction to Nick's rugged appearance.

"Yeah…"

"Well you've won our contest," one young man said. "Is this a bad time?"

"Obviously…" he retorted. "But the past couple days have been a bad time, and the future isn't looking much better, so say what you have to say."

"Well, we've come to deliver your prize," the other young man said.

"Really, what prize?"

The teenage women reached into a paper bag which Nick hadn't noticed she had.

"You've won a freshly baked pie," she said excitedly.

"Cool…" Nick said placidly, before chuckling. "You guys want a piece?"

"It was a pleasure reading your essay. My name's Alex," he started. "It really meant a lot to me."

"Good…good," Nick repeated. "You guys want to come in, and have a piece of this pie?"

"No we have to deliver the second and third place prizes still, but we really loved your work. You should teach a creative writing class at our school. Here's the number of our school," the young lady said.

"Right, thanks," Nick said.

Nick walked back inside and noticed it was only nine am. He set the warm pie onto his wooden kitchen table. The metal tin under the pie clattered against the table. He stared at the pie.

"All I am," he began to think. *"Everything I've done in my life, and I'm rewarded with a pie."*

Nick pushed his finger through the flaky crust on top, putting a small hole in it. When he pulled his finger out again he was left with a purplish goo.

"Blueberry..." Nick said aloud after tasting it. "I hate blueberry."

"My entire essay gone...Leila gone...job gone...well that's not that bad. But it is! Damn it, that's my family business. I certainly don't want it, but I don't want to leave it to some board. So yeah I'm pissed, and what am I left with? A blueberry pie...That's what my life is worth...one blueberry pie..."

"I don't even like blueberry pie! What is this? What do you want me to know? What?"

Nick got up from the table and remembered he was going to be meeting Boris at the coffee shop. He threw some clothes on himself, grabbed up the pie, and stormed out of his house. He met the streets with a glare. His gait was fast and he grumbled to himself as he went.

"Blueberry pie...I don't even like blueberry pie. That's what life is, some God damn blueberry pie. I don't even like blueberry pie...in fact I down right hate it! The universe is trying to tell me something. Well to hell with the universe...I don't like blueberry pie, and I'm sick of eating what the universe gives me. I'm not going to eat this pie!" he finally yelled. "And I'm not going to top it with some good ice cream either to hide the taste. I can't even have a glass of milk with it. The universe wants to give me blueberry pie, well fine..."

Nick came into the coffee shop and stomped his way to Boris' table. Alfred was there. Boris and Alfred sat next to one another. Nick came right up to them and said:

"I'm not eating this blueberry pie."

"Good," Boris said. "So what?"

"Ok Nick," Alfred began. "So what are you doing with a pie?"

"The universe gave it to me."

"Are you ok Nick," Boris asked.

"It's the stones," Alfred said. "My cousin Missy had stones and said it was worse then when she gave birth."

"Are you going to sit down Nick?"

"I know what I'm going to do with you," Nick said to the pie. "I've got to go; I'll talk to you two later."

"Bye Nick," Alfred said a little confused. When Nick left, Alfred continued to say, "That was odd."

"You haven't known him very long," Boris said.

Nick continued his banter with himself as he came to the Corner Pocket. He came in and there stood Pearl.

"Hi yah Nick."

"Hi Pearl," he said in passing, sitting down at the first booth. "Pearl I need a steak knife."

"A steak knife Nick?"

"Yes. Now you're in for it," Nick said to the defenseless pie. "I'll show you what the universe can do with itself. I'm going to be free from all this life orgasm shit."

Pearl came back with the steak knife.

"Are you ok Nick?"

"Never been better," Nick began. "Although, if you could step back, I need a little space."

"Do you want some honey or something for that pie?"

"No! I shall not garnish this pie!"

Nick glared at the pie, all his pain was in the forefront of his mind.

"You can't conquer me," Nick thought.

The Best Orgasms Come from the Universe

"I am no puppet for the universe," Nick cried.

He brought the knife down and cut around the edges, dissecting the crust. **He took the pieces and ate them**. Then he slammed the knife into the center of the pie.

"It's what you take from the universe's that counts," Nick said looking at the pie.

"Is that blueberry pie?" Pearl asked.

"Yeah."

"You don't like blueberry?"

"No, but the crust is always the same."

"Oh."

"I think I'm going to leave now."

"Ok, Nick," Pearl said, as if she understood what in the hell he was doing.

Nick removed the knife, cleaned it with a napkin, and handed it back to Pearl.

"Thanks Pearl," he said, reaching into his pocket for his wallet. He opened it, and noticed the card Duncan had given him.

Nick handed Pearl a five, but she didn't accept it. He put away his wallet, but kept the card, upside-down. He took his pie and head outside the diner, where he went back to walking the streets.

He turned the card over which read:

One Free Double Scoop ice cream cone

From: Universal Ice Cream

Outside Duncan's Italian Restaurant

<u>Never Expires</u>

CHAPTER FORTY-SIX

Nick entered his home and set the pie on his end table. He wasn't in the door for more than five minutes before the doorbell rang. When he answered the door, he found Griffon standing in his doorway.

"Hey Nick," he began. "I tried calling, but there was no answering message, and besides you know I hate machines."

"Yes I know Griffon, what's up?"

"Well, I wanted to thank you for buying those paintings."

"Sure."

"No, it was really great of you. I was wondering if you want to go out for a drink or something."

"I can't."

"Why not."

"I don't like alcohol."

"I didn't mean alcohol. Why do you assume by saying going out for a *drink* I mean beer."

"I don't know."

"So do you want to go?"

"Not really..."

"Why not?" Griffon asked and then he noticed the hole in Nick's wall were the answering machine was plugged in. He also noticed the hole in his window. Suddenly Griffon became very aware. "Did that pretty woman from the art gallery dump you?"

"I don't want to talk about it."

"She did, didn't she?"

"Yes..."

"You wanna fight?" Griffon asked getting on guard.

"Not really."

"Oh, well, let's go out for coffee, and you can tell me all about it."

"I can't drink coffee. It's on my list of things not to consume."

"List?"

"I don't know why I'm telling you this...Yes my list. I have kidney stones."

"Oh cool. I had them before. It really hurts doesn't it?"

"You had them."

"Yeah, but with me the stones were too far along and they had to surgically remove them. They had to go in manually. I was pissing blood for over a week, it was crazy."

"If I weren't having the week I am having, that might have disgusted me."

"So let's go."

"No Griffon."

"Come on, let's have beer."

"I don't drink beer."

"Well you should, a beer a day is good for you. It has all kinds of minerals and shit."

"You can make the greatest of facts sound repulsive."

"I know isn't it great? So come on let's get you out of here, you need to move on. Beer goes through your system really fast; it'll help you with the stones."

"I don't need to pass anymore...one was enough. I'm going into surgery next week to have the rest shot by sound waves, or something."

"Cool. So are we going to go?"

"I don't know."

"Ah, good that's better than no. What's your alternative, sit around and mope?"

"Yeah that sounds pretty good right now."

"Oh, fuck that. Let's go."

Griffon grabbed Nick's shoulder and "helped" him out the door. Griffon took him to a bar close by. Nick noticed someone he did not expect. It was Fredrick...He was surrounded by about four friends of his.

"No, no," Nick began. "I'm not going in."

"Why?"

"I can't take Fredrick today."

"Who's Fredrick?"

"He's the tall one."

"Wow, he's a big one. Have you ever contemplated how you'd take a guy that big down?"

"No, and I don't care to."

"Nick!" he heard someone yell.

"If that's Fredrick, I'm going to kill you Griffon."

"Nick, its Fredrick!" he said coming to the entrance of the bar.

"I hate you Griffon."

"Hey Nick," Fredrick began. "I just made a big deal on that book you gave me an idea for. My agent is pushing to have it made into a

The Best Orgasms Come from the Universe

movie too, and I haven't even finished it yet. Me and some buddies are celebrating. Come join us."

"No thanks Fredrick, me and Griffon were just coming in to pick up some beer and head home."

"Come on Nick, you're the reason I started writing it. It's coming out really good."

"Great Fredrick."

"Come on Nick."

"Yeah come on Nick," Griffon added.

"Fine," Nick said. "What do I have to lose?"

CHAPTER FORTY-SEVEN

As the midday turned into the evening, Nick's tolerance for company dwindled. Fredrick started getting more and more drunk, while Griffon seemingly unaffected drank to no end, and Nick nursed his one beer. Fredrick went on for hours about sports and woman mostly. His friends all laughed at his bad jokes. After Nick had enough, he turned to Griffon, and said:

"I'm going to get going."

"Ok Nick," Griffon said. "If you want."

"Where you going Nick?" Fredrick asked.

"I'm heading out."

"You aren't going to stay and discuss my book with me?"

"No, Fredrick."

"Why not?"

"I've been here for several hours, if you want to talk about your book, you've had plenty of time. I need to go home."

"I was waiting for the party to die down a bit."

"Possibly some other time."

"You hate my books," Fredrick said out of nowhere. "Don't you?"

"You're drunk, Fredrick, I'm just going to leave."

"No, Nick, I want to know. You hate my books, and you hate me," Fredrick said.

"So what if he does," Griffon added.

Nick rolled his eyes.

"Well I think you're a terrible writer Nick. You think your all high and mighty because you write about real life. Let me tell you something, you write about crap people can identify with because you don't have anything that only you believe in. You think people are just here for you to write about," Fredrick bellowed.

"Just let me leave Fredrick."

"There's nothing to you Nick. You don't have a life, you don't have anything but writing. Once someone realizes that about you, they'll leave you. You're not happy, you're sad, you are only happy when you belittle the people around you."

"You don't know me Fredrick and I'm leaving," Nick started walking away.

"The great Nick Sermon, the only hero in his story, because no one's ever in his story long enough to compare."

"Do you want a fight Fredrick? Because I'm really in no mood."

"Yeah, I want to kick your ass Nick."

"You're not worth it," Nick said. "Beating the piss out of you wouldn't accomplish anything."

"Yeah, just keep walking."

It was then that Nick turned around and walked back toward Fredrick.

"I'm not doing this because it will accomplish anything. I'm doing it because I want to."

Fredrick's eyes grew wide just before Nick smashed his fist into his stomach. Fredrick bent down in a quick rush of pain, and Nick punched him twice more in the head, knocking him to the ground.

Griffon saw his chance and jumped from his seat at the bar and punched one of Fredrick's muscular friends. Out of nowhere someone punched Nick once in the side and once in the head. Quickly Nick turned and faced his new opposition. The brown bearded man wasn't even part of Fredrick's crowd. As the hairy man punched again, Nick blocked and countered swiftly with a shot to the gut. The man sucked in a gulp of air as Nick heaved him over the bar counter. The echo of Griffon's laugh could be heard over all other sounds of combat.

Fredrick got himself up quickly and punched a random person on his way heading toward Nick. With a pointless gurgle like battle cry, Fredrick charged in at Nick with his arms extended in hopes to grab him. Nick turned to notice the new threat, moved to one side, and pushed Fredrick into the bar counter. With his enemy's side exposed, Nick took his opportunity and slammed his fists into his ribs. The mammoth man went a bit limp, and Nick tossed him over the bar as well.

Griffon was an expert brawler as well as a skilled martial artist. He fought swiftly and brutally. He'd have a seemingly ineffective fighting stance, then he'd shift his weight, and suddenly he'd send his opponent to the ground with a spinning back kick. Nick's small brawl had transgressed into a full-fledged bar fight. In the first thirty seconds of the fight, Griffon had taken down nearly six guys. Then someone grabbed him from behind, and Nick was sure he'd have to intervene. As the big guy lifted Nick's friend off the ground, someone else found Griffon's feet crashing into their face. When Griffon made contact with the ground once again, he immediately sent his elbows into the large man's ribs. As the massive behemoth loosened his grip, Griffon spun around, sending his palm into the man's collarbone.

In the second Nick took to watch the man fall like a stone, someone blind-sighted him. It felt as if all the blood was rushing to his head, as he hurtled to the ground. He jumped up and was a bit disoriented as he reached his feet. He could feel shards of glass fall from his head. A headache rushed him and everything began to spin. He could see everything spinning in the opposite direction as a fist came hurling at his face. All he could do was let his knees give way. The fist swooshed by as he dropped to the ground. He didn't know who he was dealing with, but it didn't matter, he grabbed frantically forward. If his mind was more focused he'd have known he clutched the man's ankles. What he was holding didn't entirely matter, for it had Nick's desired affect as he pulled back. The man toppled over, hitting his head hard against the ground.

Nick's eyes began to focus, and he stood to see Fredrick heading towards him. Fredrick was on him before Nick could react. Nick was hit two times before he began to block. Fredrick continued his bombardment of attacks, crashing down on Nick like an avalanche. Nick took another punch in the side, as he retaliated. He hit Fredrick three times. Then he came in for a fourth and a fifth, ending his foes offensive. In his moment of near victory, Nick sidestepped and kicked Fredrick's right knee out. Fredrick lost control of his legs and fell to his knees as if he were about to pray. Now eye to eye, Nick punched Fredrick three times close to the same eye, and finished him with an uppercut to the chin.

Nick stayed on guard. Few people were standing that took part in the fight. Even Griffon had a split lip and cut knuckle. Everyone who didn't take part in the fight, choosing to remain spectators, began to clap. Nick looked around at the destruction. He considered his two choices, one he could leave as he originally intended and go to bed in pain, or he could make amends by paying for the damages and beer.

Nick removed his shoe, and reached into it pulling out some folded money. He dropped it dramatically at the counter.

"The beer is on me," Nick said.

The bartender peeked over the bar at the money. He unfolded the bills to examine them. It totaled nearly a thousand-seven-hundred dollars.

"That's for the damages and for the beer," Nick grinned.

The beaten people started getting up from the ground after the idea of free beer registered in their minds. Nick helped Fredrick up to a stool. Griffon was still chuckling.

"That's great," Griffon said.

It took Fredrick a while but eventually he said, "You know what Nick, I love you, yah bastard. I didn't mean what I said. You're a great writer and a great man."

"I'll have to beat the crap out of you more often," Nick smiled.

"You're a good fighter Nick," Griffon smiled. "I thoroughly enjoyed sharing the field of battle with you."

"You are one crazy-ass bastard," Nick said.

After the crowd died down, the three men stepped outside. Even Nick held a beer; he figured he had a headache anyway so he might as well enjoy the bitter taste of male bonding. The night sky was all black from the cloud cover. All three of them sat at the curb of the sidewalk drinking from their bottles of beer. Between Griffon and Fredrick badgering him, Nick told both of them about his debacle.

"So what are you going to do about it," Fredrick said.

The Best Orgasms Come from the Universe

"I don't know."

"Do you love her?" Griffon asked.

"Yeah I do."

"Then you know what you have to do," Fredrick said.

"Actually I have no idea what I'm going to do. She leaves on Friday."

"Tell her you love her," Griffon said.

"I have."

"Well I'm fresh out of ideas then," Fredrick said.

There was a pause where Nick and Griffon stared at Fredrick. Then Griffon turned to Nick.

"Does she love you?"

"I think so..."

"So what the hell are you doing?" Griffon asked.

"What?"

"You should be out there making it happen. Nick you're the only man in the world I respect," Griffon went on. "You can't give up. You never give up, that's what is so great about you."

"She doesn't want me."

"Oh, I know," Fredrick said. "Ask her to marry you, chicks love that stuff."

"That would just add to my humility."

"No I think Fredrick's right," Griffon said.

"What?"

"Ask her to marry you," Griffon said. "Sometimes, when someone loves someone else, they need to show it. So tell her everything...don't leave anything out, and then ask her to marry you."

"I don't..." Nick began

"If she says no, at least you know you tried your hardest."

"I don't know Griffon."

"What do you mean, you don't know?"

"What can I say that I haven't said already?"

"Listen, if you want her, and she wants you…then what's the problem?" Fredrick questioned.

"I wish I knew. She's got a lot of pain."

"Pain…we both know pain," Griffon said. "What did I do to get you out here?"

"You hounded me about it until I conceded."

"Yeah and once you got here, look what happened."

"I got into a bar fight and got a horrible headache."

"No, well yes…but the gain out ways the loss. This little jaunt helped you to open up, and you learned something about yourself. Now you're talking to us and trying to fix the problem. You can't let her go. Pursue her…do what you have to, women love the attention …and then…and then she may concede."

"I don't want her to just concede."

"But then…she'll open up," Griffon said. "If it's one thing I know, its people with fucked up problems. What have you got to lose?"

CHAPTER FORTY-EIGHT

THURSDAY

Nick went to bed the previous night and contemplated Griffons words. In a weird way, he was right, Nick had to try. He woke up at eight o'clock with the worst headache he had ever had since college, nevertheless he forced himself out of bed and into the shower. He thought he should go to Leila at his worst time. Although his worst didn't have to smell like wet dog mixed with stale beer. He wanted to go to her at his worst to prove to himself that she loved him. If she really loved him, it shouldn't matter what he looked like. Nick knew she loved him, but he needed proof, like she seemed to. He decided to move on with his life. Fredrick had promised the night before to help Nick collect his things from his job. Fredrick owned a red pickup truck, which he loved to drive.

Nick met Fredrick downstairs and they walked to Nick's old company.

"You ready for this Nick?"

"Yeah."

"What's the pie for?"

"My friend Bruce likes blueberry," Nick said. "Oh and that reminds me."

"What?"

"Here," Nick said handing Fredrick, Duncan's card. "You can get some pecan ice cream. I really appreciate your help."

"Sure Nick."

When they entered the building, Nick could see Curt and Mick off in a corner chuckling to one another. He went up the elevator for the final time. When he and Fredrick reached the twentieth floor, everyone on the floor turned to see them. They stared as he walked to his office. Out of the columns of cubicles came out Bruce.

"Nick! Nick!"

"Hello Bruce," Nick replied.

"You're early."

"For what?"

"For work."

"I don't work here anymore Bruce."

"Actually you do," Bruce retorted.

Mary walked to him from her usual desk.

"It's true, the board can't fire you."

"Well they already did."

"Actually they tried but I spread the word around, and all the workers threatened to quit when they heard you were leaving. Although, Herbert was the real kicker, he told the board about his ideas, and he said he'd sell them to another company if they fired you, so you still have your job."

"That's all very nice of you but I don't want my job anymore."

"What do you mean Nick?" asked Bruce.

"I don't want to work here anymore."

"Why?"

The Best Orgasms Come from the Universe

"Because I've never cared about it," Nick answered. "I just didn't have anyone to trust it to, but now I do. I'm leaving the business to the three of you. Well, the two of you, and Herbert. Let him know when you see him next. I'm giving my sixty percent to the three of you. Oh and Bruce, I'm giving this pie to you as well."

"It has no crust."

"I had to eat the crust, and I'm sorry about the finger hole. It should be fine though..."

"Oh, thanks..."

"So all this work, you're just giving away the company anyway?" Mary asked.

"Yeah, it all yours, do with what you like."

"I don't know what to say..."

"Just say, wow," Nick said smiling at Mary.

"Wow..." she said back.

"What about Curt and Mick?" Bruce asked. "They don't know about it yet, and they were the ones who..."

"I know they went behind my back," he said. "I have an idea, give Herbert a call."

Nick, Fredrick, Bruce, Herbert, and Mary all went down the elevator hauling things from the office to Fredrick's red truck. Everyone filed out except for Nick. Just before he left, Curt and Mick stopped him.

"We hate to see you go Nicolas," Mick said.

"I'm so sorry about what happened," Curt added.

"Listen you guys," Nick began. "I know you are the two who sold me out, and its ok, because you're fired."

"I'm sorry Nick, what?" Curt said.

"You're fired, both of you," he repeated. "I've been waiting since I first started working here to fire the two of you."

"You can't fire us, you have no authority over this business anymore," Mick said.

"And the board said if we got rid of you, we'd still have a job," Curt continued. "And the little employee strike didn't work."

"I figured that much," Nick said and everyone came back inside. "But you see the board doesn't like you two either, so they forgot to mention, to you, about Herbert here. He had some ideas that they bought in exchange for me to be back in the business. And I am very pissed off that the two of you thought you could get me fired from the company my family built."

"Well you still can't fire us, unless the board votes on it," Curt said.

"And they aren't going to get rid of us while your still here, Nicolas," Mick said.

"Well, actually I'm not here anymore. I'm just the one passing on the news. I gave up my sixty percent to Herbert, Bruce, and Mary. So actually they have the power to fire you, I'm just the messenger."

"I don't really see why we pay you," Herbert said. "I think it's about time you were terminated."

"I concur Herbert," Mary said. "What about you Bruce?"

"I guess..."

"Nick you can't do this to us," Curt said.

"It's not me, it's them," Nick said. "I've got to go."

"The board members made us do it," Curt continued.

"Nicolas, you can't do this to us," Mick yelled grabbing Nick's shirt.

"His name's Nick," Fredrick said just before punching Mick in the nose.

"Oh dear..." Curt paused. "Please Nick, don't do this. We worked for your father, please...we were forced."

"Hey Curt," Bruce said.

"What?"

"Do you like pie?"

"What?"

It was then Bruce hit Curt with the crust-less blueberry pie.

Curt said nothing.

"Thanks guys," Nick said. "I'll see you all later."

Nick left the building and Bruce and Fredrick followed.

"Fredrick, if you could do me a favor and run this stuff to my house later, I would be most appreciative."

"Sure, I'll catch you later Nick."

Nick extended his hand, and Fredrick went forward, giving Nick a hug instead.

"Bye Fredrick."

Fredrick left and Bruce stepped forward.

"So what now?" Bruce asked.

"I don't know Bruce."

"Where are you off to?"

"I'm going to go win my woman back."

"Cool, I never knew you two were apart."

"It's a long story. I have to make a stop at Persephone's."

"So this is it, my partner in crime is splitting on the business."

"That's right."

"I guess I'll talk to you later than."

"Until then, have fun Bruce."

"You too Nick. Oh, and good luck."

"Yeah."

CHAPTER FORTY-NINE

Nick went into Persephone's store hoping to find her. Persephone was no where to be found, so he walked the aisles to wait. Then he came upon the row where his father's books were. He removed his father's last book and opened it up to the about the author section. Nick looked at the black and white picture of his father. The old man's balding scalp, thin circular glasses, and gray checkered beard reminded him of his father's last book signing. The picture was only taken six days before the signing, and twenty-two days before he died. Although, more than the book signing, the picture reminded him of the second to last meeting he had had with his father. They went out to have coffee and discuss women. In high school, Nick was very shy towards women he liked. He had many *girl-friends*, but no girlfriends. His father explained to Nick why he shouldn't be nervous towards them.

He said, "What do you have to lose by talking to them."

It was a common saying and a bit of a cliché, but it was the only wisdom Nick's father ever imparted to him. They spent the rest of the day checking out women in malls. Nick had fun, and his father did as well, or at least if he didn't, he was a really good actor. It was strange to Nick that he had never thought of that old moment until then. He continued looking at his father's picture and said:

"I met a girl Pop. She's really smart, and fun, and funny. She makes me really happy and I think she feels the same way about me. And yeah I know what your going to say...yeah she's pretty," Nick laughed. "She really pretty, she's got this thing she does with her shoulder. She smiles over it, and then shrugs with only her right side. She brings her chin close to her neck. It's heavenly Dad. That little thing makes being on this earth worth it. But right now she's not with me. And I wish you could have met her. She's great...and I'm the happiest when I'm with her. I'm afraid I might end up being without her, and I think I'll be happy without her Dad. I just don't want to be, you know what I mean? I love her and I'm in love with her. She's everything I need, she everything I want, and she's everything else. She's hurting inside, but I'll do anything for her Dad...anything," Nick paused and took a breath. "Thanks for listening...I loved you too...yah know."

Nick wiped away his tears, closed the book, put it back, and headed for a comfortable chair to wait. He sat down, and oddly enough, he fell asleep. When he awoke, Persephone was standing over him.

"Nick, were you sleeping?"

"I don't know."

"It's eleven-thirty; I called the store an hour ago, telling them I'd be late. How long have you been here?"

"I don't know, nine-ish."

"You fell asleep for nearly two hours?"

"I guess so...that's kind of weird isn't it?"

"It's not like you, have you been sleeping?"

"Not really."

"Sleep is good for you."

"Yeah I know."

"Are you ok Nick?"

"There is so much stuff...I...don't know anymore."

"Tell me..."

"There's so much..."

"Just let it out."

"Well Boris and Alfred broke up, and they are back together. Boris got angry at me because I thought Jesus would be a Pagan if he were reborn, now that I think about it, the whole reborn things is very reincarnation-ish, which isn't heaven...Anyway, Bruce tried to kill himself, but he's better now...well better meaning he has no desire to kill himself. He went away to Arizona to see his kid. They made up. My old friend Griffon sold me some paintings, because he owed some people money...and if he didn't pay they'd kill him. I got into a fist fight last night, I got kidney stones on Sunday, and my entire life was summed up by a blueberry pie and a ticket for free ice cream."

"You don't even like blueberry pie."

"I know, that's what I'm saying. Then there's work...my employee Herbert has some great ideas to make my business millions of dollars. I lost my job, and then got it back, and then got rid of it again. And then there's Leila..." Nick said with a chuckle. "Leila and I almost got arrested for destruction of property. She had a killer birthday, and she told me stuff about her past relationships. I told her how I truly felt, and we broke up."

"I know."

"You know?"

"Yeah I do..."

"What should I do?"

"Well she's going to be coming in to say goodbye to me. You could talk to her then."

"Yeah...but what about you...what's going on with you?"

"Jack and I are adopting a baby..."

"That's great, when did you two decide to do that?"

"Well, when Jack came home from his mother's, we made love, and I won't get into that, but afterwards we talked about kids. I had this friend back in college who had a baby even after the doctors said it was impossible, so Jack and I kept trying. After our day at the diner, when you accidentally brought all that stuff back, I started thinking. I thought I can't let a tragedy like that secretly control my life. So I talked to Jack about it, and we are looking into adopting a child."

"That's so great; you and Jack are going to make great parents. I especially think you'll be a great mother. Good sisters make good mothers, and you've been like a big sister to me for a long time. You're a good sister and a good friend."

"Thank you Nick, although it's kind of odd that you say that though, because I've considered you more of the big brother, than me being the big sister."

"Why, you're older, and far wiser than I am."

"Well I am older...I don't really think anyone is really wise, which is maybe what wisdom is, but it's not that. You have something most people are missing."

"What's that?"

"You've got depth and you have a kind of sureness about you. It's not because you're rich, or because you're creative, and it's definitely not because of your opinions. It's something in here," Persephone said putting her hand over Nick's heart. "It's because everything you do, everything about you, comes from the most unique place of you. Even when you falter, you never forget this, which is why you're going to live on beyond your years. And that's why you are, and always will be, my big brother."

"Thanks..."

"Nick, you're a great man."

"I'm not much without Leila."

"That's where you are wrong and that's where you have always been wrong. You are still great without her; it's just easier when she is around. Speaking of Leila, I think that's her now."

"What?" Nick turned and saw her.

"Listen Nick, she cares about you...in fact she may even love you, but you need to be prepared that she may say no."

"I know...I love you Persephone," Nick said.

"I know," she said before hugging him.

When she pulled away she was smiling.

"What?"

"You've got that look."

"What look?"

"The Nick-look."

"Is it a good look?"

"It's a really good look."

"Thanks Persephone."

"Hey Nick."

"Yeah?"

"I love you too."

"I'll see you later."

CHAPTER FIFTY

Leila walked to the back café, noticed Nick, and turned herself around.

"Leila," Nick exclaimed

Nick was hushed from all angles.

"No! You...shh!" Nick cried. "Leila please listen to me...hear me out."

"Listen Nick, I don't want to do this."

"Why can't I be with you? I want to be with you."

"I'm not what you need."

"You're everything I need. I need to love you."

"You can, without being with me."

"I do..."

"I'm not worth it Nick," Leila said.

"You are."

"I can't love you Nick..."

"I don't believe you," Nick stuttered, with tears filling his eyes.

"You don't get to write both sides of this argument," she said.

"What are you talking about?"

"You can't live without reaching other people. You're only happy when you're writing...you only love me because I inspire you. You can't see past your little world, where you can write both sides of an argument. You believe that writing is the only way you can make a difference. When you learn otherwise, you're going to be a sad miserable person, and I don't want too be there for that, and I especially don't want to be the reason you realize that. I've been hurt to many times to disappoint another person. Before I came along you didn't have a single problem. You're a nice guy Nick, but it won't last."

"Women don't want nice guys anymore...The whole starving for romance thing, was all a joke. Today's people need problems to stay together. Is that the idea? Women want someone they can improve, that's it. You think because I'm happy that I don't have problems. I need someone and all the women I've ever cared about have left me. In high school they just wanted to be friends, in college they didn't want relationships and now...now they think...I change too much... But you...you don't want to see me. You think we just found something new in one another...and when the new leaves and becomes the now...it will lose something. You think we'll stay at the same point of our moon...of our circle. You think I'll lose sight of you...but I still see you...and I thought the looking glass went both ways. I want to go full circle. I want you...We can't lose sight at the same time..."

"Take him back honey," one reader said, who had watched the entire debacle.

"I can get over this...but I don't want to. You help me be a better person. Please..." Nick said.

Leila looked all around as her eyes filled with water. She trembled a bit.

"I can't...be hurt anymore...us...I just can't..." she cried. "I've got to go..."

Leila turned away, looking at the ground, sliding the tears off her cheek. She left the bookstore, turned to her right and swiftly disappeared. Nick sat himself on the ground, looked around, and then stared off into space. The old black woman sitting next to him grinned a large smile.

"Go after her," she inserted calmly. Nick looked up, the lady reminded him of Pearl. The lady continued. "Sometimes, a woman needs to know she's worth being chased after. She has a head start...now get off your ass and get going."

Nick looked baffled a moment as he sat staring with his mouth half open. Then his entire world came back to him in hope. The epiphany lit every fire in his soul, and his energy beamed through his eyes. He jumped up from his spot of the floor, thanked the woman, and ran out of the store.

"Go get her," Persephone cheered from the café.

Nick started with an unsure quick gait, which quickened as he reached the outside. He looked at both of his sides and recalled her turning right. He sped down the crowded Thursday morning street. Everyone looked at Nick's disheveled appearance in a condescending disgust. He weaved and dodged the people, searching for Leila in the crowd. The cars on the street were backed up with hundreds of vehicles as far as one could see down the city road. After seeing no sign of Leila, Nick looked into the gray clouds and then at the people all around him. He saw their faces, and then finally he glanced down at his withered brown sandals. Then he screamed.

"I shall not disappear!" Nick bellowed.

With that Nick jumped onto the hood of a stopped taxi. He stepped up to the roof and scanned the crowds. He spotted Leila swiftly navigating the crowd in her dark blue business suit as she crossed the cross walk. Nick called out her name, and she didn't turn. In fact everyone but Leila turned, including the owner of the taxi.

"Leila...Leila! I love you!" Nick smiled as she turned to see him. She although was not smiling. "If this was easy...it wouldn't be any fun to win!"

"Get off my taxi!" the cabby yelled.

Nick jumped off and ran toward her. Everyone in their cars stared at him as he slithered his way around the vehicles.

"I want to marry you!" Nick said continuing trying to see around the cars. The street was quiet, and still as everyone listened to his exclamations. They watched because no one would ever dare to do it. "I want to live with you! I want you to slap me for all the stupid things I've done...and I want us to grow old together. And I want you to be with me for everything in-between! I want to die every night and be reborn in your arms when I wake up. I'm not a poet...but it's true. I want to make breakfast...and I can't cook! I want to get up early and buy us fresh everything-bagels. I want to write my life everyday with you in it!"

As Nick reached the cross walk, Leila was nowhere to be seen. The people standing there, just looked around, and then one uptight looking suit-wearer grinned and said:

"She went that way..."

Nick nodded and continued running in the direction the man said.

"Take me home! You're my home...it doesn't matter where we go! I only want you."

Nick said running as fast as possible. As he passed by a long stretch, a homeless man pointed down the street. Nick continued down the one way street in the opposite direction. Big red signs saying: **Wrong Way** lined the road and he continued.

"I'm going to love you for the rest of my life...but I really want to love you for the rest of our lives."

Nick turned a corner and there she was standing with her hands at her sides. He came to a dead stop.

"This is all I am," Nick said quietly. "I wanted to say this at my worst, but around you I can't do that...because you bring out the best in me. Leila I love you...will you marry me?"

Leila walked forward with the sign of tears still on her cheeks. She crossed her eyes a bit as she came into his space. She glared into his eyes a moment and then said:

"If you say nearly that much during our wedding vows...I'm going to kill you."

She smiled as Nick looked at her hair and down her face. He kissed her and it was cut short as Leila pulled away. There was a short pause.

"Your best...needs a shave," Leila grinned before kissing him again.

The drab, cold, wet Thursday seemed to envelope the two of them in a clutching mist. The two seemed centered in the universe, with the entire monotonous gray world surrounding them. In Nick's next book he ended it by saying:

"Not all stories have happy endings...it just so happens, mine does."

Brandon C. Lay

EPILOGUE

Mick and Curt...

...both left for New Mexico with all the money they had saved up. Mick got a tan, Curt got a woman. Mick died of skin cancer three years later. Curt married the woman. She in turn lived with him for half a year, and then divorced him, taking all his assets. Curt was alone and had no one. A year later he got a license to work at a casino in Las Vegas. He found Jesus, which worked out well for him. He became a religious man, and married an ex-striper. They were married by Elvis, and he lived out the rest of his days as a manager of the slot machines at the casino. He died at the age of eighty.

Fredrick...

...became a successful suspense mystery novelist. He married a short woman from France, and they moved to Spain. He died from a heart attack at the age of forty-three. And he never did remember to use that ice-cream coupon.

Griffon...

...became a biker for three years, but it didn't suit him. During that time he drove around the US of A. He settled down in Washington DC, and learned to become a body guard. He was kicked out a month later, after sleeping with his female teacher. Having no money, and after losing his taste for painting, he became a merchant marine on a ship called the S. S. Pickle. Nick lost complete contact with Griffon when he turned forty, because he jumped over board off the coast of Australia and swam to shore. He lived out the rest of his short life wrestling alligators. A day never went by, when he didn't have fun...

Boris and Alfred...

...broke up seven times, but they always managed to get back together. Boris quit writing fantasy novels, and concentrated on movie screenplays. He also became Alfred's manager, and helped to spark his career. Alfred was a supporting actor in several of Boris' comedies and dramas. The dramas weren't that great. They both died together in a plane crash flying to Scotland to shoot a big budget film. They were both sixty. Nick remained their friend until the very end.

Bruce...

...moved to Arizona to be closer to his son. He opened an expansion of Nick's old business there, and it doubled the company's profits. Bruce continued his bachelordom until the age of thirty-five. He met a beautiful Spanish woman, named Rosalyn. They were married five months after meeting, Nick was the best man. Nick and

Bruce continued there friendship across country, and visited one another frequently. Bruce and Rosalyn had two kids together, one of which they named Nick. Bruce died two years before his best friend Nick did.

Persephone...

...out lived everyone. Jack and she adopted four children. All of Persephone's children had children, and all of her grandchildren had children. Throughout all of her life she stayed very close to them. There wasn't a day that went by, when she didn't smile, excluding Nick's day of death. She lived to the age of one-hundred-seven and was never alone. She died as a Great-great-great-grandmother.

Nick and Leila...

...married outside their home in the dying days of Autumn on a Thursday. The reds, and yellows, and oranges were silhouetted by a gray sky. The leaves fell over the newlyweds like flowers from the light fog and Leila wore her princess dress. Nick's personal vows given to Leila were not nearly as long, though just as poignant. When the reception ended so did Fall. It rained for three days afterwards, and by the end all was fresh and clean for winter.

Everything wasn't simple, Nick's money ran out and he got a job as a movie reviewer for the local paper. Other than the paper, Nick was never published while he was alive. Leila continued selling wine in her sister's small shop in Pennsylvania. They were comfortably well off. They had five children together, four girls and one boy. One daughter became an actress, one a dancer, another a painter and the last traveled all over the world as a landscape photographer. Their son became a writer.

Brandon C. Lay

Nick lived to the age of seventy eight. He requested his family to throw a huge party in his honor. The party was small, due to the fact that Nick outlived all his friends except Persephone. Leila died a month after Nick, while she was visiting her actress daughter in Paris. She was buried next to Nick.

Nick's only son became a well known author under the alias Brutus and published thirteen of his own books. He then printed his father's work at a small, relatively unknown, publishing house. Nick's total works included: twenty three novels, thirty novellas, eight screenplays, nine collection of short stories, and three stage plays. With the money from Nick's books, the publishing house became the most well-known in its division. Among the numerous reviews of the collections of Nick's work, one man from the most respected writer's magazine said, "Nick is the pinnacle of all the forgotten and overlooked representative of his time." He became the example of a man that never overcame anything but his daily life. Nevertheless he was never forgotten.

Brutus Macky, Daren Hill, Aaron Burduss, Laurence and his son Jack, and Taran Aaron...

...lived forever in the heart of Nick's writing, as did everyone he encountered...

THE END

About the Author

Brandon Caine Lay was born in Massachusetts on December 29, 1985. He currently lives in Macungie PA and attends Emmaus High School until June 2004. He's been writing creatively since elementary school and has written numerous pieces of poetry.

"Other then writing, acting and movies are my biggest passion. I write very visually, because I love the idea of showing a story as well as telling one. Writing people is the most interesting for me. It's in the way we think, how we believe, and how we deal with our emotions. It's fascinating."

Brandon dreams of becoming a professional screenplay writer, director, producer, and actor for films. If The Best Orgasms of the Universe were ever made into a movie, he'd like to play Nick.

"Being creative is just so liberating."

When you swallow your pills
I think of all the people lost inside you

The pill versus the sugar Hill
Mining disaster.